AMERICAN ANTHEM
BOOK THREE

JUBILEE

B. J. HOFF

WESTBOW
P R E S S
A Division of Thomas Nelson Publishers
Since 1798

visit us at www.westbowpress.com

Published in Nashville, Tennessee, by WestBow Press, a Division of Thomas Nelson, Inc., in association with the literary agency of Janet Kobobel Grant, Books & Such, 4788 Carissa Avenue, Santa Rosa, CA 95405.

Unless otherwise indicated, Scripture quotations used in this book are from the New King James Version. Copyright © 1982 by Thomas Nelson, Inc. Used by permission. All rights reserved.

Publisher's Note: This novel is a work of fiction. Names, characters, places, and incidents are either products of the author's imagination or used fictitiously. All characters are fictional, and any similarity to people living or dead is purely coincidental.

Library of Congress Cataloging in Publication Data

Hoff, B. J., 1940-
    Jubilee / B.J. Hoff.
        p. cm. — (American anthem ; bk. 3)
    ISBN 0-8499-4391-4 (trade paper)
    1. New York (N.Y.)—Fiction. 2. Hudson River Valley (N.Y. and N.J.)—Fiction. 3. Blind musicians—Fiction 4. Pregnant women—Fiction. 5. Immigrants—Fiction. 6. Physicians—Fiction. 7. Clergy—Fiction. I. Title
    PS3558.O34395J83 2004
    813'.54—dc22
                                                    2004009467

Printed in the United States of America
04 05 06 07 08 PHX 9 8 7 6 5 4 3 2 1

AMERICAN ANTHEM
CHARACTERS

MICHAEL EMMANUEL
Blind conductor-composer. Formerly an internationally acclaimed tenor.

SUSANNA FALLON
Sister of Michael Emmanuel's deceased wife. Michael's fiancée.

CATERINA EMMANUEL
Michael Emmanuel's daughter.

PAUL SANTI
Michael Emmanuel's cousin, assistant, and concertmaster of the orchestra.

LIAM AND MOIRA DEMPSEY
Husband and wife. Caretaker and housekeeper at the estate of Michael Emmanuel.

ROSA NAVARO
Renowned opera diva. Friend and neighbor of Michael Emmanuel.

—

CONN AND VANGIE MACGOVERN
Husband and wife. Irish immigrants employed by Michael Emmanuel.

THE MACGOVERN CHILDREN
Aidan, Nell Grace, twins James (Seamus) and John (Sean), Emma, baby William.

RENNY MAGEE
Orphaned street busker who emigrates from Ireland with the MacGoverns.

ANDREW CARMICHAEL

Physician from Scotland who devotes most of his medical practice to the impoverished of New York City.

BETHANY COLE

One of the first woman physicians in America. Andrew Carmichael's associate and fiancée.

—

FRANK DONOVAN

Irish police sergeant and close friend to Andrew Carmichael.

MAYLEE

Abandoned child afflicted with premature aging disease.

MARY LAMBERT

Single mother of three children and recovering opium addict.

ROBERT WARBURTON

Prominent clergyman and lecturer. Andrew Carmichael's nemesis.

EDWARD FITCH

Son-in-law of Natalie Guthrie. Friend of Andrew Carmichael.

NATALIE GUTHRIE

Elderly mother-in-law of Edward Fitch. Patient of Andrew Carmichael.

BY MENTION OR BRIEF APPEARANCE:

DEIRDRE FALLON EMMANUEL

Michael's deceased wife. Mother of Caterina and sister of Susanna.

FANNY J. CROSBY

Hymn writer and poet.

CONTENTS

JUBILEE

*The world cries out
With a common voice:
"Is there Hope? Where can Hope be?"
To our wounded world,
God still replies
With the Cross of Calvary.*

—B. J. HOFF

To Hold a Promise

I WAS MADE HER GUARDIAN ANGEL

AND TO ME THE CHARGE WAS GIVEN,

STILL TO KEEP AND SHIELD HER FOOTSTEPS

ALL THE WAY FROM EARTH TO HEAVEN.

FANNY CROSBY

Bantry Hill, Hudson River Valley
August, 1871

Michael Emmanuel held his newborn daughter with extreme care, as if she might break from the pressure of his arms.

The shallow, even breathing from across the room told him Deirdre, his wife, had fallen asleep, exhausted by the birth process. The doctor was gone, leaving behind the nurse to look after the mother and child. Michael heard the rustle of her skirts and the occasional clatter and dull thud of things being tidied up and put away.

Night had gathered in on Bantry Hill, a sultry, humid night that hung heavy over the grounds. In spite of the August heat

1

that had scorched the valley for days, the stone walls of the mansion kept the rooms pleasantly cool.

Too cool for an infant? Immediately, Michael tested the thickness of the receiving blanket in which his daughter was wrapped. Satisfied that she was snug, he carefully got to his feet. He was eager to introduce his new daughter to the rest of the household, who would, he knew, be just as eager to welcome her.

Ordinarily, he would have taken the wide, sprawling steps on his own, his blindness no hindrance in his own, familiar home. But not this time, not with such a precious bundle in his arms.

"Nurse? Would you be good enough, please, to carry the baby downstairs for me? The others will be waiting to see her, and I don't want to risk a fall."

"Oh, of course, sir. I'd be happy to."

She came and took the child from him, leaving him with an unexpected feeling of emptiness. Already he missed the warm sweetness of her small form in his arms.

In the drawing room, as he'd expected, they found Paul, more brother than cousin, along with Liam and Moira Dempsey, the couple who had worked for Michael for years. Rosa Navaro, too, his good friend and neighbor, had been there throughout the day, waiting.

Michael thought his face would break from the fullness of a smile he could not suppress. Perhaps, though, he could be for-given a touch of drama as he parted the blanket away from his tiny daughter's face, then lifted her for all to see. He was pleased by the *oh*s and *ah*s of admiration, the excited mur-murings among them.

It was Rosa who firmly announced that the child "looks just like you, Michael! Your dark hair—and so much for one so tiny!"

Each of them had something to say, but it was Paul who most clearly voiced what was in Michael's heart. With a gentle hand on Michael's arm, his young cousin pronounced quietly: "She is your gift from heaven, *cugino*. You hold in your arms God's promise for your life, your future."

"What is her name to be, Michael?" asked Rosa.

Now he had to fight to keep his smile in place. His daughter's naming had been of little interest to Deirdre. Her indifference had been just one more wound among many.

"I don't care what you call her! I never wanted her in the first place, and you know it!"

Michael forced the memory of Deirdre's angry words out of his mind and drew his daughter closer to his heart. "Her name is Caterina. Caterina Saraid—Saraid after my mother."

There was another round of approving murmurs. Then, after a few minutes more, Michael tucked the infant snugly against his shoulder and left them. He wanted to be alone with his child.

Slowly and carefully, he made his way to the front door and stepped outside, onto the broad porch that ran the length of the house. The baby sighed against his shoulder, and he moved to cradle her in his arms, rocking her a little to and fro. The air was still warm and fragrant with the late summer roses from the gardens and the wildflowers on the hillside. No breeze stirred, and other than the usual night strummings of the crickets and the occasional screech of an owl, all was quiet.

There should have been nothing but joy and excitement in his heart on this night. A man should be filled with celebration at the birth of his first child. And indeed the incredible happiness of holding his new daughter in his arms was enough to nearly overcome all other thoughts, all other emotions. But somewhere beneath the joy was a place where an old pain dwelt, a weight of misery that even the elation of new fatherhood could not dispel.

His daughter, this small, incredibly perfect, and completely innocent infant, was unwanted—and unloved—by her own mother. As unwanted and unloved as *he*, her father.

She must never know, this baby girl sleeping so peacefully in his arms, that her mother had tried to abort her, that in a drunken rage—rage at *him*—she had attempted to lose their child by jumping from the high-pitched porch of the carriage house.

He had once thought there could be no pain more agonizing than that of living with a woman who despised him, who humiliated him at every opportunity, who continually sought to rub his face in her loathing of him. But he had been wrong. Deirdre's resentment of their unborn baby throughout the months of her pregnancy, her indifference to anything related to their child, and her refusal to even *pretend* affection after her birth was the worst pain he had ever known, the greatest heartbreak of his life.

And the greatest dread. For he knew his wife's animosity toward him and their daughter would not abate simply because the birth had been accomplished. If anything, it might become even more poisonous and vindictive.

Already she had refused to help name the child. She had also refused to nurse her, leaving them to either find a wet nurse or depend entirely on a nursing cup. In truth, had the doctor not unknowingly placed the babe in her arms after the delivery, Deirdre might not have held her at all.

Before Caterina was ever born, Michael had vowed that she would never suffer from her mother's coldness. Or her cruelty. Somehow he would have to become a buffer between the two, would have to give the child enough love that she would never suffer from neglect.

But how? How did a man become both father and mother

to his child? How would he ever compensate for what Caterina might lack from her mother? With a blind man for a father and a mother who was at best cold and indifferent, how would his daughter ever experience a normal childhood?

His eyes burned, and his heart squeezed so painfully he caught his breath. The reality of his own helplessness suffused him, and he moaned aloud to ward off despair.

As if alarmed by the change in him, the infant in his arms whimpered. Michael drew her soft warmth as close to his chest as he dared without hurting her. He attempted to soothe her, crooning softly in the language he knew best, the tongue of his Italian father. He must not give in to this hopelessness. He could not, *would* not raise his child in the shadow of fear. He must seek only the good, the best, for his daughter.

What was it Paul had said?

"She is God's promise for your life, your future."

Michael passed a gentle hand over her tiny features, her crown of silken hair . . . like his, Rosa had said. He lifted the baby to press his lips against her cheek—so soft, so sweet, it made him ache.

Suddenly, he felt a tiny hand groping, then finding his index finger and closing over it. And at that instant he realized Paul was right. Here was God's promise; here was his future . . . his child, his daughter, his life. He had no idea how he would be all things to her, all the things she would need. But he would live his life trying, being as much as he could be, doing whatever he could to make sure this promise of God was safeguarded and fulfilled.

ONE

REUNION

New York City
Late March, 1876

The first time Susanna Fallon saw Riccardo Emmanuel, she wasn't in the least surprised that he was weeping.

He had not seen his son, after all, for years. Not since the accident that had blinded Michael. It was all she could do to hold back her own tears as she watched Michael's father grasp his son by the shoulders, study him, then pull him into a long embrace.

Uncomfortable with the idea of intruding on such an intimate family occasion, Susanna had wanted to stay behind this morning. Despite the love that had blossomed and then deepened between her and Michael Emmanuel over the past months, she still found it hard to think of herself as his fiancée, not his dead wife's sister and his daughter's governess. Only at Michael's insistence had she agreed to come to the city with him to meet his father's ship. And so far she had managed to remain where she wanted to be—in the background.

Around them, all was confusion and commotion. The New York City harbor brought back memories of her own arrival in America: the fear she'd had to struggle against when she'd first stepped off the ship into the midst of the other immigrants milling about the waterfront; the tall buildings along the wharf that had seemed so forbidding; the mix of foreign tongues and English, spoken more sharply and harshly than she was used to; and the ever present runners, most of them Irish themselves, who preyed on their fellow countrymen as they hustled them off to disreputable shanties and dilapidated tenements where unscrupulous landlords would take advantage of them yet again.

Susanna shuddered and, shading her eyes with one hand, looked up at the bright March sky. Although winter still held the city in its tenuous grip, the late morning sun was clear and sharp, the bracing air full of promise that spring was on the way.

Susanna watched as Riccardo Emmanuel released Michael to draw Paul, his nephew, closer and kiss him soundly on both cheeks. Then he bent to sweep four-year-old Caterina up into his sturdy arms, tugging at a long, dark curl as she squealed with delight.

"*Bella! Mia bella nipote!*"

My beautiful granddaughter.

"But surely this cannot be your baby girl, Michael? Not this *bella creatura!* Why, she's nearly grown!"

Susanna smiled to see Caterina throw her arms around the neck of the grandfather she had never met, hugging him as if they'd been together forever. Clearly, this relationship held great promise.

Only when Michael called to her did Susanna finally step out and approach. Seeing her, Riccardo Emmanuel set Caterina carefully to her feet, then beckoned Susanna closer.

"Ah," he said softly, with a quick glance at Michael. "She is exactly as you wrote of her, *figlio mio.*"

She had only a second to speculate exactly as to *what* Michael had written before Riccardo turned to her. After only a slight hesitation, he brought her hand to his lips, his keen blue eyes taking her measure in one quick but thorough sweep. Had it not been for the unmistakable twinkle in his eye, that sharply discerning gaze might have intimidated Susanna. As it was, however, Riccardo Emmanuel seemed more intent on *charming* her than intimidating her.

He was a big man, Michael's father—nearly a head shorter than his son but of broad, even rotund, girth. Like Michael, he sported a neatly trimmed beard and wore his hair, liberally streaked with silver, somewhat longer than fashion dictated. With his weathered, ruddy skin, he looked like a man who had spent much time in the Tuscan sun.

He was—dashing, Susanna decided. Impeccably tailored, freshly barbered. How had he managed that aboard ship? And where in the world had he found a flower for his lapel?

And then there was his smile. Brilliant. Irresistible.

Susanna liked him immediately.

He lifted his head, still searching her face as he said, in surprisingly good English, "I am delighted to meet you at last, Susanna. We will spend much time getting to know each other, no?"

"I'm looking forward to it, *signor* Emmanuel."

He shook a finger at her. "No, no! None of that. You are

betrothed to my son. You will be my daughter, and so you must call me Papa." He said all this with an ingenuous smile and a certain good-natured presumption.

Well, then. In addition to being dashing, he was also adept at getting his way.

"Very well. Papa," Susanna said, aware that she was being dazzled and enjoying it immensely.

At that point, Michael cleared his throat as if vying for attention.

"We still have to take the ferry upriver, Papa. We should be going. Pauli will see to your luggage, and Susanna and Caterina and I will go with you through the registration."

Michael extended his hand then, reaching for Susanna. When he failed to find her, she moved closer and put a hand to his arm. She glanced at Riccardo Emmanuel and saw that he was watching his son with an expression of great sadness. In that instant, Susanna's gaze met his, and a look of shared love and understanding passed between them.

Then Michael's father squared his shoulders, renewed his smile, and again caught Caterina up into his arms. "So—let us tend to the necessary business and be on our way! I am eager to begin my visit!"

"And we're so happy to have you here, Uncle Riccardo!" Paul told his uncle. "We intend to make your visit so very pleasant you will decide to stay and make your home with us!"

"Ah, is that what you're up to?" said Riccardo Emmanuel, tweaking Caterina's nose. "Then the first thing you must do is to feed me as soon as possible! I thought I would most certainly starve on that ship's swill. I'm sure I've lost far too much weight."

Grinning at Caterina, he thumped his considerable stomach. "Why, I must be a mere shadow of myself by now!"

Caterina giggled and hugged him again.

After completing the registration process, Susanna and Michael led the way to the ferry while Caterina, her grandfather, and Paul followed behind. In their wake came a boy towing a luggage cart piled with Riccardo Emmanuel's trunks.

"So," asked Michael, his hand covering Susanna's on his forearm, "what do you think of my papa?"

"I think he's absolutely wonderful, and I couldn't be happier that he's come." Susanna paused. "Although it seems you may have a serious rival for your daughter's affections."

Michael lifted one eyebrow but smiled. "This is bad for me, I think. I am no competition for my debonair papa."

"Oh, I don't know. You do have a certain charm of your own."

"*Grazie*," he said dryly. "I must remember to use this to my advantage from now on. Just as soon as I discover what it is."

Susanna squeezed his arm. "You're a sweet man."

"*Sweet?*" He slowed his pace slightly. "What man wants to be *sweet?* You might just as well tell me I'm dull, I think."

"Hardly. I understand that Italian men are strong-willed, even stubborn at times. But always interesting. Never dull."

"A generalization," he pointed out, then amended, "though no doubt an accurate one."

"I'm sure that's true."

"It would seem that I am marrying a very diplomatic woman."

"Also true."

He seemed to have forgotten that they weren't alone, slowing his steps even more and nudging a little closer to her.

"Michael," Susanna warned, "your father—"

"—is no doubt pleased to see his son so happy," he said. "This *is* a happy day for me, *cara.*"

Even in profile, Susanna could see the contentment ordering

his strongly molded features. Gone—for good, she hoped—was the tightly drawn look of sorrow that had shadowed his face when she'd first arrived in New York the year before.

"That's what I want for you, Michael. *Much* happiness."

"Your love has already given me that," he said as they continued walking. "And now, to have my family all together, here—I could not possibly hope for more."

TWO

A MAN WITHOUT REMORSE

MAN IS CAUGHT BY WHAT HE CHASES.
GEORGE CHAPMAN

The world occupied by the Women's Clinic and Convalescence Center was one of squalor and despair.

Prostitutes and thugs roamed the streets of the area freely, looking for their next "clients" or victims. Derelicts of all colors and nationalities—Negro and white, Irish and Slav, Italian and Bohemian—loitered in doorways, tin cups or bottles in hand, as they called out jeers and insults to the vehicle traffic rumbling by. Even now, well before the noon hour, men and women could be seen carousing and fighting, dancing and procuring, openly debasing themselves and their companions. Only the pigs and marauding dogs spilled out into the streets in greater numbers than the forgotten souls on Baxter Street.

Andrew Carmichael was always relieved to put the area behind him. Not so much because of the unfortunates who swarmed the neighborhood—he spent a large part of his life among the outcasts of the city, many of whom were worse off than these degraded residents of Five Points. But the narrow alleys and mud-slick lanes of the entire settlement gave off a miasma of wretchedness and corruption that seemed to cling to a man like a vile web from which he could not extricate himself so long as he was inside the infamous slum.

Today, however, it was worry, not relief, that fueled his hasty departure. Mary Lambert, a woman he had been treating since back in December, needed to be lodged in a facility where she could receive far more concentrated care and attention than the understaffed women's clinic could provide. Although she had come a long way in recovering from her opium habit, Mary was still indigent and homeless, her children lodged in two separate institutions. And the clinic would have no choice but to release her sooner than later. They needed beds too badly to allow a patient to stay once she was deemed "cured."

Andrew paid the young Negro boy he'd engaged to watch the buggy, then climbed in and sat thinking for a moment. Mary *wasn't* cured, not really. Her health had been shattered, her body wasted, and opium addiction was an insidious thing. Without a place to go and with her children taken from her, she was likely to fall back into her old ways as soon as she walked out the clinic door. He had to find the means to keep her in treatment until she was much stronger—and until there was something more waiting for her than misery.

Andrew felt that Mary would benefit greatly from the treatment at Prospect House, a private clinic with an excellent, highly experienced staff. But Prospect House was expensive, and there was no one to pay the bills.

His gaze flicked over the dilapidated tenements lining the street. A pack of ragged children charged in front of his buggy, chasing one of the countless pigs that roamed the filthy streets and alleys. A bearded drunk sprawled in the doorway of one of the many flophouses, bottle in hand, seemed scarcely conscious. From the upper floor of a nearby boarding house came a shriek and then a curse, followed by the sound of breaking glass.

Andrew shuddered, then retrieved a piece of paper from his pocket. There *was* someone in a position to aid the hapless Mary Lambert—someone who was obliged to help her, who owed the woman far more than the payment of her medical expenses.

Yesterday he had obtained the address of that someone.

And today he intended to use it.

He studied his own scrawled handwriting for another moment, then tucked the paper back into his pocket and drove away.

—

The impressive brick three-story was not quite a mansion. But with its high, narrow windows, graceful columns, and tastefully landscaped grounds, it made a statement of elegance and charm. Taken with the rest of the obviously affluent neighborhood surrounding it, the residence of the Reverend Robert Warburton stood in startling contrast to the squalid slum Andrew had just departed.

He hesitated, aware that what he was about to do would take him far outside the boundaries of his professional responsibilities, not to mention his usual nature. And that no matter how he might attempt to justify his intentions, he was acting out of anger—anger fueled by the resolve to right a wrong done to a patient.

Before he could talk himself out of the idea, he climbed down from the buggy and started up the walkway. By the time he reached the paneled double doors at the front of the house, there was a fire in his knees. Indeed, every joint in his body seemed aflame. The pain from his arthritis had been relentless all morning, so vicious that perspiration now dampened his face, and he blotted his forehead with a handkerchief before lifting the brass door knocker.

Perhaps he shouldn't have been surprised by the middle-aged Negro man who opened the doors. The neatly tailored dark attire and deferential manner marked the man as a servant, though to the best of Andrew's recollection, none of the clergymen with whom he was acquainted employed servants.

But then Robert Warburton wasn't just any clergyman. It was probably safe to say that no other churchman—except possibly for Henry Ward Beecher before the adultery scandal had shaken his ministry—commanded as much respect or wielded as much influence as Robert Warburton. Through his pastorate of one of the city's largest and wealthiest congregations and his extensive writings on morality issues in politics and human services, Warburton had established himself as a public figure of no small renown. He was generally revered among the Christian community as a man of God with a heart of gold, held up as one who typified true compassion and benevolence, especially where the lower classes were concerned.

Andrew couldn't help but wonder what Warburton's most ardent admirers might think if they were to discover that the man they held in such high esteem had sired three illegitimate children, only to abandon them and their mother to their own resources in a dilapidated tenement on Mulberry Street.

—

The man at the desk rose as soon as Andrew was ushered into the library, coming to meet him with an outstretched hand and a cordial smile.

"Dr. Carmichael, is it? Please, come in. Have we met?"

Andrew was immediately thrown off guard, not only by the geniality of the other's greeting, but also by the man's appearance. He had expected something of an elder statesman, with an imposing physical presence. But the man who stood before him beaming and pumping Andrew's hand appeared to be no older than his late forties. He stood several inches shorter than Andrew, stoutly built and somewhat jowly, with a receding hairline and small, pouched eyes. His features were thick, almost coarse, his skin florid and somewhat mottled. His handshake, Andrew noted with some discomfort, was aggressive and energetic.

"Have we met, Dr. Carmichael?" the clergyman said again, finally releasing Andrew's throbbing hand.

"No, I'm certain we haven't."

"Well—have a seat, won't you?"

Warburton returned to his desk, motioning to a chair directly across from him and looking surprised when Andrew remained standing.

"Well," he repeated after a slight hesitation, "what can I do for you, sir?"

"I haven't come on my own account," Andrew said, recognizing that his tone sounded forced, stilted. "I simply wanted to make you aware of a certain . . . circumstance, one I believe you will want to remedy."

A look of uncertainty crossed Warburton's features, but the good-fellow smile remained fixed in place. "Really? And what situation might that be?"

The clergyman lowered himself into the chair behind the desk, again gesturing that Andrew should be seated. Again, Andrew ignored the invitation.

Now that he was face-to-face with Warburton, he felt a measure of doubt begin to blur his initial confidence and wondered if he had might not have undertaken a fool's errand after all.

"I'm here," he said, anxious to be done with this distasteful business, "on behalf of Mary Lambert and her children."

Warburton's expression never wavered, though he took his time in replying.

"Mary Lambert? I'm sorry, but I don't recall the name. Is she a new member of the congregation?" Warburton's smile actually widened. "The church has grown so quickly, I can't always keep up as well as I'd like."

The man's ingenuous manner grated on Andrew like a rusty file. "I believe you know who Mary Lambert is, sir."

Warburton now affected a gesture of impatience. "If you would kindly get to the point, Dr. Carmichael? I've a very busy afternoon ahead."

He was so sure of himself. It struck Andrew that taking the man down a peg or two would not be altogether unpleasant. But he hadn't come to satisfy his own resentment, acute as it was.

"Very well. I'll be blunt, Mr. Warburton. This patient of mine, Mary Lambert, and her children are in desperate need of assistance—financial assistance. It occurred to me that you might want to help alleviate their difficult circumstances, given the fact that the children I refer to are *your* children as well."

Warburton's good-natured expression suddenly flamed to a look of surprise, then outrage. He shot to his feet, the chair tottering with the force of his movement.

"Whatever are you talking about?"

Andrew clasped his hands behind his back, watching Warburton. "I am talking about a woman who bore you three children. A woman with an opium habit who is trying to put her life back together. A woman who has been receiving medical attention for some months now but who needs the care only a private clinic can provide—for an indefinite period of time. Meanwhile, her children have been taken from her and separated from one another. The boy—his name is *Robert,* as I'm sure you're aware—is presently staying at Whittaker House, and the two little girls, who were hospitalized for a time, are now being cared for at the Chatham Children's Home." He paused. "I thought you should know their circumstances."

At that moment, Warburton looked as if he might leap over the desk and assault Andrew. Instead, he lifted his chin, knotted his hands into fists, and said in a voice laced with an arrogant self-assurance, "See here, Carmichael—I don't know what sort of a swindle you're attempting, but if it's money you want, you'd do well to remember that I'm a pastor, not a rich man. However, even if I *were* wealthy, I'd hardly fall for whatever absurd scheme you've concocted. I'll have to ask you to leave immediately."

This wasn't going well. Andrew had never been one for confrontation, and even though his anger had compelled him to come here, it was now beginning to interfere with his intent. Not that he was taken in by the other man's outrage; Warburton was furious, all right, but his fury was that of a guilty man unexpectedly exposed, not an innocent man wrongfully accused.

Even so, had he really thought that he had only to face Warburton with the evidence of his wrongdoing and the man would be so stricken with remorse that he'd immediately move to make restitution?

Robert Warburton's defiant stare made it clear there would

be no softening of this man's heart, even toward a woman who had borne him three children or toward the children themselves. Indeed, Andrew sensed that Warburton had already turned his back on his mistress and his children, had put them completely out of his life, and was altogether capable of erasing the memory of them.

Despite Warburton's lack of response to the accusations, Andrew had no doubt whatsoever about the truth of what Mary Lambert and her son—*Warburton's* son—had confided to him. For one thing, Mary had revealed things about the clergyman that would have been known only by someone close to him, such as the fact that Warburton suffered from diabetes and an occasional flareup of gout.

Andrew had managed to verify the status of the clergyman's health through two of his professional colleagues, but only with some difficulty. There was simply no way that someone like Mary Lambert would have been privy to such information unless she had been well acquainted with the man himself.

No, however facilely Warburton might deny the truth, Andrew had no doubt but what the man was guilty of exactly what Mary had charged.

It was equally clear that Warburton would do whatever it took to make certain no hint of scandal touched him.

Revulsion rose in Andrew's throat. It was difficult to understand how a man could set himself up as a preacher of God's Word and a teacher of God's way—and still continue to live with such a blight on his soul.

But it wasn't his place to judge, he reminded himself sternly. And there was nothing to be gained for Mary or the children by pursuing this exchange any further.

He studied the other man's flushed features, then said, "My only reason for coming here, Warburton, was to make you aware of a deplorable situation in which you apparently played a crucial part. I had hoped that for the sake of the woman you've ruined and the three children who are also suffering the consequences of your behavior, you might accept your responsibility and do the decent thing for all of them. I can see I was wrong."

He paused, catching his breath against a stab of pain that radiated all the way up his arm. "If you should have a change of heart," he said, "you can reach me at my office."

He turned to go, but Warburton quickly rounded the desk and grabbed Andrew's throbbing arm hard enough to make Andrew lose his breath.

"If you have any intention of spreading this outrageous story, Carmichael, I strongly advise you to forget it."

Andrew shook off the other's grasp. "You needn't concern yourself on my part, Warburton. *I'm* not your problem."

A vein pulsated at the clergyman's temple. "Then don't give me reason to become *your* problem, Carmichael. Because if I hear so much as one word of this preposterous tale repeated, I can promise you'll regret it."

Andrew stared at the man. "You're *threatening* me?"

Something flared in Warburton's eyes. Then, as if he'd thought better of what he meant to say, he took a step back, his features clearing slightly. "A man in my position has to protect his reputation."

Suddenly his countenance settled into the same benign, good-natured expression with which he'd first greeted Andrew. "I'm sure you understand what I mean, Dr. Carmichael. After all, you are in a similar position, are you not? Your profession also demands the highest caliber of integrity. Men like ourselves cannot guard our character too carefully, now can we?"

The man *was* threatening him.

Something cold wound its way through Andrew at the hint of menace that lingered behind the other's genial gaze.

Momentarily at a loss, he turned away without a word and headed for the door, despising the painful stiffness in his limbs that prohibited any facsimile of a dignified exit, yet too eager to escape the corruption of his surroundings to delay another moment.

—

In his haste to reach the front doors, Andrew nearly collided with a woman entering the house. He mumbled his excuses, then stopped to stare. Even without the hooded wrap she had worn upon their first meeting, he recognized her: the mysterious woman who had appeared at his office late one winter afternoon months before, seeking treatment for Mary Lambert and her children.

The woman hesitated just inside the entryway, her eyes wide with obvious recognition. Just as she opened her mouth as if to speak, her gaze flicked past Andrew to the hallway behind him, and from her expression he realized that Robert Warburton had followed him out of the library.

Again the woman's gaze went to Andrew, her startled expression changing to one of appeal.

Understanding dawned, and Andrew knew she must be none other than the wife of Robert Warburton. He nodded to her, their eyes meeting and holding for only seconds before she dropped her gaze and passed by him.

Shaken, Andrew hurried down the walkway to the buggy.

What kind of woman, he puzzled, would approach an unknown physician in search of help for her husband's mistress and illegitimate children? Had her visit to his office been the altruistic action of a wife intent on compensating for her hus-

band's sins? Or had she meant to protect Warburton's reputation by attempting to conceal the consequences of those
same sins?

Whatever her motives, he reflected, she had saved the life of
Mary Lambert and perhaps the lives of her children as well.
Without intervention, they would probably not have survived
the winter.

Something told him, however, that the man he had just
confronted would not thank his wife if he were to learn of her
extraordinary efforts—whether those efforts had been on his
behalf or for the welfare of the woman with whom he'd been
unfaithful.

THREE

An Exciting Morning at Bantry Hill

There are gains for all our losses.
There are balms for all our pain.

RICHARD HENRY STODDARD

The last person Paul Santi expected to see when he opened the back door off the kitchen on Friday morning was Conn MacGovern's daughter, Nell Grace.

He gaped at the vision she made, standing there in the doorway, a basket in her arms, the morning sun behind her gilding her auburn hair. She was like a painting. A poem. A song!

How fortunate for him that Moira Dempsey was occupied upstairs. Otherwise the housekeeper would have opened the door.

Finally, he realized he was staring. "*Signorina*—Miss MacGovern! *Buon giorno*! Come in, come in!"

23

He held the door, allowing her entrance. Once inside, she smiled at him, then quickly lowered her gaze. "I brought a gift for the poor wee girl. The one that's ill," she said, lifting a cloth from the basket so Paul could see.

He found himself peering into the amber eyes of a white-and-apricot spotted kitten. The creature's stare was surprisingly direct, seemingly unafraid, and openly curious.

Paul glanced up to find Nell Grace MacGovern studying him. "For Maylee?" he said.

She nodded. "'Tis one of the barn kits. We—Mum and I—thought perhaps she'd be good company for the child. Little girls almost always take to kittens, it seems."

Paul couldn't take his eyes off her face. *Bella!*

"Will she be allowed, do you think?"

"Allowed?"

The girl invariably had this effect on him. All she had to do was come near and he immediately became—how to say it?—"tongue-tied." His wits seemed to escape him. Either he stood mute and dry-mouthed or else he babbled like a great *stupido*.

"To have the kitten," the MacGovern girl prompted.

He did love to hear her speak! Truly, that Irish lilt was lyrical. Like a crystal stream splashing over small stones. *Si*, like music.

Again, her expression told Paul he was staring.

"Ah! The kitten. *Si*—"

He stopped. *Could* Maylee keep the kitten? He remembered Dr. Carmichael saying the child's resistance to illness was not as strong as that of a healthy child due to the cruel affliction that wasted her. Did cats carry germs? He had no idea.

The MacGovern girl looked so hopeful. He hated to disappoint her. Yet, the doctor had insisted that they must be very careful.

"We will speak with Miss Susanna," he finally said. "She takes charge of Maylee's care. She will know. And she will most likely be delighted with your thoughtfulness. We will go right now and find her."

The girl's face brightened.

He took the basket from her and gestured toward the door.

She smiled at him, and for a moment Paul felt like dancing. But he could only smile in return—the foolish, vacant smile, he feared, of one who had taken leave of his senses.

It was as he had told Michael some months ago: the thunderbolt had struck him at last. He could only hope it would not leave him such a fool forever. To be in love was a wonderful thing. He knew this, even though he had never been in love before. Love was supposed to be a grand adventure, a wondrous, exciting thing. He knew this as well.

What he had *not* known was that love might also render him a man without his wits.

At that moment Gus the wolfhound poked his head through the partially open door, then lumbered the rest of the way into the room, no doubt in search of Caterina. The big, fawn-colored hound—easily as tall as a grown man when he reared on his hind legs—started toward them, his tail whipping in circles. The kitten mewed, and the wolfhound stopped, his attention caught by the basket dangling from Paul's arm. He took a step back, then loped forward.

Paul tried to stop him, but Gus poked his big head into the basket, eliciting a demonic shriek from the small creature inside.

"Gus, get away—" Paul started to caution.

The kitten shot out of the basket, skidded across the slippery surface of Moira Dempsey's recently mopped floor, and hurled herself against the base of the pie safe before leaping onto the baking table.

The wolfhound charged in pursuit, barking as if he'd treed a squirrel.

Paul shouted a retreat, but Gus merely tossed him a look over his shoulder and continued to circle the table where the kitten crouched, back arched, claws digging into the wood as she hissed and spat at the dog.

The wolfhound howled back at her, then thumped one mighty paw onto the table, dangerously close to the small creature's neck. In a whoosh, the kitten catapulted from the table, over the wolfhound's back, and fused herself to the doors of the cupboard, where she clung, glaring behind her at the wolfhound.

The MacGovern girl hurried to retrieve her, but the kitten simply scaled the cupboard until she reached the very top, where she began to skulk from one end to the other, gloating down at the frustrated wolfhound.

Moira Dempsey chose that instant to come clomping through the door, fire in her eyes and a blistering stream of Gaelic on her tongue.

Paul groaned. Nell Grace MacGovern's face froze in terror. The wolfhound barked at the kitten, then turned to snap at Moira Dempsey, whom he had never much liked. The kitten hurtled from the top of the cupboard to the sideboard of the sink, landing smack in the middle of the crock of bread dough Moira had set out to rise.

—

Susanna got to the kitchen as quickly as she could when she heard the commotion. Her first thought had been that Caterina and the wolfhound had been up to mischief again. As a pair, they could be counted on to deliver trouble wherever they went—and Moira Dempsey typically blamed Susanna for any disruption. But Caterina had stayed the night with Rosa Navaro, her godmother, and was nowhere on the premises.

The scene that greeted her was such that she could only stand and stare. Across the room a small, yowling creature rose out of the bread dough, kicking and flailing the air with its paws. Like a miniature *golem* from the Hebrew legends, formed of clay and a secret spell, it struggled to free itself from its glutinous prison.

Gus the wolfhound yelped and snarled, jabbing his big head toward the sticky little creature as if to thwart its escape. Nell Grace MacGovern stood wringing her hands and gaping at the bread dough, with Paul pivoting from her to the hound, clearly stymied as to what to do.

Meanwhile, Moira Dempsey splayed her hands on her hips, scolding them all as only Moira could, the Irish shooting from her mouth like a barrage of hot coals.

Susanna turned to look as Michael entered, holding a sheaf of papers in one hand, raking his hair with the other hand as he added a spiel of Italian to Moira's run of Gaelic. *Something to do with trying to work in a lunatic asylum,* Susanna thought.

It occurred to Susanna to be grateful that Papa Emmanuel had taken the buggy to collect Caterina from Rosa's house. One more agitated Italian male in the house right now might be one too many.

She put a hand to her fiancé's arm. "'Tis all right, Michael. Really. Just a small . . . incident with—I think it's a kitten."

"A *kitten?* All this noise from a kitten?" He paused. "*What* kitten? We have no kitten."

Susanna shooed him out of the kitchen, promising to get the situation under control "in no time," breathing a sigh as he went.

Moira seemed to have turned the full blast of her fury on the kitten itself for the moment, shaking her apron at it and screeching like a demented harpy. As if the housekeeper's harangue had sounded a clarion call, the poor creature suddenly gave a bloodcurdling wail and launched itself from the sideboard onto Moira's shoulder, from where it slid effortlessly down the gaping front of the woman's apron.

The MacGovern girl brought her hands to her face in a look of sheer horror. Paul had gone quite pale, his eyeglasses slipping almost all the way down his nose, no doubt from the perspiration dampening his face.

Moira whirled around in a mad little dance, trying to shake the kitten loose. But the creature apparently felt protected at last, even playful, as it began to pitch from side to side beneath the bodice of the woman's apron, eliciting a series of squeals and shrieks from the Irish housekeeper.

Good sense overcame a sense of hilarity as Susanna moved to loosen the ties of Moira's apron and in the same motion catch the kitten as it tumbled free. Taking the indignant little creature to the sink, she began to sponge it with a damp towel.

It took some doing, but Paul managed to coax Moira out of the kitchen, then came back to remove the reluctant wolfhound, leaving Susanna and Nell Grace to cope with the kitten and restore order to Moira's kitchen.

Susanna could not help but wonder what it would take to restore a measure of calm to Moira.

Only when Paul explained that the troublesome creature was meant as a gift for Maylee and would, if allowed, be taking up permanent residence did Susanna give way to the simmering amusement that had been threatening to explode almost since she first walked in on the bedlam.

Her good judgment dictated that under no circumstances should the fierce little feline be allowed to stay. But the thought of the pleasure such a gift would bring the ailing Maylee—instantly followed by the idea of the temperamental Moira Dempsey at the mercy of the small goblin—urged her to abandon, just for this occasion, her more practical nature.

"I think the kitten will be a lovely gift for Maylee," she told an incredulous Nell Grace, who stood cuddling the now clean and contented wee creature against her shoulder.

"She can't be allowed outdoors, of course—she'll have to be kept very clean. And we'll need to keep her claws closely trimmed. But with a little care, I'm sure she won't be a problem."

She smiled to herself as she recalled Moira Dempsey's demented dance.

—

Susanna stood just inside the doorway of Maylee's room, enjoying the girl's pleasure and excitement as she sat in the middle of her bed, holding the spotted kitten on her lap. Surely this unusual, delightful child deserved all the happiness available to her.

Maylee was a tiny, delicate girl who even from this short distance appeared more like a fragile old lady than the eleven-year-old child she actually was. The victim of a bizarre prema-ture-aging disease, Maylee already exhibited the telling signs of the disease's escalation. Her wispy white hair scarcely cov-ered her scalp. Her skin was dry, wrinkled, and unnaturally mottled in some places with "liver spots." Her joints were almost always badly swollen these days, and Susanna knew she lived in considerable pain most of the time. Yet when one asked after her health, Maylee invariably replied that she was "feeling very well today."

Abandoned by her parents while still a toddler, Maylee had spent almost her entire childhood in one of the city's institutions until Michael learned of her existence from Dr. Carmichael and eventually arranged to have her moved to Bantry Hill. Susanna liked to think that they were providing Maylee with something she'd never had: a real home. Certainly, the entire household had pitched in to help with the child's care in an effort to make her remaining time on earth—which according to Andrew Carmichael would almost certainly be brief—as pleasant as possible.

Even Moira Dempsey seemed to have developed a surprising tenderness for the girl. In spite of a routine that kept her constantly busy, the housekeeper had, from the beginning, taken charge of helping Maylee bathe, as well as seeing to the special diet that Dr. Carmichael had prescribed. More than once, Susanna had marveled at Moira's uncharacteristic gentleness with the girl; she clearly doted on her.

For Maylee's part, she seemed to have no conception of herself as a victim, although Susanna couldn't help but think of her as such: the victim of a merciless, punishing disease for which there was no known cure, not even medications to alleviate the worst of its plundering. Maylee, however, was unfailingly cheerful, genuinely appreciative of the smallest thing done for her, and, as Michael was quick to point out, an inspiration for them all.

Indeed, Michael seemed to have formed an uncommon bond with the girl over the past few months. Susanna knew he was determined that the ailing child should not suffer from loneliness in addition to everything else. He took special care to spend time with her each day, and his visits were more than duty calls. Susanna hadn't missed how pensive he seemed after being with Maylee and how attentive he was when she felt strong enough to take her meals with them.

It was disappointing that Caterina, at only four, was really too young to be a close friend to the older girl. Not that she didn't make an effort—she often played board games with Maylee, and sometimes the two enjoyed teatimes together with their dolls. But the age difference was significant, and no matter how conscientious Caterina tried to be, the gap between them most likely would not be breached.

Maylee had made another friend, however, one closer to her own age. Renny Magee, the young girl who had come over from Ireland with the MacGovern family, was spending more and more time with Maylee, who seemed to find her an entertaining companion. They spent many hours together talking and reading, with Renny almost daily bringing small items from outdoors to amuse Maylee.

Vangie MacGovern had no idea exactly how old the Magee girl might be—she had been alone, singing for her supper on the streets of Dublin, when Conn MacGovern found her—but both Vangie and Susanna had concluded she couldn't be more than twelve or thirteen. She was slight, exceedingly thin, with an unruly thatch of dark hair, a small space between her two front teeth, and a wiry energy that seemed in direct contrast to Maylee's gentleness. But unusual as the combination might appear to be, the two were apparently becoming great chums.

At the moment, however, a different combination drew her attention. Nell Grace MacGovern—as lovely a young woman as Susanna had ever seen—was sitting on the bed next to Maylee, showing her how the kitten liked to be held and stroked. At the side of the bed, Paul stood watching Nell Grace with an expression that could only be described as *adoring*.

Michael had alluded to the fact that Paul had been struck by "the thunderbolt" in regard to Nell Grace. Watching them now, Susanna had to concur. It seemed to her, in fact, that Michael's gentle cousin had not only been struck, but was still reeling from the impact. His dark eyes, which usually glinted with amusement behind his spectacles, now held a slightly dazed expression, and his slight, youthful body leaned toward the girl like a sunflower toward the light. And when Nell Grace turned to look at him in response to something he'd said, Susanna smiled to herself.

Clearly, this was a thunderbolt with a double edge.

FOUR

An Uneven Measure

That man is great, and he alone,
Who serves a greatness not his own,
For neither praise nor pelf:
Content to know and be unknown:
Whole in himself.

Owen Meredith (Lord Bulwer-Lytton)

The day finally drew to an end, but it seemed to have taken an interminable time getting there.

Susanna and Michael sat before the fire in the drawing room, even though it was conceivably improper for them to be sitting here by themselves so late at night with everyone else abed—except possibly Paul, who was wont to roam about until all hours. Susanna reasoned that this was the first time today she and Michael had been alone, and they were both too much in need of the quiet and a few precious moments spent together in peace to fret about a proper chaperone.

Besides, even now they were busy. Michael had offered to

help wind several skeins of yarn into balls for the blanket Susanna was knitting as part of a layette for the MacGovern baby, due to arrive near the end of April.

"There," she said, inspecting the looped ends of the skein draped over Michael's hands.

"This is all I have to do?"

"Mm. Just keep your hands as they are. Not too far apart. Not too close."

She took the loose end of the yarn and wrapped it around four of her fingers several times, then around the middle, and began to work the yarn, keeping a watchful eye on her helper's hands.

"How am I doing?" Michael asked.

"Wonderfully. Consider this a permanent position from now on."

"Ah. I learn quickly, no?"

"You learn quickly, yes."

Amused, she watched him smile as he continued to gently lift and dip his hands in a kind of rhythm while Susanna wrapped the yarn into a ball. In one way or another, it seemed that anything in Michael's hands turned into music.

"What color will this blanket be?" he asked.

"White. Most everything will be white."

"Everything? What else are you making?"

"Hopefully, an entire layette. Don't let that slip to Mr. MacGovern, though. I want this to be a surprise for Vangie."

"Ah. And how is she?"

Susanna reached to move his hands a little closer together. "Like that, Michael. You have to keep the tension the same."

She started winding again. "Nell Grace is concerned. She told me this morning that her mother hasn't been feeling all that well for days now. Vangie *does* look tired," she went on. "And much too pale."

Susanna supposed they really shouldn't be talking about Vangie MacGovern's condition. In truth, she probably ought to be downright uncomfortable discussing the subject with Michael. And yet it always seemed so uncommonly natural, so easy, to tell him anything. Everything.

She had never thought about it in quite this way before, but it occurred to her now that Michael had become her closest friend. Odd. She had never had a truly *close* friend before, not even her sister. And now that she'd finally found such a friend, he turned out to be her future husband. She thought it might be a very good thing indeed to be marrying her best friend. On the other hand, until they *were* married, it also made it somewhat more difficult to observe the proprieties.

Observing those proprieties hadn't been a problem until they fell in love with each other. Indeed, her initial feelings about Michael when she'd first arrived in New York had comprised distrust and suspicion. After all, he was the husband of her late sister, Deirdre, who in her letters had written almost nothing good of the man she'd married.

Susanna allowed herself a long look at Michael, his dark head bent over the dancing yarn, intent on doing even this homely task to the best of his ability. She shook her head in disbelief that she had ever given credence to Deirdre's rantings about his "selfishness" and "brutishness." Deirdre, who had never had a thought in her short life for anyone but herself.

But Susanna had believed those letters. And she would never have come to live at Bantry Hill were it not for two circumstances. One was that little Caterina, left motherless after Deirdre's accident, desperately needed a caretaker. And the second was the bitter reality that Susanna needed a home. After the death of her parents, facing the prospect of either a loveless marriage or working for strangers, she'd decided it would be better to care for her only surviving family member, her young niece—even if her niece's father was a brute.

But he wasn't a brute, of course. Far from it. And Susanna would be forever thankful she'd made the decision she had. For she had come to love Caterina as if she were her own child—and Caterina's father more than she'd ever thought she could love—

"You've slowed down," Michael observed, ever sensitive to changes in her mood. "Am I doing it wrong?"

"You're perfect," she told him, picking up the pace again—and acutely aware that it would be best to change the subject.

"I wish you could see Paul with the MacGovern girl," she told him. "He's absolutely enchanted with her."

Michael chuckled. "I don't have to *see* them. Pauli speaks of little else these days. And what of Miss MacGovern? Do you think she likes him?"

"Oh, indeed! She has the most marvelous eyes, you see, and when she turns them on Paul they positively shimmer. It couldn't be more obvious that they're very taken with each other. And they do make a handsome couple."

"Ah. You have this all figured out, it seems."

"And something else—" she went on. "Did you notice how many questions your father was asking about Rosa at supper this evening? He certainly took his time fetching Caterina home from Rosa's house. I wouldn't be at all surprised if your papa isn't a bit smitten himself."

Michael raised his eyebrows. "Papa? And Rosa?"

"Rosa Navaro is an extremely attractive, intelligent woman, Michael. And she and your father would have much in common, what with both of them being from Tuscany and loving music as they do. Think about it."

Obviously, he was doing just that. "Papa and Rosa," he

finally said, shaking his head. "Would my father have—appeal—for a woman like Rosa, do you think?"

Susanna looked at him. "Your papa is absolutely natty. And yes, I should think women would find him most attractive." She paused, unable to resist. "And there's the Italian factor as well."

He frowned. "The Italian factor?"

Susanna smiled to herself. "Well, some seem to think there's a certain irresistible appeal about Italian men . . ."

His hands stopped moving. "Oh? Irresistible, eh? And . . . what do *you* think?"

"Well—oh, Michael! Be careful. You're losing the—"

He grabbed at a loop to avoid dropping the yarn, but too late. The remaining loops slipped from his hands to the floor. He bent to retrieve it and Susanna reached to help, dropping the ball she'd been winding in the process. They bumped heads, laughed, but quickly sobered when Michael reached for her, touching her face and drawing her to him for a brief kiss. And then another. Susanna's gaze went over the darkly handsome Tuscan face, the black hair shot with silver, the quick smile that never failed to make her heart leap—as it did now.

"I believe I like this work," he teased. "Anytime you would like me to help, you've only to ask."

Flustered, Susanna tried for an even tone of voice. "You can help me untangle this mess is what you can do. Hold out your hands again."

He smiled and, like an obedient schoolboy, sat patiently as she draped the yarn over his hands and began to work through the snarled strands.

"What is this you are doing?"

Susanna and Michael both jumped at the sound of Riccardo Emmanuel's booming voice as he walked into the room.

"Papa," said Michael. "I thought you would have been asleep long ago."

Michael's father seemed to fill up any room he entered. He stood before them now, arms crossed over his sturdy chest, an imposing figure in a crimson dressing robe and matching nightcap.

"What are you doing?" he asked again, frowning as he stared at Michael's hands.

Michael kept his head bent over the yarn. "I am supposedly helping Susanna," he said lightly, "although I think I'm more trouble than help."

"May I get something for you, Papa Emmanuel?" Susanna asked him. "Some warm milk and biscuits, perhaps?"

He declined her offer with a wave of his hand. "No, nothing." He paused, still frowning, and only then did Susanna realize that he was, if not angry, at least annoyed.

Her instincts told her to leave the two men alone. "Well, I believe I'd like some for myself. Michael?"

He nodded. "That would be nice, *cara*. If you don't mind."

Susanna didn't mean to eavesdrop as she left the room, but Riccardo Emmanuel had the kind of voice that couldn't be ignored. She was no more outside the drawing room than she heard him proclaim, "I must tell you, *figlio mio*, it disturbs me to see you so. I hope you are not giving in to the blindness."

"Giving in?" Michael's tone was definitely puzzled. "What do you mean, Papa?"

Susanna stopped, unable to walk away until she heard Riccardo Emmanuel's reply.

"I find you sitting here, in front of the fire, working the yarn like a woman when I would expect to find you concentrating on your music."

Michael didn't respond right away, and when he did,

Susanna could still hear the confusion in his voice, as well as the slight thickening of his accent that invariably came when he spoke with either his father or Paul. "My music? But, Papa, always I work with my music. I spend hours every day—"

"*Uffa*! Your music should be the most important thing in your life, Michael! It is God's gift to you. You should have no time for trivial things such as—yarn."

There was a long silence. Susanna heard the sofa creak under Michael's weight as he shifted and stood. "Forgive me, Papa. I don't mean to be insolent, but you are wrong."

His father made a sound as if to interrupt, but Michael stopped him, his tone respectful but firm. "*Susanna* is the most important thing in my life, Papa. Whatever time I can spend with her is not trivial."

"Of course, of course! I understand about Susanna! She is a wonderful young woman, and you are most fortunate to have found her. But *you* must understand, Michael, that you are a very important man. A genius! Yet you have stopped using your voice, forsaken the opera, your singing—"

"Did I not explain all that to you in my letters, Papa?"

"*Sì*, you did, although I won't pretend to understand. Michael . . . only God can give a man such a voice. Do you truly believe that He would not want you to *use* that voice? Is this how God would expect you to use the gifts He has given you? Helping a woman roll *yarn?* Unthinkable!"

There was a long silence. Then, "I told you, Papa. I left the opera because it was . . . an obstacle, a hindrance to my faith. It was no longer a good thing for me. But I haven't abandoned my *music.* Surely you must see this. I work very hard. With the orchestra, the composing—"

With relief, Susanna heard his father's tone change to a reasonable note.

"I know, I know, Michael! Still, I see you—hiding away here, in this cold, dark place, like a—a hermit! Writing the music is good, *sì*, and your work with the orchestra is to be commended, but—your *voice*, Michael! To no longer sing—"

"I *do* sing, Papa," Michael said quietly. "I sing in worship. I sing for Caterina and Susanna, and sometimes I also sing with the orchestra. I sing . . . for *God*. And I'm not hiding away here. This is my home. I am at peace here. Finally, I am at peace. Please, Papa, this is not something I wish to debate with you. I made my decision, and I believe God led me to that decision. Please, you must try to understand."

His father said something in Italian, with Michael answering in kind, and at that point Susanna stepped away from the door and went on down the hall.

This was not about yarn, she realized. Nor was it about her. At first she'd felt guilty, mortified that Michael's father was blaming her for encouraging Michael to squander his time when there were more important things he should be doing. But now she sensed that Papa Emmanuel's pique had been triggered not so much by what Michael was doing as by what he was *not* doing. It had to do with Michael's turning his back on the stage, on the celebrity that had once been his. In the process, in Riccardo's mind, he had disobeyed—and disappointed—God.

More to the point, he had disappointed *Riccardo*.

Susanna ached for Michael. She knew how painful it must be for him not to have his father's approval or understanding. He loved his papa intensely. Even an ocean apart, they had remained close over the years. Now, to learn that after all this time, his father didn't accept the path he had chosen, that indeed he disapproved of that choice, perhaps even believed that Michael had betrayed his gift—this would cause Michael a terrible anguish.

Still, it was good that his father was here. Only by being with Michael on an everyday basis could Riccardo come to realize what a strong man—what a truly *remarkable* man—his son had become over the years.

Michael and his father loved each other—of that there could be no doubt. Surely this time together would not only help deepen that love, but would also restore Riccardo's pride in his son as he came to better understand the choices Michael had made and his reasons for making them.

But, please, God, let Michael not be too wounded in the process.

FIVE

MAKING MAYLEE SMILE

FRIENDSHIP IMPROVES HAPPINESS,
AND ABATES MISERY, BY DOUBLING OUR JOY,
AND DIVIDING OUR GRIEF.

JOSEPH ADDISON

The best things about Bantry Hill, at least in Renny Magee's estimation, were its endless opportunities for exploring and the limitless treasures to be found within a hand's reach. To a girl accustomed to big-city slums—first in Dublin and then in New York—the open countryside held an irresistible appeal.

For the first few months of their resettlement on the river, Renny made it her business to spend nearly every free minute investigating her new surroundings. Now that the weather had grown milder, she could extend the scope of her kingdom, climbing trees the likes of which she'd never seen in Ireland, examining footpaths that led into forests so dense the daylight couldn't break through, scouting the wildlife—red foxes and black squirrels, owls that lulled her to sleep at night and delicate gray doves that woke her in the morning. She climbed massive rocks so high the view made her dizzy, and she walked crumbling stone bridges where the moss and lichen of another century had stamped their patterns for all time. She spied on giant elk and deer and every now and then engaged a moose in a staring match.

She had even gained a bit of familiarity with the Big House itself.

At first, the blind man's mansion had been off limits. Both Vangie and the MacGovern had cautioned that Renny was not to go near the place unless invited. With the arrival of her new friend, Maylee, however, the situation changed. Because she and the wee girl—who in truth looked more like a little old lady than the eleven-year-old girl she actually was—had struck up well together from the first, Renny was soon invited to the Big House on a regular basis. So far these visits had taken place entirely in the frilly downstairs bedroom where Maylee had been ensconced, but Renny held hopes that she might one day see the rest of the rambling old mansion that reminded her for all the world of a castle in a storybook.

Today it was late afternoon before she arrived for her visit with Maylee. She'd taken time to collect a pouch of colored stones and an armful of pussy willow branches. Maylee liked to touch the catkins, and she would add the stones to the rest of her collection.

Inside the house, Renny found her friend waiting eagerly, sitting in the big rocking chair by the window with her new kitten on her lap. Renny darted a look to the bed where, sure enough, several books were laid out for her choosing.

She could scarcely wait to make her selection, but first she handed Maylee her "treasures," as the other girl called them. As always, Maylee's smile grew larger with each stone and branch she examined.

"Oh, Renny! These are the best ever treasures! Thank you!"

Although Renny pretended to shrug off the other's gratitude, in truth she was highly pleased. She liked doing things to brighten things up a bit for Maylee. The younger girl asked for nothing, but Renny had soon learned that these little gifts from outdoors or a tune played on the penny whistle would invariably bring a smile.

And making Maylee smile had come to be of special importance to Renny, who couldn't imagine what it would be like to be in the other girl's place. It seemed cruel beyond all understanding that someone so young should be afflicted in such a way. Miss Susanna had explained about Maylee's "condition," about the strange disease that somehow speeded the process of aging so that, although Maylee was only eleven years old, her body was much like that of an elderly woman.

At times Renny thought she could almost see her friend growing weaker and more frail by the moment. Lately, she had felt a kind of desperation to bring whatever pleasure she could to the ailing girl. But it seemed almost like trying to stem a hemorrhage from a mortal wound. She had the sense that at any moment, despite her best efforts, the flow of blood might accelerate and drain the very life away from its host.

She shook off her gloomy thoughts when Maylee raised the question Renny had come to anticipate during each visit.

"Well, you're ready for a new book, Renny. Which one do you want to start today?"

Renny took her time making up her mind, finally settling on a book of fairy tales. Maylee had many books, some of which had been given as gifts while she was still at the children's home, others given to her by Miss Susanna or the blind man's cousin, Mr. Santi. Renny favored the small set of Bible stories with lots of pictures, though she also was partial to the books featuring animals that talked or particularly hateful people who got their comeuppance in the end.

"Oh, you'll like that one, Renny!" Maylee said, indicating the volume of fairy tales. "The brothers Grimm wrote some of the very best stories of all!"

Renny thumbed through the first few pages. "'Twas written by brothers?"

Maylee nodded. "Brothers from Germany. It's called 'collaborating', Miss Susanna said."

"What's called collaboratin'?"

"When two people write a book together. Go ahead and start. I like to hear you read."

Renny cracked a small smile, trying not to show how pleased she was. "Could be because you taught me how, I expect."

Maylee was always telling her how quickly she learned and what a good reader she was by now. Renny still remembered the first time Maylee had loaned her a book in return for some stones and ferns Renny had brought her from the woods. Too ashamed to admit to the other girl that she didn't know how to read, Renny had simply taken the book with a mumbled thanks and made a hasty getaway. When she returned the book a few days later, Maylee insisted on sending another home with her.

For days afterward, each time Renny returned a book, Maylee pressed another upon her until finally, confused by the girl's generosity and at odds with her own pride, Renny had burst out with the lie that books were really of no interest to her, that she had more important things to do.

She cringed now as she remembered how Maylee's pointy

little face had fallen, almost as if Renny had struck her. But after a moment she had simply tilted her head in that funny way she had and, with a long look at Renny, said, "Can't you read, Renny? Is that why you don't want the books?"

Something in that steady, kindly-natured gaze had made it impossible for Renny to deny the truth any longer. Her face burning, she confessed her secret.

Instead of looking down on her, as Renny expected, Maylee had taken it upon herself that very day to begin teaching her, assuring Renny that "as clever a girl as you are, you'll be reading everything in sight in no time."

Renny wasn't one to boast, but in truth she had learned quickly. And the more she read, the more she wanted to read. By now she and Maylee had a well-oiled system in place. Renny collected items from outdoors she thought Maylee would enjoy: pine cones, sprigs of greenery, shiny stones from the river, and anything else she thought would appeal to her friend. In return, Maylee would listen to Renny read, helping her where it was necessary, then send her off with a book or two until next time.

Thanks to Maylee, Renny no longer had to work to conceal her humiliation. Now she could take turns with Nell Grace and Vangie reading three-year-old Emma a bedtime tale, and when the MacGovern was ready to relinquish his newspapers at the end of the day, she could pore over them the same as he, although not quite so quickly.

Maylee's teasing voice called her back from her thoughts. "Renny? Where have you gone? I asked if you'd play your tin whistle for me."

Renny nodded and pulled the penny whistle from the back pocket of her skirt. She had finally, albeit reluctantly, given in to Vangie's insistence that she do away with both pairs of her boy's trousers and don a skirt. In Renny's estimation, skirts were a big bother. Trousers were ever so much more comfortable for exploring and just about anything else—but Vangie had it in her head that since Renny was "growin' up," it was unseemly to run about "dressed like a raggedy plowboy." In truth, she had grown tall enough over the past few months that the one skirt she had brought from Ireland and the boy's trousers she had scrounged on the streets of New York were noticeably too short. So Vangie had had her way—as was generally the case.

Renny brought the whistle to her lips and began to play. Maylee was fond of the hornpipes and the jigs, and by the time Renny leaped into the latter she was dancing to the sound of her own music and her friend's chiming laugh. The kitten, however, had gone skittering across the room to hide under the chest of drawers.

—

At the sound of Renny Magee's tin whistle and Maylee's laughter, Michael smiled and stopped just short of the door to listen.

What a treasure young Renny had been to the ailing Maylee. With her music, her lively antics, her attempts to bring the outdoors inside—and her friendship—the Irish orphan girl had enriched Maylee's life and brought a note of joy to a child who presumably had known little before now.

Michael had quickly grown fond of both girls, appreciative of the youthful cheerfulness they'd brought to Bantry Hill.

As for Renny Magee, he had already concluded that the girl was musically gifted. She could do some extraordinary things with a common tin whistle, and the rhythmic stomps that punctuated the lively tune confirmed what Susanna had told

him—that the girl had "flying feet" when it came to the old
Irish dances.

According to Conn MacGovern, who had brought the girl
with him when he and his family came to work on Michel's
estate, Renny was inclined to be "saucy" and perhaps "too
clever by far." But Michael had heard the note of affection in
the big man's voice when he spoke of the girl and wasn't fooled
by the feigned criticism. Conn MacGovern was fond of Renny
Magee, even if he did disdain to show it. And according to
Susanna, Mrs. MacGovern had more than once declared the
girl a "fine helper" and a "good child at heart."

As he stood listening to the music of her tin whistle, it struck
Michael that he just might be able to use the talents of this
mercurial "good child" to his own ends—or, more accurately, for
the purpose of his *American Anthem's* first performance. That
would happen this summer, during a concert at Central Park
celebrating the country's one hundredth birthday.

He wondered how open Miss Renny Magee, former street
busker and vagrant entertainer, might be to performing in
front of a far larger audience—say that of a few thousand
people gathered to celebrate the centennial of the United States
of America.

SIX

A Deceptive Contentment

BLESSED ARE THE SOULS THAT SOLVE
THE PARADOX OF PAIN,
AND FIND THE PATH THAT, PIERCING IT,
LEADS THROUGH TO PEACE AGAIN.

G. A. STUDDERT KENNEDY

Vangie MacGovern was enjoying a rare afternoon of peace and quiet.

As she sat in the sturdy, padded rocking chair at the open window of the bedroom, letting out hems on the twins' trousers, she caught herself whispering the same prayer over and over: a prayer of thanks for bringing them to this place called Bantry Hill, a place that only their Lord could have provided for them.

The day was uncommonly warm, one of those disarming afternoons when the trees were dotted with the first few speckles of blossoms soon to open and the air held a tempting hint of springtime. Had it not been for the nagging headache and the discomfort of her swollen limbs, she might have been lulled into a nap.

The house was completely quiet, a rare occurrence indeed. Nell Grace had taken Emma for a walk, and Vangie's husband, Conn, had taken the twins with him to clear some of the brambles and weeds from the fence line. Of course there was no telling Renny Magee's whereabouts, but most likely she had gone to the Big House for a visit with her friend Maylee.

Vangie leaned back, for the moment giving in to the aching heaviness in her abdomen and legs. Despite her increasing discomfort during the last weeks of her pregnancy, she lived with a sense of quiet joy these days. Indeed, were it not for the ongoing concern about Aidan, her eldest son, and when he might arrive in America, things would have been near perfect.

But surely Aidan would come soon, hopefully before the new babe arrived. How grateful Vangie was that her Conn had finally swallowed his pride and written Aidan, asking him to joint them in America—and that Aidan had swallowed his own pride and accepted. What a gift it would be to have their *first*born under roof with their *new*born at the same time—and her two grown menfolk finally at peace with each other.

She put a hand to her middle, thinking about the babe due to be born in just a few weeks. *This* child would be born into a real home, not a foul-smelling basement in the Liberties of Dublin or a tumbledown shanty off an alley in New York, but in a snug, clean house on a lovely piece of land where the only things one could see for miles were rich, fertile fields, the mighty river, and rugged mountains covered with forests. The younger children loved it here and she knew Aidan would love it too.

Their house was small but cozy and nicely furnished with

everything she and Conn needed to make a comfortable home for their family. She smiled at the thought of her husband. At last Conn had a job he loved, working for Mr. Emmanuel, taking care of the grounds and the horses and other livestock.

The children were thriving, the twins growing like healthy young colts, going to school and helping their father about the place. Little Emma, their youngest, had grown into a happy, spirited little tyke who scampered all over the place, especially delighting in chasing the chickens and playing with the cats in the barn. She was well out of didies by now, and that would be a help when the new wee one arrived. As for Nell Grace, the girl seemed to be well content, though lately she'd had to assume more and more of the household tasks in Vangie's place.

Vangie couldn't think what she would ever do without the girl—or without Renny Magee as well. *That* one never ceased to surprise her. Renny seemed to be everywhere at once. When she wasn't working in the stables with Conn, she might be found helping Mr. Dempsey about the grounds. Other times she would go roaming through the woods or up on the hill, "exploring," or collecting items to take to the poor ailing child, Maylee, who lived in the Big House.

Only in the evenings, when the family had settled in for nightfall, were Renny's whereabouts predictable. Then she could almost always be found hunched over the table, removed from the rest of them as she pored over one of Conn's newspapers or yet another book lent to her by Maylee.

It was as if the girl could not get enough of the books. Nell Grace had been the first among them to realize that Renny couldn't read. Vangie still felt ashamed that she'd been too involved to notice. But what with the harrowing crossing, James's illness aboard ship, and the ongoing struggle just to survive once they arrived in New York, there had been no *time* to notice, no time for anything except for work and more work. When Nell Grace finally called Vangie's attention to her discovery, the child, Maylee, had already undertaken the task of teaching Renny Magee to read.

They had become fast friends, those two. Strange friends. One would have thought that Renny—the older—with her all her restless energy and gumption, might have seen fit to lord it over the younger Maylee. But in many ways, the more fragile Maylee seemed the elder of the pair. Vangie had not been around the ill child all that much, but she found it a bit surprising how Renny Magee, who was as stubborn as she was independent, invariably gave in to her.

Vangie ached for the girl, yet sensed that Maylee would abhor her pity. And sure, it was nothing like pity that Renny Magee brought to the friendship. Miss Susanna had remarked more than once on how well the two got on together, and Vangie had seen for herself that they gave each other something that might have otherwise gone lacking for each. In a way that perhaps only the Lord could understand, they *blessed* each other.

Almost lightheaded from drowsiness now, her vision clouding as it was wont to do lately, Vangie set the sewing aside and closed her eyes. She would rest, she decided, but only for a moment.

—

The house was quiet, the deep, heavy shadows of late afternoon drawing in when Renny Magee returned from her visit with Maylee.

She found it odd that she would be the first one home at the end of the day. Most often Nell Grace and wee Emma were in the kitchen when Renny walked in. She looked around, then went to the sink and pumped a cup of water, downing half of it before realizing something else was amiss. Her gaze went to the cookstove. It was cold. No potatoes cooking, no stew simmering, no water heating for tea.

A glance at the sink and the table showed no sign of preparations for supper.

All this and an uncommon silence . . .

Renny slammed her cup down, wiped her mouth on her sleeve, and hurried out of the room, toward the back of the house.

She found Vangie dozing, slumped forward in the rocking chair by the bedroom window, her sewing bag on the floor.

Should she wake her? Vangie hadn't been sleeping well lately. She was too uncomfortable, she said. Still, she would be upset if the family came back to a cold stove and an empty table. Even now, when she was heavy with child and not feeling well, Vangie MacGovern took her responsibilities as woman of the house very seriously.

It seemed strange that Nell Grace hadn't started the supper. But then Vangie usually got things going and let Nell Grace tend to the rest.

Renny stood there, trying to think what to do. Finally she spoke Vangie's name. When there was no reply, she crossed the room and stopped in front of Vangie, whose arms were wrapped tightly around her abdomen.

Renny spoke her name again, louder this time, and Vangie raised her head. Her face was puffy and red, her features drawn. She stared at Renny with hollow eyes, as if she didn't really see her.

Fear squeezed Renny's spine like an icy hand. "Vangie? Are you all right?"

For an instant Vangie's eyes seemed to clear. She opened her mouth as if to speak but gasped and threw her head back against the chair. "Renny—get Conn! Tell him to . . . come!"

Renny saw the blood then. It was thin and watery, but it was blood all right, trickling down Vangie's legs and turning to a pool at her feet.

She began to shake. Oh, she was cold—she'd never been so cold! She stared at Vangie, unwilling to leave her alone, yet not having a thought of what to do. Her head felt like mud, her legs like useless sticks beneath her.

Vangie reached out with one hand as if to push her. "*Go!*"

Renny whirled and ran. She shook so hard as she charged through the house, she thought her bones would surely shatter like glass. Her chest was on fire, for she had no breath. She bolted out the door and onto the lawn—stumbling, nearly falling, straightening, and screaming for the MacGovern as she went. Screaming for *anyone* who would come.

—

Nell Grace heard her before she saw her. Renny Magee, running straight at her and Emma, shrieking like a wild thing.

Nell scooped Emma into her arms and began running as well. "What is it, Renny? What's wrong? Is it Mum?"

Renny stopped, nodding and gasping for breath, her thin chest heaving. "There's blood! I think she's in terrible pain! She said your da should come right away. Oh, she's bad, Nell Grace. She's in a bad way and no mistake!"

Nell Grace didn't hesitate but drew Emma tightly against her. "I'll go to Mum," she said, breaking into a run. "You go get Da!" she called back over her shoulder. "He and the boys are at the fence down by the creek. Go as fast as you can, Renny! Tell Da to come at once!"

Renny was already on the way. She had caught her second wind now, and her legs took on new strength as she ran. She seemed scarcely to touch ground as she went flying over the field and down the hill toward the fence line, calling out to Conn MacGovern as she went. She couldn't shake the image of Vangie clutching at herself, as if she were trying to hold herself together, the pain racking her face, the blood . . .

She took a furious swipe at her eyes and kept on running, willing herself not to think about the blood, not to think about anything but reaching Conn MacGovern.

SEVEN

At the Edge of the Storm

I HEAR ALL NIGHT AS THROUGH A STORM

HOARSE VOICES CALLING, CALLING

MY NAME UPON THE WIND—

JAMES CLARENCE MANGAN

Vangie thrashed her arms and legs, struggling to stay afloat as one red wave after another pounded her and pulled her under. Fierce pain gripped her, but more frightening than the pain was the angry, unknown sea in which she found herself.

Flashes of lightning, jagged and razor sharp, pierced the water, illuminating the raging current that swept her away from shore. She was caught up in a vortex, an undertow that threatened to drag her below even as the storm whipped her about, tossing her over the waves like an empty fish basket.

Between rolls of thunder, she heard her name called and looked back toward shore to see Conn and Nell Grace crying out to her. Miss Susanna from the Big House was there, too, with Mrs. Dempsey, the housekeeper, right beside her.

But where were the children? Wee Emma and the twins?

She reached out for Conn, as if he could somehow pull her back to the safety of land. But even as she thrust out her arm, she knew she was too far out for rescue.

She turned away, gasping when a babe suddenly appeared in view, bobbing and rocking as if he were riding the waves. A tiny infant, wrinkled and red, with only a wisp of hair but with great, sad eyes, his little arms and hands beckoned her forward, coaxing her to come now, come away from that other place, away from those calling her name—

An enormous wave slammed at her, hurled her up and over, as if she were but a weightless thing. As the sea dropped her again, Vangie glanced back toward the shore one more time. Conn's face was contorted with what appeared to be fear—or grief—as he continued to cry her name over and over again. Nell Grace was sobbing, her hands covering her face.

There were other voices, some she knew and others she didn't recognize. She thought they might be praying, but they were soon lost when an tremendous roll of thunder came barreling in on her.

Her legs felt so heavy, her arms as well. Any moment now she would surely be dragged to the ocean floor or flung wildly into the storm and lost at sea.

She ceased her efforts to turn back to shore, her strength too far gone to fight her way through the relentless fury of the storm. Besides, the babe with the sorrowful eyes seemed to be pleading with her to come to him. Aye, *him*—sure, the infant was a boy! And he so tiny and helpless! He needed her more than the others, his eyes seemed to say, more than those she was leaving behind.

—

Susanna took one look at Vangie MacGovern and wanted to run from the room. The woman was obviously in excruciating pain. She didn't even appear to be conscious. At best, she was out of her head. Her usually lovely features were swollen almost beyond recognition, her eyes open but unfocused and so shadowed they looked to be bruised. She lay moaning and muttering, sometimes calling out or shrieking.

She looked as if she might be dying.

Was this what childbirth was like?

Susanna jumped when a clap of thunder shook the small house and a wicked bolt of lightning arced outside the window. For once, Susanna was thankful to have Moira Dempsey nearby. She felt helpless entirely, but the irascible housekeeper had already begun snapping orders to Mr. MacGovern and Nell Grace, sending them from the room while she turned back to examine Vangie with a confidence born of experience.

"Ach, this one needs more help than I can give, and soon!" she said, straightening and turning to Susanna. "Her waters have broke, and the babe's tryin' to come. And somethin's bad wrong."

"But the baby's not yet due."

"Due or not, it means to be born. Tell my man to go for a doctor. Someone should have sent long before now."

Susanna tried to think. "Dr. Kent is the closest, but he's never recovered from his stroke. There's no one else nearby."

Moira cast a look at the woman writhing on the bed, then turned back to Susanna. "I fear this babe will not be born at all, at least not alive, without a doctor." She paused. "I'll do what I can, but she's in for a long, hard time of it. I've never helped with such a birth, but I'll warrant the babe is turned wrong to begin with. And she has the look of one with the poison runnin' through her."

Susanna had no idea what the older woman meant about "the poison," but the look in Moira's eyes sent fear hurtling through her like a splash of icy water.

"What—how can I help?"

Occupied with elevating Vangie's upper body, Moira scarcely glanced at Susanna. "You shouldn't be in here at all," she said. "You're naught but a maiden. No need for you to watch this."

Susanna really didn't *want* to "watch this," but she'd be no help to Vangie MacGovern by playing the coward. "No, I'll stay. There might be something I can do."

The housekeeper turned now, her sharp gaze raking Susanna's face. "'Be keepin' those children out of here, then. And the man as well. They shouldn't see her so."

Another slam of thunder struck just then. Vangie cried out, and Moira turned back to her, tossing instructions over her shoulder. "We'll be needin' plenty of hot water and towels. And if you think they'll come, send my man to the city after those doctor friends of yours. They'll never get here in time, but even so, we ought to try."

Susanna couldn't help but think that if someone had only sent for them sooner, Bethany Cole and Andrew Carmichael would have been well on their way by now. She knew they would come, for they were friends as well as physicians. Andrew had come in the middle of the night, after all, when Caterina was so terribly ill with the croup. But it would take hours for them to get here from the city. And watching Vangie MacGovern, she had a sick thought that neither Vangie nor her baby could wait for hours.

Ashamed of her own cravenness, Susanna knew she had to

get out of the room or be ill. "I'll—have Nell Grace fetch some water and towels. Then I'll go and find Mr. Dempsey. There's that new telegraph office at Tarrytown. Perhaps he could get a wire off to Dr. Carmichael. That would save a great deal of time."

"If he can rouse the fool what minds the place," Moira grumbled as she heaped more pillows and a quilt under Vangie's torso. "From what I've heard, he's in his cups more often than not."

Susanna closed the door behind her as she left the room. In the kitchen she forced a smile for the anxious faces turned toward her, but she feared her voice was less than convincing as she attempted to reassure them. She managed to persuade Nell Grace to stay out of the bedroom, but Conn MacGovern would have none of it. Before Susanna could even protest, he was on his way back to his wife.

Once outside the cottage, she practically ran the distance to the house, heedless of the rain and the muddy water splashing onto her skirts. Heedless of everything except Moira's words, which continued to echo ominously in her head:

"They'll never get here in time . . ."

EIGHT

THE FADING CRY

LITTLE CHILDREN, TEARS ARE STRANGE
UPON YOUR INFANT FACES,
GOD MEANT YOU BUT TO SMILE
WITHIN YOUR MOTHER'S SOFT EMBRACES.

SPERANZA (LADY JANE FRANCESCA WILDE)

Bitter cold engulfed Vangie, numbing her limbs and stealing her breath, while flashes of lightning bore down upon her in dizzying succession. Torn and battered by the force of the wind and brutal waves, she felt exhaustion take over and knew she could no longer keep herself afloat.

The cries from the shore were growing fainter now, the face of the wee baby boy fading from view. He was wailing, crying out for her, and Vangie extended her arms to him, knowing even as she did that the distance between them had widened and she had no real hope of reaching him. She hadn't the strength to go forward or backward, could do nothing but give in to the wind and let the sea carry her where it would.

A terrible grief seized her, but she was too spent even to weep as the storm made one last crushing assault on her. She had lost them all, lost her loved ones left waiting on the shore, lost the tiny babe now gone from her sight—the infant son, *her* son, taken from her before she ever knew him. She could still hear his fading cry, a litany of loss, and it intensified her grief.

Suddenly, without warning, the wind seemed to turn. The angry roaring of the sea began to subside. The lightning dimmed, and the very air grew thick and still. Vangie felt herself lifted and held secure, cradled in the waves that only a moment before had threatened to destroy her. Released from the numbing cold, a gradual, renewing warmth began to spread over her.

But nothing eased the hollow anguish of her soul. Vangie was sure she could still hear the babe calling out for her. She searched her line of vision for the infant boy who had been there only a moment before, but there was no sign of him. Her arms—her *heart*—felt empty and bereft as the gently rocking waves carried her back to shore.

The weak cry of the babe seemed to echo over the water. He was near, as close as a whisper breathed softly upon her cheek . . . and yet beyond her grasp.

"Mother . . . Mother . . ."

No, this wasn't the cry of a babe, the voice of an infant. This was the imploring voice of a man, a man hidden in the mists that had settled over the sea at the edge of the storm.

"Mother . . . Mother, 'tis Aidan."

Not a babe, but Aidan, her firstborn son, a man grown.

And he, too, far beyond the reach of her flailing arms.

—

"Toxemia," Bethany Cole said, her voice tight as she straightened from her examination of Vangie MacGovern. "And the baby is breech."

Andrew Carmichael nodded, tossing his suit coat and rolling up his shirt sleeves. "Let's get a table brought in here. I don't want to move her."

"You're going to do a caesarean? Here?"

"I don't have a choice," Andrew said. "She's bleeding, and she's going to start seizing any moment. It's too late to try to turn the baby." He looked around him, assessing the resources available. "Why didn't they send for us sooner? She must have been this way for hours."

"Apparently they didn't send for Susanna and Mrs. Dempsey right away either." Bethany shook her head. "They're recent immigrants, don't forget. Everything is strange to them, and probably frightening. They most likely didn't know what to do. Actually, there wasn't much they *could* do. Susanna said the closest doctor is recovering from a stroke and may not return to his practice. That's why they sent for us."

Andrew expelled a long breath. "Well, she's scarcely conscious. This could hardly be a worse situation." He didn't so much direct his words to Bethany as to himself. He felt exceedingly frustrated by the circumstances and more than a little anxious about the treacherous delivery he was about to undertake.

He ran a hand across the back of his neck, knowing what he had to do but reluctant to do it. "I suppose I should speak with MacGovern."

"Andrew?"

He looked at her.

"Do they have a chance? Either of them?"

Did they? He didn't know how to answer her. He knew himself to be capable, but this would be no ordinary delivery. A breech birth. Toxemia. A mother nearing forty years. He shook his head. "The risk is as great for one as the other," he said. "I'll do everything I can, but we both know that ultimately it's in God's hands."

"Yes," Bethany replied quietly. "I know. Well, I suppose you should talk with Mr. MacGovern now. And Andrew—I expect they'll want to send for a priest."

He swallowed, finding it painful against the raw dryness of his throat. "Yes," he said. "They'll want to do that."

He turned and started for the door. There were times—and this was definitely one of them—when he wished God had called him to the ministry. Or the mission field. Anywhere but medicine.

—

Bethany brushed a shock of dark hair away from Andrew's face, then blotted the perspiration from his forehead with a towel. She had never been more impressed with the man who was her partner in medicine—as well as being the man she loved—than during the long ordeal with Vangie MacGovern. Even in circumstances that could not have been much more trying, she could only watch him with admiration.

His long, lean face was set in intense concentration, his hands quick and sure. Working on a table that was solid but not quite large enough, with only the most rudimentary of necessities—including kerosene lamps for light—on a patient who was clearly in a mortal state, he performed a caesarean delivery that was nothing less than astounding in terms of brevity, control, and skill.

From the moment Bethany placed the towel soaked with chloroform to the mother's face until Andrew made the quick, deft incision, then lifted the tiny infant from the patient's open womb, he never faltered. Bethany knew his hands were giving him grief throughout the process—there was no mistaking the swollen joints and redness of his skin—but he remained steady, as calm and seemingly confident as if he had performed this sort of surgery numerous times under the same primitive conditions.

He was, in her eyes, magnificent.

He gave the baby's bottom a smart slap, which produced only the weakest of cries. Then he handed him into Bethany's waiting arms, draped by a warm towel.

This was by far the smallest infant Bethany had ever seen. "Will he be all right?"

She had to ask, even though she anticipated his reply.

"I honestly don't know," Andrew said, beginning to suture. "Cleanse him as well as you can, but try to keep him securely wrapped as much as possible. Massage his limbs, but very carefully." He glanced up. "You know what to do. There's only so much we *can* do."

The door opened just then, and a tall, silver-haired priest stepped inside. Andrew frowned and shook his head, lifting a hand as if to indicate "not yet," then went on suturing the incision. The priest nodded and moved to stand in a shadowed corner of the room.

After Bethany had washed the infant, she wrapped another prewarmed towel around him, hugging him close to her heart as she rubbed his tiny legs through the thickness of the cloth. He began to wail, a frail cry like that of an abandoned kitten.

As she cuddled the child, she watched her fiancé close the

incision, then lift the still unconscious Vangie MacGovern from the table onto the bed.

Her throat threatened to close when she saw Andrew motion for the priest. The man stepped out of the shadows and came to stand beside the bed.

Andrew glanced at the exhausted mother, then at the infant in Bethany's arms before he responded to the priest's unspoken question.

"I don't know," he said, his voice weary, his shoulders slumped. "I expect the mother would want last rites for them both."

Bethany drew the infant boy a little closer, as if she could strengthen his thin, fluttering heartbeat by pressing his tiny form closer to her own heart.

When the priest gently lifted him from her arms, it seemed that the baby's feeble wail continued to echo deep inside her own spirit.

NINE

VALE OF SHADOWS

LEAD ME THROUGH THE VALE OF SHADOWS,
BEAR ME O'ER LIFE'S FITFUL SEA . . .
FANNY CROSBY

By midafternoon the next day, Susanna faced an unsettling certainty—that the previous night had changed her forever. It had evoked a formerly unknown fear that now threatened to shake a fundamental conviction about herself and what she wanted from life.

How would she ever again entertain the thought of giving birth without remembering Vangie MacGovern's swollen form, her distorted features, and the agonized cries that reflected a torment unlike anything Susanna had ever imagined? After this, how could she ever bring herself to give Michael the family he so desired?

He had made no secret of the fact that he'd always longed for a "house filled with children." He had grown up as an only child and was emphatic about not wanting the same kind of childhood for Caterina. Papa Emmanuel, too, often made mention of how *he* looked forward to more grandchildren, even hinting at the possibility that those grandchildren might be the very inducement that would keep him in the States.

As Michael's wife, Susanna would only naturally be expected to share this desire for a family. And up until now, she *had* shared it. Before last night, however, she had never given much thought to what exactly was involved in bringing a baby into the world. Even though she'd grown up on a dairy farm, her parents had done their best to keep her and her sister Deirdre fairly unenlightened about such things as mating and giving birth.

For the first time, Susanna realized that perhaps her mother—for it had been mostly her mother's doing, as she recalled—had done her no favors by sheltering her so closely. What she had witnessed with Vangie MacGovern might not have been such an immense shock had she been better prepared. Uninformed as she was, she had been badly shaken by last night's events. Indeed, she was still struggling to suppress the fear they engendered, along with her disgust at herself for reacting as she had.

She crossed her bedroom and sat down on the side of the bed, unable to stop thinking about Vangie MacGovern. Such suffering—and the poor infant might not even survive. Simply watching Bethany and Andrew with the MacGovern family after the delivery had confirmed her own suspicions that the baby's grasp on life was tenuous at best.

As for Vangie herself, Andrew Carmichael had not attempted to minimize the seriousness of her condition, although it seemed to Susanna that he considered the mother's survival more likely than the infant's.

Incredibly, as if there had not been agony enough for the MacGoverns during that dreadful night, in the early hours of the morning had come the devastating news that their oldest son, en route to America, had been lost at sea.

Susanna shuddered, her own personal anxieties receding in the face of the tragedy that had fallen upon the MacGoverns. How much more must that poor family bear? How much more *could* they bear, Susanna wondered, sick at heart for them all, but especially for Vangie, who might yet have to face the terrible blow of losing not only her firstborn son but her newborn as well.

And that was assuming Vangie survived to learn of her loss.

—

By sheer force of will, Conn MacGovern sat still as a stone, watching his wife sleep. He wanted nothing so much as to flee the small room that reeked of sickness and despair. The despair was his own, for Vangie was as yet unaware that the life of their tiny infant boy was in jeopardy and that they had already lost their eldest son to the sea.

Conn felt as if he were being torn in half, willing Vangie to come to while at the same time dreading the moment when she would revive.

If she revived.

And if she did, would she survive the dire news he must lay upon her? Weak as she was, the loss of Aidan, their firstborn and ever so dear to her heart, might be the final blow that would destroy her, even before she learned that death might also await the new babe.

He tried to reason with himself that perhaps, if the wee boy should live—perhaps that might strengthen Vangie's will enough to make *her* want to live.

As quickly as the thought arrived with its fragile trace of hope, just as quickly did it flee, leaving Conn's spirit as bleak and chilled as before. Even the doctors could not say whether the babe would last through the day.

How could he not fear the worst? Although Mrs. Dempsey had had some success in getting the infant to suckle from a knotted cloth soaked in sweet cream with a little sugar water, the babe appeared desperately frail, his blue-veined skin thin as paper and just as fragile. Even his wail was pitiful, as weak as that of a sick pup.

To lose two sons, their eldest and their youngest—why would he think that Vangie could bear it, in her own dangerous condition, when he wasn't at all convinced that *he* could?

He had tried to be strong, to cling to his faith, ever since his first glimpse of the babe after the birthing, and even after the word came about Aidan. No doubt Vangie's counsel would be the same steadfast reminder as was her custom to offer in a dark time such as this: "What seems a disaster when left to our own means," she would say, "can be turned to a glory when touched by our Lord." Or something to that effect.

But Vangie was the one with the faith of a saint, not himself. He did his best not to bring shame to his Savior, but the dear Lord knew his faith was a feeble thing indeed compared to Vangie's. She was the one who kept them all from flying apart when things were bad. Like any man, he liked to think he was the bedrock of his household, strong enough and brave enough to meet whatever might come. But in truth, Vangie was *his* bedrock. His flame-haired darling feared nothing. Well . . . except perhaps for bats and spiders.

His spirit groaned to think of ever living a day without her.

Oh, sweet Savior, what would I do . . . what would any of us do if You were to take her from us? Please, Lord, have mercy, not simply for my sake, but for the children. How could I possibly care for them all and give them what they need without Vangie? How would they ever manage without their mother?

Struck with terror at the direction his thoughts had taken, Conn felt he would surely strangle. He squeezed his eyes shut and began to knead his temples with his hands, hoping to relieve the ache that wreathed his skull.

The rain had finally ceased, but the wind was still up. Dazed with exhaustion and nearly numb with fear, he thought at first the faint moan was naught but the wind rustling through the great pines that ringed the property. But when it came again, he opened his eyes to see Vangie watching him.

He shot out of his chair and bent over her, catching her hand in his.

"Conn . . ."

Her voice was thin, scarcely more than a tremulous whisper, but to Conn it sounded like music. "I'll go and get the doctors, love! You must lie very still now."

"No . . . wait. The babe, Conn . . . is the babe—is he all right?"

Conn swallowed, squeezing her hand carefully. "He . . . he's a wee thing, love, but a fighter. Sure, he'll be fine in no time at all." He stopped, studying her. "How did you know we have ourselves another boy, Vangie?"

She gave the slightest shake of the head. "I just . . . knew. I dreamed about him. I . . . think I saw him."

Conn knew he should go and fetch the doctors, but still he clasped her hand, unwilling to leave her. "Well, your dream was right enough, love. And won't he be needing a proper name now? We'd not quite decided on that, so we'd best—"

Suddenly, she shook her hand free, grasped his arm and pulled herself up, clinging to him.

"Vangie, you mustn't—"

"Aidan! Oh, Conn, I dreamed of our Aidan, too! Has there been any word of him?"

Conn's blood seemed to halt its flow. His heart pounding, he sat down beside her on the bed, supporting her with his shoulder as she continued to cling to him. Her eyes burned with the flame of fever, and her hand on his arm was like a claw.

"Vangie, you mustn't do this, you must not strain yourself so—"

She ignored him, beginning to ramble as if she hadn't heard. "He was calling for me, Conn . . . on the sea. There was a storm . . . he kept calling but I couldn't reach him! At first I thought it was the babe, but it wasn't. It was Aidan! Oh, Conn, he was calling out for me, and I couldn't—"

She stilled, her sunken eyes enormous against the pallor of her skin. "Conn?"

His name on her lips was harsh and laced with fear.

It was too soon to tell her . . . she wasn't strong enough . . . it might drain what little strength was left in her . . .

He tried to calm her, knowing as he did that Vangie, even weak as she was, could strip away all his pretenses like the skin of an onion and look into his soul. She knew him too well. She had seen what he could not say. Much as he longed to, he couldn't lie to her. Not now. Not ever.

"What is it?" she said, her feverish eyes searing his own, her grasp tightening on his arm. "The babe?" She twisted to better study him, and the panic in her gaze wrenched Conn's heart.

"No. 'Tis as I told you, Vangie. The babe is holding his own."

Her eyes darkened, and Conn saw her struggle, saw her dread of hearing the worst, her inability *not* to hear it.

"Aidan?" she finally choked out.

An entire world of grief hung over the name of their son like a shroud.

"So it *is* Aidan, then. Tell me," she said in a tone dull and thick with knowing.

Conn tried to pull her closer, but she gave a fierce shake of her head and lifted a hand to restrain him. "*Tell* me," she said again, her voice turning hard.

He was the one who had had to tell her each time they'd lost a child—the tiny girl who had died before being birthed, the infant son who had not lived past his first week. And each time, seeing the raw pain in her eyes and the terrible desolation that hung over her for weeks afterward, he had thought he could never bear to see such sorrow looking back at him again.

But this was a harder thing entirely, a far worse agony to thrust upon her. To lose one's firstborn—to watch him grow to manhood, love him and care for him for nearly twenty years, and then know he was gone forever—could there be a more grievous loss?

If only that loss could have been prevented . . .

But I begged him to come. For the sake of your mother, I told him, you must come so you and I can be reconciled and bring her some peace . . . and so we can all be together again as a family. She is fading here without you. You must come . . .

Worse yet was the bitter awareness that, had he not been so hardheaded, had not been such a bane to the boy all of those years of his young manhood, perhaps Aidan might have come across when *they* did, instead of waiting.

But he could not think of that now. That was *his* grief. He could not make it hers. Somehow, for now, he must put aside his guilt, his torment, and help her bear her own.

She was waiting, watching him, her blue eyes hot and shadowed with fear.

And so he told her, trying to ignore the part of himself that
he could feel dying with every word he spoke.

—

In the kitchen, dim in the late afternoon light filtering through
the small windows, Renny Magee sat watching Nell Grace try
to feed her new baby brother with a knotted cloth dipped in
sugar water.

The poor sickly little thing was doing its best to suckle, and
Nell Grace actually seemed encouraged, but Renny wondered
if her hopes might not be ill-founded. Ever since the priest
had been summoned in the night—and soon afterward sent
for the blind man to come and pray with him—she had feared
the worst for the wee boy.

And for Vangie MacGovern as well, though Renny tried
hard to shut *that* thought out of her mind. As yet she couldn't
bring herself to think about Vangie dying. She *wouldn't* think
about it.

The kitchen was hushed, as was the rest of the house. The
twins and Emma had been put to bed. Miss Susanna and the
Irish housekeeper had gone back to the Big House to see to
Maylee and the blind man's little girl.

Two hours or more had passed since Conn MacGovern had
shut the door of the bedroom, where he watched over Vangie.
Only the low voices of the blind man and the priest, who had
again come together to pray, and the sound of Nell Grace's
crooning broke the silence.

Renny didn't like the quiet. It made it harder to ignore her
own troubled thoughts. Because she wouldn't allow herself to
worry about Vangie, and since Nell Grace had taken charge of

the wee babe, there seemed no escaping the sickening waves of guilt that rode over her at frequent intervals.

If the MacGoverns' eldest son had only used his passage to America instead of giving it over for her, he would be alive now.

If Aidan MacGovern had come across with the rest of his family—if Renny had stayed in Ireland, where Conn MacGovern had wanted her to stay—then the dread news about their son's death would not have arrived this day. He would not have died in a shipwreck.

It was *her* fault. Hers. Never mind that Aidan MacGovern had chosen not to make the crossing with his family. Never mind that Conn MacGovern had failed to convince his son that he was being foolish entirely by letting a raggedy busker girl use the ticket in Aidan's place.

If she, Renny Magee, had not begged to come with them, grabbing at her chance for free passage as if it were her ticket to life itself, then perhaps the MacGovern lad would have changed his mind that day on the docks.

He might have, after all. Wasn't that so?

But the boy *hadn't* come across, and she *had*, in his place, and now Aidan MacGovern was dead. And even if Vangie survived her sickness and the birth of the babe, she might still die. She might die of the grief.

Renny's gaze went to the two men in the shadowed corner. The big blind man stood with a hand on the silver-haired priest's shoulder. Their eyes were closed as they continued to pray, but Renny could sense the sorrow in the blind man's face. He was a good man—a kind man—according to Maylee. Sure, and he must be, to spend the hours that he had praying for Vangie and the babe as if they were family.

Renny knew she should be praying too. She had tried, earlier, only to stop when the few words she'd managed to force up from the barrenness inside her spirit sounded wooden and meaningless entirely. How could she pray about the dreadful things that had happened? What was there to pray *for*?

Besides, it seemed wrong somehow to pray about the MacGoverns' tragedy when she might have been at least partly responsible for *causing* it.

Without warning, a fierce cry from the bedroom shattered the quiet of the house. Renny jumped and turned toward the bedroom door, as did everyone else in the room.

The sound of Vangie's mournful keening stabbed Renny's heart like a dagger. All the pain of the night before and the long, sorrowful day now came thundering down on her like an avalanche, pinning her beneath it and crushing her with its weight.

She stumbled from the chair and, without so much as a look in the direction of Nell Grace or the two men in the corner, made a lunge for the door, practically throwing herself outside, into the night.

She didn't care where she went, as long as she couldn't hear the sound of Vangie MacGovern's heart breaking.

TEN

WHERE SECRETS DWELL

WHERE ONCE SHE WALKED WITH GRACEFUL STEPS,
SHE FALTERS NOW AS BLIND.
SHE WALKS THE WAY OF HOPELESSNESS ·
WHERE GUILT AND SECRETS WIND.

ANONYMOUS

Andrew Carmichael had seen only one patient with symptoms similar to those of Natalie Guthrie. And since he had not been the lady's physician at that time, but only a medical student tagging along behind the great Dr. Cyrus Cooper, he had gained little from the case other than the disillusioning awareness that some illnesses can frustrate even the finest of physicians.

Late this afternoon, he had been summoned to the home of Edward Fitch, where Mrs. Guthrie lived with her son-in-law and his family. The heir to Fitch's Department Store and a highly successful attorney in his own right, Fitch was also a

former patient. Since recovering from a severe case of diph-
theria a few years past, the man had been quite outspoken in
attributing his rather startling recovery entirely to Andrew's
care.

Andrew, who had simply been filling in during another
other doctor's absence, had done his best to convince Fitch
that the man owed his recovery to the grace of God more than
to any "miraculous" cure effected by himself. In truth, there
was little *any* physician could do in the face of such a virulent
case other than to employ the usual treatment—which was
often ineffective. The grateful attorney, however, had chosen to
believe that Andrew had worked some sort of a providential
healing in his behalf, and no amount of protests to the contrary
could change his mind.

Consequently, Fitch had referred a half-dozen or so wealthy
friends to Andrew's practice. A few had made generous dona-
tions to hospital wings or children's homes at Andrew's request,
when they would have otherwise paid *him* exorbitant fees.
Although not entirely comfortable with spending his time
attending to the wealthy, who could afford any physician in
the city, Andrew wasn't so foolish as to ignore the benefits of
having a few patients who could afford to pay their bills on
time—and make an occasional contribution to needy institutions as well. So when Edward Fitch's carriage arrived for him
late Friday afternoon as arranged, he had gone willingly
enough, leaving Bethany to see to their one remaining home
visit for the day, an elderly widow on Houston Street.

Between Fitch and his mother-in-law, Andrew had by now
made quite a few calls to the opulent, but not ostentatious,
mansion. Although the residence itself seemed to sprawl over
an enormous piece of real estate, it gave an unexpectedly warm
impression of graciousness and family living. Andrew found

himself relatively comfortable when he called, and he had come to like and respect the heavy-shouldered attorney who resided there. He had quickly learned that the perpetual frown on Fitch's broad face in no way indicated bad humor, but was more the expression of a man who was always thinking, his mind constantly turning ideas over for inspection. Fitch gave himself no airs. In fact, were it not for the reputation of his family and the genteel elegance of his home, one would never have recognized him as a man of wealth and influence.

Fitch rose from his chair behind his desk as soon as Andrew entered the study. The two men shook hands but wasted no time on pleasantries.

"How is she?" Andrew asked.

Fitch shook his head. "It's been a difficult week. And today—well, she's worse than I've seen her for some time. Earlier this morning she was so nervous she was in a shake. Pacing the upstairs like a caged cat, not eating—she wouldn't even speak to my wife or the children." He paused, looking at Andrew. "Her mood changes without any warning whatsoever. One hour she's in a fever; the next she's so enervated she can scarcely communicate with any of us. That's how she is now— or was, last time I went up to check. I tell you, it's as if she's simply—falling to pieces."

Andrew couldn't argue with Fitch's observation about his mother-in-law "falling to pieces." That seemed to be exactly what was happening to Natalie Guthrie, and for no apparent reason.

But there *had* to be a reason. Apart from her obvious weight loss, which was only to be expected since her appetite had drastically decreased, she seemed to be in good physical health. Yet emotionally and mentally, the woman was clearly deteriorating.

"When I was here last week," he said, "you mentioned a

family vacation, to get her away from the city. Have you broached the subject with her yet?"

Fitch's expression turned sour. "You'd have thought we were trying to put her out in the street. She became almost hysterical. She used to love going to the lodge. Now she won't even entertain the thought of it."

He stopped, giving a shake of his head. "I'll admit I'm almost at my wit's end with her. And so's my wife. Why, the children are actually *afraid* of her. I can't bring myself to have her institutionalized, but she's having a disastrous effect on our home life."

He was looking at Andrew as though hoping for an answer, a solution, but Andrew had none. He had become more and more convinced that Natalie Guthrie's illness was emotional or mental in origin, but as to its specific source or treatment, he had no idea.

"I wish I had an answer for you," he told Fitch in all sincerity. "But I'm afraid I can only advise you to seek help from a specialist. Someone who focuses on . . . disorders of the mind."

Fitch scowled. "You mean one of those alienists? I'd never convince my wife to expose her mother to such a person. She believes it's all quackery. And I'm not so sure but what she's right."

Andrew tried for just the right words, for he understood the man's distrust of psychiatric treatment in general, even if he didn't entirely share it. Among the "better families" such as the Fitches, mental and emotional illness were subjects to be whispered about, not discussed openly. And physicians who aspired to treat those conditions were looked upon with either distaste or distrust. *Quackery* was a common epithet applied to those who practiced any kind of psychiatric care. Andrew himself had questions about some practices, yet knew of patients who had definitely benefited from attention to their mental state.

"Mr. Fitch—"

"Edward," the other corrected.

"Edward, I wish you and your wife would at least consider the possibility of psychiatric treatment. I'm at a loss as to what else to do for Mrs. Guthrie. And we both know she's getting worse, not better."

"Andrew, you're the only person outside the family who can even come near her these days. She won't leave the house, she won't accept callers—she won't even come downstairs if the children have friends in to play. Even if I could convince my wife to enlist psychiatric help for her, Mother Guthrie would most likely bar herself in her room and not come out."

Andrew knew Fitch wasn't exaggerating. He was certain he could arrange for a house call from one of the psychiatrists in the city, but that would avail nothing if Natalie Guthrie wouldn't see him.

"Well, let's go up," he said. "Perhaps I can at least calm her a bit."

—

Natalie Guthrie's condition appeared even more wretched than it had upon Andrew's last visit, two weeks previous. Despite her son-in-law's description of her earlier excitability, the woman slumped in a chair by the fireplace looked as if every last ounce of strength had been drained from her. A sickly pallor had replaced her usually flushed complexion, and her hair clearly had not been dressed that day. Her hands rested limply in her lap as if the bone structure had been liquefied and rendered useless. There was no hint of the self-possession or prideful posture that, according to her son-in-law, had once charac-terized her demeanor.

Her expression brightened only a fraction when Andrew

entered the room, and her greeting was a lethargic, low murmur of his name.

He went to her and took her hand, which he found to be cold. She made no effort to return his clasp. "How are you, Mrs. Guthrie?"

She looked at him with dull eyes. "I am . . . very tired just now, Doctor. Very tired."

Andrew nodded, studying her dry skin, her slack jaw. It struck him that Natalie Guthrie had given up. There was simply no life about the woman; she was virtually fading away.

But why?

Edward Fitch stepped up just then. "Mother Guthrie, is there anything I can have sent up for you and Dr. Carmichael? Some tea perhaps?"

She gave a faint shake of her head but made no reply.

"Andrew?"

"No, thank you. I'll just visit with Mrs. Guthrie for awhile."

Fitch glanced from one to the other, then excused himself and left the room.

"I'd like to examine you, Mrs. Guthrie. Why don't I have your daughter come in?"

She gave an idle wave of her hand. "Not today, Doctor. I don't want to be examined today."

Andrew tried to feign sternness with her. "You didn't want to be examined last time either. How can I help you, Mrs. Guthrie, if you won't even allow me to monitor your condition?"

To Andrew's dismay, she began to weep. He stooped low and took her hand. "I didn't mean to upset you, Mrs. Guthrie!"

She shook her head, the tears streaming down her cheeks. "I know you mean well, Dr. Carmichael," she said, her voice low and thick, her words coming slowly and in a monotone, "but you can't help me. You mustn't waste your time coming

here. Please don't bother with me any longer. Just . . . give me
something to help me sleep, won't you? Some laudanum or . . .
perhaps something a little stronger. I'm sure that's all I need."

She had made this request before, and once—only once—
Andrew had complied with a light sleeping potion, enough for
two nights. But he sensed that giving her anything stronger
could be a treacherous mistake. He knew all too well how an
innocent act, even on the part of a well-intentioned physician
who meant only to help, could turn a patient onto a path that
led straight to destruction.

He also knew this was no time to allow his sympathy for the
woman to override his better instincts. "I'm afraid I can't do
that, Mrs. Guthrie," he said, straightening. "I don't believe it
would be the best thing for you right now."

Unexpectedly, the dullness that had glazed her eyes only a
moment before was replaced by a flash of anger. The woman's
chin came up, her jaw tensed, and in that instant Andrew caught
a glimpse of the pride and a certain air of condescension that, in
a previous time, might have distinguished the woman's bearing.

"What exactly does *that* mean, Doctor?" Her voice was
surprisingly firm all of a sudden. Firm and even haughty.

Andrew recognized that this Natalie Guthrie might once
have had the hubris to intimidate her own physician. He
wasn't about to let this unexpected show of strength divert
him, however.

"Merely that a palliative isn't going to solve your problem,
Mrs. Guthrie. I'm interested in seeing you well again, nothing
less."

She stared at him. "And you don't trust me with laudanum,"
she said woodenly. Again her entire countenance changed. As
quickly as it had come, the imperious dignity had fled. Her eyes
glazed with tears, her shoulders slumped, and her chin fell.

"I will never be well, Dr. Carmichael," she said, not looking at him. "I want only to be less a burden to my daughter and her family. Caroline is the very best of daughters, and Edward is as good to me as if I were his own mother. But they don't know what to do with me, and the children—" She broke off, shuddering. "—the children avoid me. I believe . . . I believe I must consider going away. An . . . institution, perhaps, or even . . . I don't know . . ."

She had begun to ramble and seemed to be growing more agitated.

"Mrs. Guthrie, that's not an answer," Andrew hurried to say. "And it's not what your family wants for you. They love you. They want to help you—"

"I'm not worthy of their love! They can't help me! And neither can you!"

With a strength that surprised Andrew, she half rose from the chair, her hands gripping the arms as if to steady herself. Even in her agitation, she was deathly pale and trembling visibly.

Andrew moved, meaning to catch her if she fell, but she groped her way to her feet and stood staring at him, wringing her hands, her eyes darting everywhere but at him. "I'd like you to leave now, doctor. Obviously, you're not going to do anything for me, so please go."

Andrew sensed the woman was on the verge of hysteria, that arguing with her or trying to placate her might merely serve to increase her distress. Besides, he had nothing to offer her at the moment but a solicitude that to Natalie Guthrie must seem empty and worthless.

But in that moment as they stood facing each other, the thought struck him anew that this woman, once so stately and self-controlled, was being destroyed from within. And not from any mortal physical ailment, for he had exhausted every test at his disposal for some insidious illness. No, whatever blight had descended on Natalie Guthrie might be every bit as malignant as a cancer and as brutal as a punishing disease, but he was convinced it had taken deep root in her soul and was now spreading over her entire being, eating away at her body, mind, and spirit.

To his silent despair, he had to admit that she was right—that he couldn't help her, except perhaps through his prayers. All he could do, it seemed, was assure the woman that he had no intention of giving up, that he was committed to her healing. She responded with an agitated twist of her hands, and after another moment Andrew left the room and went downstairs to take his leave of a badly disappointed—and exceedingly frustrated—Edward Fitch.

ELEVEN

THE JOURNALS

OUR DEEDS PURSUE US FROM AFAR,

AND WHAT WE HAVE BEEN MAKES US WHAT WE ARE.

JOHN FLETCHER

By the time Andrew returned to the office, he was beyond tired. His joints had been aching since morning, his hands and wrists badly swollen. He'd even begun to wonder if the salicylates were losing their effectiveness. Had he used them so long and so frequently that their benefits were diminishing?

And if that were the case, then what was he to do?

He was too weary to think about that tonight. Yet he couldn't help but recall the plaintive expression on Natalie Guthrie's face when she asked him to give her "something to help me sleep."

Something to make the misery go away . . .

How well he knew that longing. And because he *did* know it

so well, he also knew why he dared not give in to the disturbed woman's plea.

Andrew sighed as he turned the key in the lock. He would just collect the newspapers and go on upstairs to his living quarters to rest awhile. Please, God, let there be no late-hour emergencies tonight. He badly needed a full night's sleep.

He stood in the open doorway to the office waiting room, looking around. Everything looked perfectly normal, just as he'd left it. Yet as he closed the door behind him, he was seized by the peculiar sensation that something was different, something was wrong.

An irrational sense of invasion stirred in him.

So strong was the sensation that he delayed entering. When he finally crossed the room, he glanced at the counter that divided the waiting area from the offices and examining rooms. Because both he and Bethany had decided they could do without a receptionist, at least for the time being, only the two of them had access to the files and other papers neatly stacked in place on the desk. Their appointment pads were still open to today's list of patients. Clearly, nothing had been disturbed.

But even though he saw nothing out of place, Andrew still couldn't shake the unsettling feeling that something was amiss.

He went to the larger of the two examining rooms and found the door open. He was certain he'd closed it. Out of habit, he always closed the doors to both examining rooms and his office when he left the premises.

The last of the day's light was gone, so the room was dark. Andrew lit one of the two gas lamps on the wall, then turned to face the room.

The first thing he saw was the window on the back wall. Someone had broken it from the outside. Shattered glass was strewn on the counter below and across the floor.

An evening breeze filtered through the shards of glass left intact, cooling the room. Andrew's first thought as he looked around was that one of the countless stray dogs that continually roamed the city streets was responsible for the chaos. But dogs didn't break windows, and no dog could have left behind such destruction and debris. Only human hands could have plundered the room with such violence.

The examining table had been thrown onto its side, and trash from the waste barrel had been pitched every which way about the room. Cabinet drawers had been overturned, their contents strewn onto the floor, along with towels and surgery pads and instruments.

His gaze went to the storage cabinets above the counter. Their doors hung open, the locks broken and thrown aside.

Andrew stumbled the rest of the way into the room and found the medicines that he kept locked inside the cabinets—including narcotics and anesthetics—now in total disarray. Some bottles had been overturned, others broken.

For a moment Andrew could only stand in shock, staring at the ruin before him. A vessel at his temple began to throb with pain. He whipped around, his heart hammering at the idea of what might be lurking at his back.

Nothing was there, and the ominous silence told him he was alone. Whoever was responsible for this wreckage had come and gone.

Fear traced the length of his spine as he stood staring into the hallway and beyond, into the waiting room.

He was shaking like a palsied old man as he turned back to the cabinets and began to rummage through the medicines, trying to recall the contents. Even though his hasty, nervous inspection was far from precise, he was almost positive nothing had been taken.

Why, then, had the room been ransacked?

He went to the second examining room and found much the same scene he'd left behind him. Here, too, the cabinet doors had been forced open, the shelves cluttered with broken bottles and spilled powders.

Slowly, fighting for his breath, Andrew began to back away, trying to think what to do. His first thought was an almost overwhelming sense of relief that Bethany was out of the office. Who knew what some larcenous thug or half-wild addict might have done to her had she been here?

But this couldn't have been the work of an addict looking for drugs . . . nothing had been taken!

Completely bewildered, Andrew stood leaning against the frame of the examining room door rubbing his right shoulder, which was on fire with pain. Then his gaze went to the open door of the private study he and Bethany shared—the door he always closed behind him.

His heart hammered against his rib cage as he walked toward the darkened room. After lighting the lamp on the wall, he saw his fears realized. His desk was a shambles—papers tossed everywhere, the drawers emptied and their contents strewn about. Books ripped apart and tossed from the wall shelving.

Mindless destruction.

Somehow he managed to still the shaking of his hands. He dropped down onto his knees and riffled through the debris. Patient notes, unpaid bills, correspondence—everything seemed to be here, though much of it had been crumpled and torn.

His journals.

Panic squeezed his heart and churned his blood as he looked around, then slowly got to his feet.

He had kept the journals most of his life—year after year of daily entries that tracked his time at medical college and then his experience in private practice, first in Scotland, next in the States. Accounts of his successes and his failures. The cases over which he had puzzled and agonized. The patients who had both frustrated and challenged him. His struggles and his sorrows. His health problems. His growing love for Bethany. Intensely personal and private, more spiritual in nature than merely a day-by-day accounting of his life, those journals revealed the very *essence* of his life.

And its secrets. Including his earlier drug addiction, known by no one here in his adopted country except Bethany. Not even Frank Donovan, his closest friend, knew the terrible secret of that other, dark period of his life.

It was all there, in the journals.

And the journals were gone.

Only God knew who had taken them.

Or why.

The fabric of his deepest fears fell away, revealing in all its horror the long-confined but never quite suppressed dread that some day, somehow, his past would be found out and he would be known for what he had been: an addict. A weak, pathetic addict who had risked everything—and nearly lost every-thing—for the sake of the narcotics that imprisoned him and held him captive.

Cold rushed in on him like a howling wind. Over the thun-dering of his heart and the roaring in his head Andrew thought he could hear the door to his hard-won peace—and any hope for future happiness—close with a resounding thud.

—

Half an hour later, Andrew was still trying to dismiss his urgent desire to go to Bethany. He wanted to be with her—he *needed* to be with her. But he didn't want to alarm her. Besides, her landlady would certainly frown on the impropriety of his presence in Bethany's flat without a chaperone, especially after dark.

He knew it would be best to wait until morning to talk with her here, at the office. But oh, how he craved the soothing effect of her presence, her warmth, her good judgment, at this moment.

Instead, he decided to summon Frank Donovan. He needed a policeman, but not just any policeman. Frank was not only his friend, but was acknowledged even by his contemporaries to be one of the shrewdest and most dependable officers on the force.

There was no denying that things were not quite as comfortable between them as they once had once been. In truth, Andrew still smarted a bit from Frank's thoughtless opinion about Bethany's "unsuitability" as a wife, his assumption that she wasn't likely to be as devoted a wife as she was a physician.

That argument had been months ago. Frank had said too much; Andrew had taken offense; and for several weeks the two had avoided each other. Lately, however, they had taken to having a chat whenever they happened to meet, and Frank was again stopping by the office for an occasional cup of coffee. Most of the time things seemed almost back to normal.

Even if that had not been the case, Andrew knew this was no time to let pride get in the way of common sense. He would send one of the newsboys who lived on the streets to find Frank and fetch him here.

Frank would know what to do.

It occurred to him that he would have to tell Frank about the journals—and that in turn would necessitate telling him at least something about what was *in* the journals.

Andrew recoiled at the very thought.

A man knows when he has another man's respect, even his admiration. Andrew had long been aware that, in spite of his friend's barbed sense of humor and his bluff demeanor, Frank held him in high regard.

What would he think once he learned the truth?

As he went to find a messenger, Andrew was surprised how much it hurt to think of losing Frank Donovan's respect—or possibly even his friendship.

TWELVE

Secrets of a Good Man

For the thing I greatly feared has come
upon me, And what I dreaded has happened
to me.

JOB 3:25

Andrew felt sheepish admitting, even to himself, how Frank Donovan's presence in the building eased his mind.

The big Irish policeman could be annoying, no doubt about it, with his ruthless sense of humor and his brash, jaded opinion of human nature. But at a time like this he was all business—deadly serious, with a keen, incisive way of assessing a situation for what it was. It didn't hurt that he emanated a kind of coiled strength, a powerful physicality that could explode any second with dire consequences. While this quality could be downright intimidating to those on his "bad side," Andrew found it reassuring to his own situation.

"You all right, Doc?" Frank said, taking off his hat and tossing it onto the counter in the waiting room.

Frank had spent only a few minutes inspecting the wanton damage of the office. Now he leaned against the counter in the waiting room watching Andrew, who had finally given in to the pain in his legs and sunk down onto a nearby wooden chair.

Andrew was anything but all right, but he merely nodded.

"Well, I'd say you got yourself an enemy. Any idea who it might be?"

Andrew looked up. "Are you saying this is not just a case of breaking and entering?" Even as he said the words, he already knew the answer.

Obviously, Frank did too. He traced his mustache with an index finger, his dark eyes boring into Andrew. "No, I'm not thinkin' it is. Who's got it in for you, Doc? Any ideas?"

"You must see this sort of thing all the time—vandalism and the like. Why do you think this might be—anything different?"

"What do *you* think it was?" Frank said, his gaze never wavering.

"A patient who thinks his bill is too high, perhaps?"

Andrew's attempt at lightness failed badly. Frank's arched eyebrow made it clear he was not amused.

"So what's gone missin'?" Frank asked. "You said there was no sign of any medicines taken. No other valuables?"

"Not that I could tell," Andrew said, massaging his swollen knuckles. "Everything seems to be here except . . . some journals from my office."

Frank frowned. "Medical journals?"

"No," said Andrew with a slow shake of his head. "Personal. Quite a few, actually. They go back a number of years."

"A kind of diary, then?"

Andrew nodded. "Yes. I expect you'd consider it foolishness, but I've always kept an accounting of—things that happen in my life."

Frank was studying him—*measuring* him—with a speculative expression. "I don't find any foolishness about you, Doc, and that's the truth. So, why would somebody be interested in these journals, then? And do you have a thought as to who that somebody might be?"

Andrew looked at him. "No." At Frank's skeptical look, Andrew said again, "I've no idea, Frank. Really. And as for—"

He stopped, humiliation washing over him.

"Doc?"

Andrew put his head in his hands and pressed his fingers against his aching temples. "There are some intensely personal things in those journals, Frank," he said without looking up. "Things I'd not want . . . anyone to know."

There was a long silence. Then, "Tell me something, Doc. Whatever is in these journals, could it hurt you at all?"

Andrew looked up, then dropped his hands to his knees. "Oh, yes, Frank. It could hurt me a great deal."

Frank pushed away from the counter but remained standing where he was, arms folded across his chest. "Well, see here, Doc. I don't need to know what's in those journals to help you get them back. But it might make my job a sight easier if you could at least give me an idea as to who might want to hurt you."

"Who—"

"Don't you see, Doc? Somebody's gone to a lot of trouble here." Frank made a sweeping gesture to take in the waiting room and the entire expanse of the office.

"But if you're right and nothing was taken save for your journals, then I'm thinking they made the mess simply to put a scare into you or at least rattle you a bit. And as for the journals themselves, from what you're tellin' me, they'd not be worth much to anyone but you."

He stopped. "Unless someone is looking to hurt you. Maybe embarrass you somehow, if there's anything of a nature in those journals that would lend itself to that."

The ache in Andrew's skull now escalated to a nearly unbearable pain. Between the headache and the fire in his joints, he found it almost impossible to think clearly.

But he could reason well enough to take in the awful truth of Frank's words.

"It wouldn't just embarrass me," he said, his voice strangled. "It could ruin me."

He heard Frank Donovan draw a long breath, knew the man was waiting for him to say more. When Andrew remained silent, Frank finally offered what he undoubtedly intended as an encouragement, but it only served to make Andrew more miserable as he realized that he couldn't afford *not* to confide in his friend.

"Well, we can't have that, I'm thinkin'," Frank said with a forced cheerfulness. "You're a good man, Doc—one of the few in this wretched city, I'll wager. You don't deserve to be treated so. I'll take care of this—never you worry."

Frank sounded awkward—and uncertain.

"Frank—"

"Just don't fret yourself, Doc. I said I'd handle it."

"Frank, listen to me."

Again Andrew lowered his head to his hands. He didn't look at his friend, couldn't bring himself to face the disappointment and disillusionment—and the disgust—that would surely register in those dark, merciless eyes when Frank learned the truth.

THIRTEEN

OLD KNIFE, NEW PAIN

WHO MADE THE HEART, 'TIS HE ALONE
DECIDEDLY CAN TRY US.

ROBERT BURNS

Andrew told Frank everything. He told him about his former drug addiction, making no attempt to soften his words when he described what he had once been, how low he had fallen, what a shameful wretch he was at that time. It occurred to Andrew that it was as difficult to relate his ugly story to Frank as it had been to tell Bethany.

But he went on, faltering only once or twice as he recounted how the addiction had been precipitated by a well-intentioned physician and instructor at the medical college who meant only to ease the agony of Andrew's rheumatoid arthritis. The hardest part came when he forced himself to describe, in some detail, what it had been like to give up the opium.

"You can't imagine," he said, his voice low. "No one who hasn't watched it or gone through it can begin to understand what it's like."

Frank broke in. "Doc, I've known my share of addicts. Don't put yourself through this. You owe me no explanations."

Andrew regarded his friend, tempted to take his suggestion, to stop right now and say nothing more. But that seemed too easy. For some inexplicable reason, he felt he needed to hold nothing back.

"You've known addicts, but have you ever watched one try to escape from the addiction?"

Frank hesitated, then shook his head. "No. Can't say that I have."

"I want you to know it all, Frank—every ugly, sickening detail. Maybe then you'll understand what those journals can do to me. Because it's all there, in black and white."

Frank said nothing, but his lean face went hard, and Andrew saw the mix of anger and pain glinting in his eyes.

"When an addict goes through withdrawal, he loses his personality, his self-respect, and whatever dignity is left to him, which in most cases is none. Sometimes, he loses his mind as well. He's nothing but a shell of a human being. The pain eats at your insides until you're a howling animal. You beg for the opium. You plead. You threaten. You pray to die. Every nerve in your body feels as if it's being stripped bare and set ablaze. Even your *brain* is pressed and squeezed beyond endurance. The pain—it's like nothing I can put into words."

He stopped. "And the worst of it is, you even lose the . . . the *shame* of what you've become. You lose everything, and yet you'd give up your soul for just one more time, one more hour, with the very poison that brought you to where you are."

"But you beat it, Doc," Frank said quietly.

Andrew shook his head. "Oh, no. I didn't beat it, Frank. An addict is never really cured. Just . . . rescued. God rescued me—is still rescuing me. Hour by hour, He sees me through a day. That's how it will always be for me. For the rest of my life."

Just as he had explained his deliverance to Bethany the night he asked her to marry him, he went on to relate to Frank how God had worked a miracle of healing through the caring heart and endurance of a friend, Charles Gordon. His roommate at medical college had eventually recognized Andrew's addiction and virtually forced his unwilling friend to accompany him to his family's home, where he proceeded to lock them both inside an attic room. For two weeks, Charles had prayed with Andrew, cared for him, and suffered with him through every stage of the torturous and demeaning withdrawal from the drug.

To this day, Andrew could scarcely bear to think of the abuse he heaped on his friend during that horrendous time. And yet his roommate had refused to give up on him. And because Charles persevered, Andrew had finally emerged from his private hell.

By the time Andrew reached the end of his account, he was so totally exhausted, so emotionally and physically drained, he could barely force the last few words out of his mouth. In the long silence that followed, he actually fought for his breath as if his heart and his lungs had been crushed.

He squeezed his eyes shut. "Everything I've told you . . . and more—it's all in the journals. It's all there."

So surprised was he to feel Frank's strong hand on his shoulder that he actually jumped, but he still couldn't bring himself to look up.

Frank cleared his throat. "Does Lady Doc know?"

Andrew nodded. "Yes, Bethany knows."

"And I'll warrant she thinks no less of you for it. Am I right?"

The memory of Bethany's quiet reassurance whispered at the edge of Andrew's mind as he shook his head. "Don't insult me, Andrew," she had said. "It would be a poor kind of love indeed that would allow the past to destroy the present and the future. It doesn't change the way I feel about you."

"Nor do I, Doc," he heard Frank Donovan say in a voice unnaturally soft and laced with an uncommon warmth. "Nor do I."

Andrew lifted his head. "What?"

"I think no less of you, Doc. In truth, though I'm sorry to hear you went through such a terrible time, I might even be a bit relieved to know you're not without a wart or two of your own, given the fact that I've so many."

Andrew stared at him, watching the familiar, thoroughly Irish smile spread slowly across Frank's features.

"You fuddled me something fierce, don't you know? It was never all that easy, seeing you as some kind of a blessed saint."

"Good heavens, Frank, I never intended you should think of me as any such thing!"

Frank's expression sobered. "But still, you're the best man that's ever crossed my path, and that's the truth. I expect that's why I had somewhat of a hard time with you—at first, that is. I kept looking for you to judge me."

Andrew uttered a humorless laugh. "I'd be the last to judge you, Frank—or anyone else, for that matter."

"Aye, in time I came to see that about you. All the same, Doc, mind what I say: You're a better man than you think, I expect. And sad to say, 'tis been my experience that there's no lack of scoundrels out there looking to bring down the really good men. No lack at all."

Frank dropped his hand away from Andrew's shoulder, pulled up a chair nearby, and straddled it, facing Andrew. "Now, then," he said, swiping a hand through his dark red hair, "I expect you've at least an idea or two about who might be behind this nasty business. So tell me what you think, Doc."

Andrew felt somewhat dazed—dazed and immensely grateful as it gradually dawned on him that both the woman he loved and his closest friend now knew the ugly truth about his past. They knew—and neither condemned him. Neither had turned away from him.

Once again, it seemed that God had poured His grace out upon an undeserving sinner's head.

The long, ragged breath of relief he pulled in was in itself a fervent prayer of thanks. He began then to tell Frank about Mary Lambert and her children. And about Robert Warburton, the well-known, much revered clergyman who had fathered those children—and threatened Andrew during a heated confrontation at Warburton's residence.

As he spoke, he saw Frank's mouth tighten, his eyes grow cold.

"But I can't actually believe Warburton has anything to do with this business," Andrew cautioned. "The man's threat was contingent upon my revealing what I know about him and Mary Lambert. But I've kept my silence, other than to tell Bethany and now you. I've given Warburton no reason to fear me."

He paused. "Besides, the man is a pastor. Even if he thought I'd spoken out about his affair, surely he wouldn't stoop to something so—sordid."

Frank's dark eyebrows shot up, then he scowled. "Doc, you'll pardon my saying so, but you can be terrible green sometimes. Didn't you just tell me this Warburton fella sired three illegitimate children?"

Andrew looked at him and nodded, feeling the heat begin to rise from his neck to his face as he realized what Frank was getting at.

"And didn't you say he treated this woman disgraceful and then abandoned her and their children?"

Again Andrew nodded. "I'm sure of it."

"And you don't think a man like that would stoop to something sordid?"

Frank shook his head, and Andrew felt thoroughly embarrassed now to realize how naïve he must seem to his friend.

"I take your point," he said before Frank could chastise him again. "I suppose it's possible."

"It's not only possible; I'd just about bet my badge on it, Doc," Frank said, getting to his feet and scooting the chair back to its original place. "A blighter like himself might not dirty his own hands in such a way, but there are those who wouldn't mind doin' it for him."

Andrew also stood. "Frank? What are you going to do?"

"I'll have to study on it for a bit," Frank said. His gaze flicked over Andrew. "You go upstairs now and get some rest, Doc. I'll bring a couple of the boyos over first thing in the morning, and we'll help you clean up."

Frank started for the door, then turned back to retrieve his hat. "Oh, and Doc? Watch your back, mind? Something tells me this isn't over."

He was almost out the door before Andrew stopped him. "Frank—"

The other man waited.

"Thank you."

Frank gave a wave of his hat and closed the door behind him, leaving Andrew to marvel, not for the first time, that the Lord had chosen to bless his life with such friends as Charles

Gordon and Frank Donovan. He hated to think where he would be without them.

———

The first article appeared three days later in the *Herald*. Andrew had finally settled himself at the kitchen table with a cup of tea and a piece of buttered bread for breakfast. He was thumbing through the pages of the newspaper when a letter to the editor caught his attention. After taking in the first few words, he set his cup of tea to the table with a trembling hand and read on.

Gentlemen,

It is with no small measure of distress that I feel it necessary to write this letter, in order to bring a matter of scandalous proportions to the attention of our unsuspecting populace. Were this not an issue that could endanger countless numbers of innocent people, I would choose to keep my silence rather than bring to light a situation that might better remain in the dark, where other unspeakable acts of like nature commonly dwell.

In this case, however, my great concern is to send a warning to those who might unknowingly fall victim to the unconscionable behavior of a practicing physician in our midst, a person of some reputation and distinction. The individual to whom I refer has under his care a significantly large and varied patient list, ranging from the shadowy and questionable inhabitants of the more squalid tenement sections of the city to the more respectable elements of our society.

This physician, who shall for the present remain nameless, while maintaining the appearance and pretense of being a qualified and conscientious medical doctor with only the good of his patients at heart, is in reality an addicted user of opium—a shameful, abominable narcotic.

Who can tell how many may have already fallen victim to the less-than-proficient skills and questionable morality of this individual?

Competent medical care is not only the right of every upstanding citizen; it is also a necessity. When one's physician, however, masquerades as an equal to those esteemed men of the healing arts while indulging himself in a degrading, despicable habit known to have enslaved its users by the hundreds—nay, by the thousands—a habit which causes erosion of all morals and the eventual devastation of the mind and body, it calls into question the trustworthiness of other members of his profession.

There is no telling what harm this particular "physician" could possibly inflict upon his innocent patients or the damage he might bring upon his noble profession. Just as shocking, if not more so, is the fact that he has recently associated himself with one of the disturbing number of female practitioners bent on carving out a place for themselves among the serious, conscientious members of the medical community.

I write with the genuine concern of a resident of our city who can not in good conscience stand by in silence, for to do so is to encourage an insidious and potentially disastrous situation.

A concerned citizen

Andrew forgot his bread and tea. He sat motionless, staring at the newspaper page in front of him, his breath coming labored and shallow.

Deep inside him, something dark and cold and ugly began to tear and open, like a once-healed wound newly stabbed and savaged by the same knife with a different blade.

Clearly, the vandalism in his office had merely been the forerunner of an even more devastating attack. Now the real evil had been unleashed.

FOURTEEN

DINNER FOR TWO

SHE BID ME TAKE LOVE EASY,

AS THE LEAVES GROW ON THE TREE;

BUT I, BEING YOUNG AND FOOLISH,

WITH HER WOULD NOT AGREE.

W. B. YEATS

Susanna stopped the moment she stepped into the dining room and found no one there. The room was aglow with candlelight, the table set with the best china, sparkling crystal, and snowy white linen. At each end, blue violets spilled from white china bowls.

But only two places had been set.

Puzzled, she walked the rest of the way in and looked around. "What in the world . . ."

Her question died on her lips as Michael came into the room. Susanna took a second look at him, suddenly glad she'd changed into her blue silk instead of relying on one of her everyday ginghams. He had obviously gone to some trouble with his own appearance. His gray jacket was informal but, as always, perfectly tailored for his tall form, and he'd donned a pearl-hued cravat that lent a touch of elegance. His dark hair, which lately seemed to be taking on more and more silver, had been brushed into as much control as was possible, given its natural unruliness.

"Susanna?" he said. He invariably sensed her presence in a room—a fact which never failed to please her.

"Michael, what's going on? Where are Caterina and your father? And Paul?"

"Papa and Caterina dined early, while you were at the MacGoverns'. Papa is seeing to Cati's bedtime. And Pauli is attending the birthday party for his friend Enzo this evening, remember?"

He touched her shoulder and, with the accuracy of one who was perfectly sighted, pulled her chair out and waited for her to be seated.

"So, we're dining alone?" she said.

He nodded and took the place to her right, at the head of the table. "*Si*, it is only the two of us tonight. And since that makes it a special occasion, I planned a special meal for us—a traditional Italian supper."

Susanna looked at him. "*Moira* cooked a traditional Italian supper?"

He smiled and shook his head. "No. Papa and I did most of it. I wanted to surprise you."

"You and your papa? Well—I *am* surprised. But your father should be eating with us if he helped to prepare the meal." It occurred to Susanna that Michael's father had been puttering about Moira Dempsey's kitchen quite a lot since he'd arrived at Bantry Hill. Or at least it seemed that way. With Michael being one of the few exceptions, anyone who dared invade

Moira's domain could count on being bullied off the premises. Either Riccardo Emmanuel had managed to ingratiate himself with the Irish housekeeper, or else he had somehow employed a few bullying techniques of his own.

"We prepared more than enough for Papa and Cati to indulge themselves earlier," Michael said. "They seemed pleased, so I hope you will be too."

He found her hand and covered it with his. "I wanted us to have an evening alone for a change. It seems as though we're always hurrying to do something, you in one place, I in another. And always there are others with us. Especially over the past weeks."

"I know. But there's been nothing to do for it except—manage. What with Maylee needing more attention lately . . . and Vangie's illness . . . and looking after Caterina, and then with your father here—of course, he's wonderful with Caterina—"

"I'm not complaining, Susanna," he interrupted. "It's just that I've missed you. I need to have you to myself now and then."

Susanna's heart turned over as she studied the dark, handsome face she'd come to love. "I've missed you too," she said softly. "And this is nice, Michael. I'm glad you thought of it."

Now that the surprise was wearing off, in fact, Susanna found herself exceedingly pleased. It was a rare occasion indeed these days when she and Michael found any time alone to just sit and talk for a few minutes, much less to enjoy a leisurely meal together. They worked together on the music, of course, but with Michael, work meant work, with little time spent on conversation. Besides, they were usually a trio, not a duet, for Paul almost always worked with them.

Just then young Rebecca MacBride, a local girl who sometimes helped Moira in the kitchen, appeared, balancing a tray with a soup tureen and bowls. Susanna discreetly slipped her hand away from Michael's and spoke to the girl before she left the room.

One taste of the smooth, clear broth and Susanna looked up. "Michael! This is delicious. What is it?"

"*Stracciatella*," he said, tasting his own. "Papa used to make this when I was a little boy. It's really just eggs and broth and cheese. A little parsley, some semolina. I'm glad you like it."

He took another spoonful of soup, then said, "So, how is Mrs. MacGovern getting along now?"

Susanna delayed her reply. These days, it seemed that any discussion involving Vangie MacGovern and her family was one marked not only by sadness and concern, but also by unanswered questions. It was difficult to gauge Vangie's condition, other than to observe that it wasn't good.

"Vangie is still—I don't know how to describe her, Michael. She's so awfully sad, of course. And physically, what with the difficult time she had—"

"With the birth," he put in.

"Yes." Susanna didn't like to think about that part of things, much less speak of it with Michael. She feared he might sense the apprehension that had taken root in her since the night she'd witnessed Vangie's ordeal.

Michael was keenly sensitive; he missed little, especially where she was concerned. Susanna would hate for him to learn that she was such a coward as to be frightened at the idea of bearing a child.

She *wanted* Michael's child—she truly did—and she knew she ought to be willing to give him as many children as he wanted. He was a wonderful father to Caterina. The thing with Michael was that he genuinely enjoyed being a father and treated the role not so much as a responsibility, but more as a joy, a delight.

If only she hadn't seen what Vangie went through . . .

"Where have you gone, *cara?*"

"What?" Susanna looked up to see him frowning, obviously waiting for her to go on. "I'm sorry. I'm really worried about Vangie, Michael. She doesn't seem to be regaining her strength as she should. But it's more than that—it's as if she's dead inside. She doesn't talk unless she absolutely has to, even to Mr. MacGovern. And the baby—she seems almost . . . indifferent to him. He's not thriving a bit, the poor wee thing."

She stopped. "Moira says a baby can sense when he doesn't have the mother's full attention or affection. It's a terrible situation, and there doesn't seem to be any help for it."

Again Michael found her hand—and again the MacBride girl interrupted them, this time to exchange their soup bowls for two small plates holding a variety of cheeses.

"You really cannot do anything more than you're doing, Susanna," he said after the MacBride girl exited the room again. "Andrew says the shock of losing the older son will most likely delay the physical healing."

Susanna sighed, pushing a piece of cheese around on her plate. "I keep thinking that if Vangie could only warm to the new baby, perhaps that would be the first step in healing her *heart.*"

Michael nodded. "*Sì*, you may well be right. There is something about a child, a new baby—"

Again he reached for her hand. "We've never talked very much about our own children, *cara*. What are your thoughts?"

Susanna froze. *Not now,* she thought, struggling for a way to change the subject.

She expelled a quick breath of relief when Rebecca returned to collect their cheese plates and proceeded to serve the main course—delicately herbed roast chicken and a bowl of small potatoes in a white sauce with parsley.

"You do realize," she said lightly after the MacBride girl was gone, "that you may have to roll me out of the room after this meal? I'm eating twice as much as I should."

"Good. Papa thinks you're too thin."

Unreasonably irritated by this offhand remark, Susanna bit down a response. Lately it seemed that Michael's father found quite a few traits in her that didn't meet with his approval. She was too young to understand world events—and therefore Riccardo tended to ignore any comment she might offer on the subject. She spent too much time doing household chores—she should let the staff take care of the menial tasks so she could spend more time with Caterina. Her presence tended to divert Michael's attention from his work—perhaps Paul's assistance would be less distracting. On the other hand, she needed to spend more time developing her own musical gifts—so she could be of *more* assistance to Michael.

And now she was too thin—as if she needed to have that particular fact pointed out.

"Susanna? Papa meant nothing. Don't be offended."

"I'm not," she said too quickly.

"You should know," he went on, "that my mother was, shall we say, a *substantial* woman. Like Papa. He thought she was the most beautiful woman in the world. He is, perhaps, a somewhat old-fashioned Italian male in the respect that he appreciates, ah . . . ample-figured women."

"But your mother wasn't Italian. She was Irish," Susanna pointed out.

"True, but they spent most of their time in Italy. Papa sometimes joked that the Tuscan sun had boiled most of the Irish out of her blood."

Susanna made no reply.

"You *are* offended," Michael said after a moment. "I shouldn't have repeated his remark. I apologize."

"Really, Michael, don't worry about it. It's not as if your father isn't right, after all," she said, trying for a note of lightness. "Rosa has offered the same observation."

He stopped eating and raised his head with a look of displeasure. "I hope you will ignore both of them, then." He smiled. "To me, you are perfect just as you are."

Again he paused. "We should change the subject. Why don't we return to the pleasant topic of children? *Our* children."

Susanna looked at him, swallowed hard, but tried to keep her tone level. "I don't think I'm . . . comfortable with that, Michael. We're not married yet, after all."

She sounded priggish and artificial even to herself, but she was determined to deflect this conversation. She simply wasn't ready for it, not yet. He would hear the unease in her voice and be disturbed, perhaps would even be impatient with her.

"But we are betrothed." He hesitated. "You don't think it proper for us to discuss having children?"

"It's just that Rebecca will be in and out to continue serving, don't you see? Wouldn't it be better to wait for another time?"

"Ah, *sì*." Seemingly satisfied with her answer, he patted her hand. "Could we at least discuss the date for our wedding, then? Don't you think it's time we settled on it and announced it?"

His expression, endearingly boyish, even eager, warmed Susanna's heart. "I expect we should, but how on earth do I plan a wedding with everything else that's going on right now?"

"You don't," he said easily. "We let Rosa plan the wedding. She has already offered, no?"

"She has, yes, but even with Rosa taking charge, I can't possibly be ready before—fall, at least."

He arched an eyebrow. "I was thinking of next month."

"Next month? Michael, you know very well that's impossible! I couldn't begin to—"

A corner of his mouth turned up.

"Oh! You're teasing me again."

"*Sì*, but not altogether. I would marry you tomorrow if it were possible." He leaned toward her, his intention to kiss her patently clear.

Rebecca MacBride picked that moment to return, carrying a large plate of fruit and a smaller one of fruit tarts.

Susanna warned Michael off by clearing her throat and saying, "Good heavens, Michael, how many courses are we to have?"

He shrugged. "Papa and I might have gotten a little carried away."

"Well, I won't fault you for it. Everything is wonderful."

"We'll have our coffee in the drawing room," he told Rebecca, adding under his breath for Susanna's benefit, "where we will also discuss a date—in the near future—for our *wedding*."

FIFTEEN

WITH THE WORLD SHUT OUT

WE TWO CLUNG TOGETHER—WITH THE WORLD
SHUT OUT.

ETHNA CARBERY

They sat together on the drawing room sofa. Michael reluctantly kept a discreet distance between them, sensing that Susanna might shy away from any real closeness with him tonight.

He found the thought particularly painful in light of his high hopes for the evening.

She had been distant for days now. He hadn't questioned her about it, instead had pretended he didn't notice.

But how could he *not* notice? It wasn't so much that she was avoiding him, but more that when they were together she seemed, if not exactly reserved, then at the least preoccupied, as if she always had something on her mind.

Something besides him.

The truth was that her uncharacteristic remoteness had been part of the reason he'd planned a private supper for tonight. He'd hoped not only to secure her undivided attention and set a firm date for their wedding, but also to discover whatever might be responsible for the peculiar way she was acting.

He realized it might be nothing more than the time she spent in caring for Caterina and looking after the many household and family affairs—including her efforts on behalf of Maylee and the MacGovern family. Not to mention the hours she spent each week helping him and Paul with his own music and the program music for the orchestra.

Still, he couldn't help but wonder if there was something more. He hoped it wasn't his father. The remark about her being "too thin" had clearly annoyed her. He should never have mentioned it. But Susanna had been withdrawn for days, not merely tonight, so any thoughtless comments on his father's part—or his own—couldn't be entirely responsible.

"Susanna? Before we discuss our wedding plans, there's something I need to ask you. And I want you to be very honest with me."

Even before he ventured the question, he could almost feel her tense.

"You seem—remote of late," he said carefully. "I'm wondering if something is wrong? Have I done something?"

There was just the slightest delay before she replied, only enough to let him know she was thinking about how to frame her answer.

"No. No, of course, not, Michael. There's nothing wrong."

"What is it then?"

"Nothing, really. I . . . suppose I've just been busy."

Her voice was thin, less than convincing.

"Susanna, I can't help but think it might be more than that. Hm?"

There was a long silence in which Michael found himself holding his breath. Was she already regretting her decision to marry him? Questioning her feelings for him? Had he rushed her into a relationship she now regretted?

He heard her sigh, and his chest tightened.

When she finally spoke, she sounded hesitant and strained—even somewhat ill at ease, as if she were trying to avoid something unpleasant. "I don't know exactly. I'm sorry if I haven't been very good company. Perhaps I am preoccupied. Lately, there's been so much to do. And there seems to be so much . . . unhappiness . . . all around us."

She paused. "With Maylee's condition growing worse and all that's happened to the poor MacGovern family, it's difficult to be . . . lighthearted. But it has nothing to do with you, Michael. Truly, it doesn't. I suppose it's simply affected me more than I'd realized. I'm sorry if I haven't been myself."

He let out an unsteady breath, unable to let himself completely relax, yet relieved to hear that he wasn't the problem.

"Don't apologize," he said. "I know it's been a difficult time for you. And no doubt I've put too much on you. I've let you do more than you should."

"No, Michael! It's not that. I do what I do because I want to, because I can't . . . *not* do it. I suppose I'm just a little tired."

He heard her attempt to force a little more brightness into her voice and realized that perhaps she *was* simply overtired.

"What can I do to make things easier for you, *cara*? I'll hire more help—"

"No, please don't, Michael! It would only mean more people about the house, and I honestly don't want that. Really, you're making far too much of this. I'm perfectly fine. Don't worry so."

He moved closer to her and took her hand. There was no response to his touch, but still he coaxed her closer. "It might be that we should at least consider hiring a nurse for Maylee. In the meantime, I'll see if Andrew—or Dr. Cole, perhaps— can come more often. Not only for Maylee, but for Mrs. MacGovern and the infant as well."

He hesitated. "And, Susanna? Please don't let Papa upset you. He means well, but he doesn't always think before he speaks. He adores you—I know he does."

He felt her tense, but only for a moment. "And I've grown very fond of him, too, Michael. Really, I have. I'm just not quite used to his ways yet. He's so . . . different from you."

He laughed a little. "Papa is different from anyone and everyone."

He took a deep breath, sensing that she'd begun to relax, at least a little. "So, then, you do still want to marry me?"

"Michael! You know I do. Why would you ask me such a foolish question?"

He drew her closer and pressed his lips against her temple, allowing himself to savor the warm softness of her skin, the sunny scent of her hair—Paul had told him it was the color of warm honey—the sheer happiness of holding her in his arms. "Then marry me soon, Susanna," he whispered. "We can be married here at the house. A simple ceremony—you said that's what you wanted, no? Nothing large or complicated. What do we really need, after all? Just you and I and our family."

He heard the smile in her voice. "A pastor, too, I think."

"Sì, all right. A pastor."

"And I'll need a gown. Nothing elaborate. But even so, it will take time."

He feigned a groan. "How much time?"

"Well, time for fittings, and the actual sewing—and alterations. It can't be done overnight, Michael. You see? One can hardly rush a wedding. You'll have to be patient."

He heard the note of teasing in her voice and felt something deep inside of him finally relax. She suddenly sounded happy—happier than he'd heard her for days.

"How patient?"

"Well . . . perhaps by late summer."

"That's months away!" he groaned.

A thought occurred to him. It would be just like her . . .

"Susanna . . . *cara*? Are you quite certain that you really want a simple wedding—a small ceremony? You're not just saying that because you believe it's what I want? Because of my . . . earlier marriage?"

She stiffened in his arms. "Your marriage to Deirdre has nothing to do with my wanting a small wedding, Michael," she said. "I simply don't want a large, showy ceremony with a lot of people. Only those closest to us." She paused. "I thought we'd agreed on that."

"*Sì*, we did. I merely want to make certain. I want you always to tell me what you want, Susanna, so there will be no misunderstandings between us. More than anything else, I want your happiness. Your happiness and your love."

He felt her hesitate, but then she surprised him by slipping her arms around his neck and drawing his face down to hers. "You will always have my love, Michael," she said softly. "And my happiness will be making *you* happy."

Michael thought his heart would explode. Gently, he framed her face with his hands, kissed her forehead, then found her lips. He kissed her and felt her breath quicken with his as he kissed her again, dizzy with the euphoria of her closeness.

He wished he never had to stop, wished he could keep her this close . . . closer . . . always. Suddenly, she released him, pushed him away. In that instant he heard his father's sharp voice and shot to his feet, bringing Susanna with him.

"Michael! Some wonderful news! You must listen to this! *Scusi*, Susanna, but this is very important!"

Shaken, Michael heard Susanna's gasp and knew she was mortified by his father walking in on them, finding them in such an intimate embrace. He reached for her hand and found it trembling.

He was both embarrassed for her and irritated with his father, who might have had the forethought to knock before bursting into the room.

On the other hand, he realized with some self-consciousness, it was he, not his father, who had put Susanna in this awkward position.

He felt Susanna try to tug free of his hand as if to flee the room, but he kept a firm grip. "No, stay," he said, his voice low. "Please."

"*Sì, sì*, Susanna! You must stay and hear this too!" His father sounded unaware that he'd interrupted a most private moment. Or if he did realize it, he didn't seem in the least contrite.

"Here, now—listen to this," said his father. "From the newspapers. It seems that Giocomo Conti is planning a new production of *Lucia di Lammermoor* next fall. And this is what you must hear, Michael. In this interview, Conti states that he will settle for no lesser tenor in the part of Edgardo than 'the legendary Michael Emmanuel!' Here, there's more—listen to this: 'I shall do everything in my power to coax the great Emmanuel out of his premature retirement. I mean to have him as Edgardo. No one else will do.'"

Michael heard the rustle of pages as if his father were waving the paper about in the air.

"You see, Michael? This is what I have been trying to tell you. Even the great Conti knows you are without equal. He refuses to allow you to waste your gift. You belong on the opera stage, and he does not intend to let you forget it!"

Michael took a long breath, striving for patience. "Papa—I made my choice, and I have never regretted it. You know this. We have talked about it many times. I have no intention of going back to the opera. Not ever."

"You are not pleased that a musician of Conti's stature would demand you for his own production of *Lucia*? Do you not understand the magnitude of such a compliment?"

"Of course I understand, Papa. And I am honored that he thinks so highly of me. But I have no interest in doing this. It is no longer a part of my life."

Michael felt Susanna squeeze his hand and knew a quick rush of gratitude for her understanding. She, more than anyone else, grasped why he had left the world of opera and why he would never return.

"*Insensato!*" his father exploded. "Foolish! God created you with a voice unlike any other. A voice of angels! And you throw it away as if it is nothing but filthy rags! I do not understand you, *figlio mio!* I do not understand you at all!"

Michael gripped Susanna's hand even more tightly. "I've sorry if I've disappointed you, Papa. But it's not as if I haven't tried to explain."

He could almost see his father shaking his head and waving a hand in the air.

"Explain, explain! There is no explaining how you could so carelessly discard such an opportunity. Such a great gift!"

And then he was gone, and Michael was left to feel an

uncommon weight of guilt and anger. Guilt that he couldn't be
what his father wanted him to be. And anger that he should
feel guilty for following God's voice instead of his own.

—

Susanna watched in astonishment and indignation as Riccardo
Emmanuel whipped around and went stomping from the
room, slapping the newspaper against the palm of one hand.
How dare he treat Michael as if he were nothing more than an
obstreperous child? It was bad enough that he had degraded
both of them by charging into the room unannounced, coming
upon them in a moment meant only for the two of them. But
to excoriate Michael for taking a path not of Riccardo's
choosing, when Michael meant only to be obedient to God's
will for his life—that was outrageous.

She fought to dismiss her own embarrassment. For
Michael's sake, she mustn't let him know that his father had
thoroughly humiliated her. But in truth, once again they had
opened themselves to temptation by being alone so late,
unchaperoned—and, admittedly, so in need of each other. Still,
she wished it hadn't taken Riccardo Emmanuel to point out
their folly.

"I'm sorry, Susanna," Michael said, his voice hoarse. "I
should never have put you in such an awkward position. This
is entirely my fault. Papa—I doubt he understands how difficult
it is for us, living under the same roof, loving each other, yet
compelled to avoid any real . . . intimacy. It won't happen
again, I promise you."

Susanna reached to put a hand to his lips. "Don't apologize,
Michael. You weren't alone in this, after all. I am just as responsible as you. I'm sorry for the way it must have looked to your
father. If there's any fault in our behavior, it falls to both of us."

Oh, Father, forgive me for allowing this situation to develop in the first place.

She studied him, wondering if she should actually voice what she was thinking. "I'm far more concerned that he's hurt you, Michael. This matter with the newspaper—he was just excited. I'm sure your father didn't mean to denigrate your work, Michael. He's very proud of you. You must make allowances. He doesn't understand."

"He never has. I fear he never will. I've tried to explain, but he doesn't hear me. He doesn't want to hear me, I think."

"He is proud of you and your music, Michael—all that you've accomplished," Susanna repeated gently. "But he's also very proud of your voice. I think he's even in awe of it, and I can understand that. So am I. But he hasn't been here, to know what it's like for you, and so it's difficult for him to accept the choice you made. He'll come around eventually. You'll see."

He gave a short nod, but Susanna could tell he was still dubious.

He drew her closer, clasping her shoulders. "Susanna, I am truly sorry that he embarrassed you. I apologize for that. But I won't apologize for the way I feel about you, for wanting to be with you. I can't help being impatient to make you my wife."

Susanna searched his face, saw the depth of his emotion— the love and the desire shadowing his strong features—and realized they mirrored her own. "And I'm impatient to *be* your wife, Michael," she said softly. "But you have a child to consider. We have to guard our reputations, not only for ourselves, but for Caterina's sake. We've known each other less than a year, after all, and Caterina's mother was my own sister. In August, it will be a year since I came to Bantry Hill. I think we must wait at least until then to marry."

His expression and the long breath he expelled told her he

was conceding. "I don't like it, but I suppose you are right." He dipped his head a little. "August, then. But no later."

"No later."

With one large hand, he cupped the back of her head, touching his lips to hers ever so gently, then brought his cheek to hers. "Susanna? Please understand—it isn't just physical need that makes me coax you to marry me soon. It's much more than that. I want to be with you. All the time. I want to know that you're my wife, that we belong to each other. I want you beside me every moment, in everything I do. I'm so eager to begin our life together, to be a family . . . you and I and Caterina . . . and *our* children. You do understand, don't you, *cara*?"

Susanna moved back just enough to bring a hand to his bearded cheek. "Yes, Michael. I understand. And I want . . . what you want. I truly do."

Even if what he wants is children?

For just a second, she felt the anxiety return to her in a flash of memory, an image of Vangie MacGovern in agony, a rush of fear and shame.

Then her gaze went over his face, loving the strength, the nobility of his features, the faint lines that webbed from his eyes, the humor and kindness about his generous mouth. And in that moment she knew that she loved this man so deeply, so completely, she would spend a lifetime giving him whatever he wanted from her.

Including a *houseful* of children, if that was his desire.

SIXTEEN

WITH CONCERN FOR THE GOOD

PEACE DOES NOT MEAN THE END OF ALL OUR
STRIVING. JOY DOES NOT MEAN THE DRYING OF
OUR TEARS.

G. A. STUDDERT KENNEDY

Early the next afternoon, while Caterina was taking her nap, Susanna picked up the section of newspaper Michael's father had discarded in the library the night before. Papa Emmanuel had left it folded open to the article he had found so exciting the night before. She merely scanned the piece, since she already knew its contents. In truth, it brought an unpleasant taste to her mouth as she recalled her embarrassment from the night before and the scene the article had prompted between Michael and his father.

She opened the paper and flipped through another few pages until she found the editorial section and settled in to read the letters to the editor. She read this section regularly, in part because they were sometimes so foolish as to be amusing, but also because they pointed out legitimate issues that needed to be brought to public attention.

By the time she neared the end of the first letter, however, and found the reference to the "shocking" association with a "female practitioner," Susanna's heart was pounding painfully against her rib cage.

Surely she was jumping to conclusions. But was she? How many physicians in the city of New York worked in partnership with a woman?

But the writer *couldn't* be referring to Andrew Carmichael! How could anyone accuse him of such a horrible thing? Why, the Scottish physician was goodness itself. Next to Michael, Susanna had never met such a godly, kindhearted man.

She stood there, her eyes locked on the appalling accusation. Even if it weren't aimed at Andrew, weren't readers likely to believe it was? Just look at how quickly *she* had latched on to the assumption.

An accusation like this could be disastrous to a physician. It could *ruin* the man!

She grabbed the paper and hurried out of the room in search of Michael, almost certain he knew nothing of this as yet. If he did, he would have told her. If he didn't—and if indeed the letter was directed toward Andrew Carmichael— Michael needed to know. The two men had formed a close friendship over the preceding months.

It was possible, of course, that Michael would likely think her foolish for suspecting the letter referred to Dr. Carmichael.

And she fervently hoped he would be right.

When at home, Michael made it a regular part of his daily routine to visit with Maylee early in the afternoon. He found the child wise beyond her years and her company a true pleasure.

As was usually the case, he found her door open. He rapped softly on the frame before entering.

"Oh, Mr. Emmanuel—I'm here, by the window! I just saw Mr. MacGovern take the black stallion out for a run. Isn't he wonderful?"

"Mr. MacGovern or the black stallion?"

Maylee giggled, and Michael walked the rest of the way into the room. He loved to make this child laugh. She had had so little reason for merriment in her brief, difficult life that to hear her break into genuine delight was a gift to his own heart.

"Do you have time to sit with me, Mr. Emmanuel?"

Michael felt for the chair across from her and sat down. "That's why I came, my young friend. And how are you this morning?"

He heard the slight delay before her reply. "I'm feeling very well, thank you."

Michael smiled a little. "Do you know, you always give me the same answer, Maylee? Now then, tell me—how do you really feel?"

"I feel . . . happy, Mr. Emmanuel," she said quietly. "Bantry Hill is so very beautiful, you see, and everyone has been so kind to me. It makes me happy just to be here."

Pleased, Michael leaned forward a little. "And it makes me very happy to hear you say that."

She was silent for a time, and Michael could almost hear her thinking.

Then, "I've been wanting to ask you if it's all right if I call you as others do—*Maestro*. 'Mr. Emmanuel' doesn't seem to suit you, but you're much too old for me to call you by your given name," she said, her tone altogether serious. "It would be disrespectful, I think."

Michael smiled at her directness. "I *am* very old."

"Oh, I'm sorry. I didn't mean that you're *very* old—"

Still smiling, Michael warded off her apology. "I'm teasing you. You may call me whatever is most comfortable for you, Maylee."

"All right, then. I'll call you *Maestro*, although I'm not exactly sure what it means."

"It's a word most often used for a conductor or a teacher, sometimes an expert in one of the arts, most especially music."

"That makes it sound just a little stuffy."

"Ah. Stuffy. That makes me feel even older, I think."

"But not as old as I, *Maestro*."

Michael winced at her soft reply. He extended his hand to her, and when he felt the small, fragile hand clasp his—the dryness of the skin, the fragility of the bones—he had to struggle to conceal the dismay that rose in him. "Is there anything I can do for you this afternoon, Maylee? Anything you need?"

She didn't answer right away. When she did, the brightness was back in her voice. "There *is* something."

"You've only to ask."

"Would you say a prayer for me? Like you did yesterday?"

"But of course." Michael leaned forward and extended his other hand to her. He was careful to apply only the slightest of pressure as she entrusted both her delicate hands to his much larger ones.

So dainty, these small hands, so tiny and fragile. The hands of a child, yet with the frailty of the aged.

Misericordia, Signore, misericordia.

Mercy, Lord, mercy.

"*Gesu*, Lord and Savior," he prayed, "I thank you for my

young friend, Maylee, for bringing her to us here, to our home, and for the inspiration of her faith, the light she has brought to Bantry Hill. Please may you wrap your love around her and carry her through the hours of this day, close to your heart . . . warmed by your grace. Let her heart sing with hope through the day—through all her days. Never may her spirit bow to anything but your majesty and your holiness, *Gesu*, and may her soul know no, ah . . . no boundaries save the fortress of your love. Amen."

Maylee echoed her own *amen*, the sweetness of her voice warming Michael's heart.

After a moment, he pressed her hands ever so gently, then stood. "I must go to work now," he said. "I hope you have a good day, Maylee. Is your friend Renny Magee coming to call?"

"I think so. I hope so."

Michael started for the door, turning back when she said, "Mr. Emmanuel—*Maestro*?"

"*Sì*?"

"I—may I ask you a question?"

"You may ask me anything."

"Can you . . . *see*—in your mind?"

"In my mind?" Michael smiled and nodded. "Yes, I can."

"Well, then, what do you see when you pray?"

Michael hesitated, momentarily confused. "I'm not sure I understand."

"I wondered . . . can you see Jesus? When you pray, I mean. Can you see Him?

"No one sees Jesus, Maylee, except for the Father," Michael said, still puzzled. "Why do you ask this?"

Her reply was slow in coming, her voice quiet. "Because when you pray, I can almost imagine that *I* see Jesus. That's why I like it so much when you pray. It's as if He's right here, in the room with us."

Michael swallowed. "And so He is, child," he said softly. "So He is."

—

Michael was at the piano in the music room when Susanna found him, working on a theme she recognized from one of the chorales in his *American Anthem*. She hesitated before entering the room, willing to postpone her unsettling errand for a moment to enjoy the music.

Something was new about the piece, which Susanna and Paul had already notated several times. The motif was the same, both haunting and beguiling, but the harmonies were different. Richer, somehow. Susanna always marveled at how Michael could take a piece she believed was perfect and, with a little tinkering, make it even more wonderful.

Papa Emmanuel was surely right that his son had a gift, a gift from God.

What he couldn't see was that Michael, far from squandering the gift, was working hard to offer it back to the Creator in the most faithful way possible.

She gave a little sigh, but then the music ceased as Michael called out her name. Pushing back the bench and rising to his feet, he turned toward her with a smile. She sighed again as she went to him.

—

Moments later, after listening to Susanna read the letter from the *Herald*, Michael stood with one hand on the mantel, the other kneading the back of his neck. His face was creased with concern, but he remained silent.

"Michael? I'm sure I'm being foolish, thinking this could be directed at Dr. Carmichael."

When he still made no reply, Susanna went on, her words rushing out. "Since the two of you have become friends, I thought you needed to know about it, in the event that someone is trying to start some sort of trouble for him."

"I'm afraid it *is* about Andrew," he said quietly, his profile hard and still.

Stunned, Susanna stared at him. "What makes you think that?"

With a deep sigh, he turned slightly toward her. "Andrew confided in me some months ago that there was something . . . regrettable in his past. Something of a most serious nature. I believe he was about to tell me the entire story. He seemed to think, since he and Dr. Cole have become not only Caterina's physicians but ours as well, that we should know about . . . whatever it is. I told him it wasn't necessary, that we needed to know nothing more than what we already did—that he was an excellent physician, and a friend, and that we trusted him as such."

He stopped, indicating that Susanna should sit.

She sank down onto the chair by the fireplace. She suddenly felt as chilled as if a cold wind had swept the room.

Michael remained standing, his voice heavy, as though burdened with a great weariness. "This is a very ugly thing, this letter. It would seem that Andrew has an enemy. A dangerous enemy."

"Whoever wrote this is insinuating that he's an opium addict! Surely, you don't believe that!"

He shook his head. "I don't know what to believe. But certainly I'd not believe anything in that letter unless Andrew were to tell me it was true. And I have no intention of asking him about it."

"As if he doesn't have enough trouble, with that awful arthritis he suffers from. Bethany worries so about his health."

Michael didn't answer right away. When he finally spoke, he seemed to be speaking to himself as much as to her. "I understand that his condition is exceedingly painful, at times even debilitating. I suppose there's always a possibility that because of the pain—"

He stopped, letting his thought drift off unfinished. "We can't speculate about something so important. If there's any truth to this letter—and I'm not saying I believe there is—but if there is, I know Andrew will explain it to us. Until then, we will say nothing of it to anyone else."

"I couldn't agree more. But it's impossible for me to imagine Andrew Carmichael indulging in such a vile habit! He's such a fine man, Michael."

"He is indeed. On the other hand, none of us is so strong we cannot fall. But whatever is behind this, it's clear that someone means to malign him. Even if this letter is nothing but lies, such accusations could destroy a physician's career. We need to pray for him."

"I simply don't understand why anyone would want to harm such a good man. I can't believe that Andrew Carmichael has ever hurt another human being."

Michael shook his head. "Surely, you are not so naïve as that, Susanna. We both know that good men aren't exempt from the effects of evil."

"No, of course not. But it seems so different when something like this happens to someone you know. And respect."

"*Sì*, that's true. Well, Andrew and Dr. Cole will be here tomorrow evening. Perhaps he will want to discuss the matter with us."

"I can't think what we'll say to them," Susanna said, getting to her feet.

"We will simply let them know we care and want to help however we can. Susanna, before you go—"

He reached out a hand, and Susanna went to him.

"About last night," he said. "There was no time this morning to talk with you. But I know you were deeply upset—"

"Oh, Michael, please—forget about last night! I'm perfectly fine. It was you under your father's gun, not I."

She saw him wince at her thoughtless choice of words. "I'm sorry. I didn't mean it that way."

He shook his head. "No, that's how it felt. But that's not what kept me awake last night."

She looked at him more closely, seeing for the first time the evidence of sleeplessness—the dark shadows under his eyes, the faint pallor of his skin. "What, then?"

"I think—no, I *know* I did you a disservice last night, and it bothers me very much."

"A dis—what are you talking about?"

"I should never have put you in the position I did. Being alone with you, behaving as I did—it was wrong." He inclined his head in a brief, formal bow. "I ask your forgiveness."

Susanna studied him, touched by the genuine contrition so obvious in his expression, his posture, his tone of voice. Sometimes she forgot just how *gallant* Michael could be. For all his worldwide travel and experience, and for all the renown and celebrity he had once enjoyed—and despite what his father and others might view as his "Americanization"—Michael was still very much of the Old World. At unexpected moments, he could display a courtly, even quaint, sense of propriety.

Susanna loved him for it. She also knew it would be a mistake to take his apology lightly. He had in no way compromised her virtue. He had not, last night or at any other time, made the slightest attempt to seduce her or lure to her into an improper situation. There was no denying that she'd been embarrassed by his father's unexpected and brash appearance. But being alone with Michael—and in his arms—had been as much her doing as Michael's.

Even so, she knew that his distress was real, that she should be careful in her reply. "It's not necessary to apologize, Michael. But thank you for caring enough to be concerned."

He lifted her hand then and touched his lips to it, a gesture that never failed to make her legs go weak while endearing him just that much more to her.

"I promise you can trust me to keep a closer guard on my feelings from now on," he said solemnly, still holding her hand to his lips.

Then he flashed that quick, boyish smile of his and added, "But only until August."

On that note, Susanna reclaimed her hand and hurried from the room, aware of the need to keep a close guard on her own feelings.

SEVENTEEN

A TIME TO FIGHT

THAT MY WEAK HAND MAY EQUAL MY FIRM FAITH . . .
HENRY DAVID THOREAU

W ithin the week, it was painfully clear that the letter to the editor in the *Herald* was affecting the practice of Andrew Carmichael and Bethany Cole.

Fridays and Mondays were ordinarily their busiest days of the week. It wasn't unusual to find the waiting room filled to capacity on either morning. But when Bethany arrived at the office on Friday morning, she found only two patients waiting, both of whom appeared too destitute to be choosy about where they went for treatment. The patient count had been light yesterday as well, although neither she nor Andrew had remarked on it.

She greeted the patients, telling them they'd be called shortly, then went to find Andrew. To her surprise, he was seated behind his desk with Frank Donovan standing across from him. The latter seemed uncommonly serious when he greeted her. Andrew, too, had no welcoming smile, but then he'd been desperately solemn and tense ever since the ugly letter had appeared in the *Herald.*

"Frank saw the letter too," Andrew said with no preamble. "He's convinced it was written by Warburton—or that he *had* it written."

Bethany glanced at Donovan and nodded. For once she agreed with the caustic Irish police sergeant.

"I still can't believe a clergyman would be capable of something like this. It boggles the mind, to think of a man of Warburton's prestige stooping to anything this low." Andrew stopped when the policeman uttered a sharp sound of derision.

"Many's the man who's plowed a crooked furrow in a straight field, Doc," said Donovan, crossing his arms over his chest. "Now tell me, what's the name of this woman Warburton was mixed up with?"

Andrew looked at him. "Lambert. Mary Lambert. But, Frank, you can't bring her into this! She's still too fragile."

Donovan pulled a sour face, then bent and splayed both hands on top of the desk. "Listen to me now, Doc. This bounder has brought bad trouble on your Mary Lambert as well as yourself. She more than likely knows the man better than anyone knows him, including his missus. And I can tell you that a woman who's been wronged by a man like Warburton is usually all too eager to pay him back."

Andrew shook his head. "Frank, Mary's not like that. And she's not well yet—"

Donovan's jaw tightened even more.

"Doc—have I ever tried to tell you how to do your job when you're sewin' someone up?"

"No, of course not, but—"

"Then don't be tellin' me how to do mine. I aim to take care of this nasty business, but you've got to trust me to do it my way. Now, where do I find this Lambert woman?"

Andrew hesitated another second or two. Then, "At the women's clinic on Baxter. I'd hoped to get her out of there before now, but there's no money to pay for a better place."

"And where are the younguns?"

Andrew frowned and leaned forward. "You leave the children out of this, Frank."

"I will if I can. But I want to know where they are, Doc."

"The boy's at Whittaker House," Andrew said after a heavy sigh. "The two little girls are at the Chatham Children's Home."

Donovan nodded, then straightened and left the office, his hat tucked under his arm.

Bethany turned toward Andrew, who sat holding his head in his hands, looking exceedingly weary. Her heart wrenched with worry to see him so . . . defeated. And after what she had learned of addiction while treating Mary Lambert, she couldn't help harboring another concern. In light of this heinous attack and the effect it was having on their practice—on their *lives*—what if he simply gave up? Was there a possibility he could succumb again to his addiction?

She shook her head, as if to throw off the ugly thought. It sickened her that she had even allowed it into her mind for an instant.

"Andrew, he's right," she said. "We're in over our heads with this. Let Sergeant Donovan handle it his way."

He raised his head. "Frank can be . . . ruthless, Bethany. Even the other men on the force keep their distance from him."

She laid a hand gently on his shoulder. "Maybe that's what

it will take to put a stop to this nightmare, Andrew. And he's right about Mary Lambert. She would know more about Warburton than anyone else. She might be able to tell Donovan something that will help."

"But Mary is still so—"

"Andrew! Will you please just this once think of yourself instead of everyone else?"

He reared back as if she'd thrown a rock at him.

Bethany fought to curb her impatience. One of the reasons she loved this man was for his goodness, his genuine concern for others. But he could also be impossibly naïve, and right now he needed to face facts.

"You're in trouble, Andrew! You need *help*. Robert Warburton knows you can ruin him if you choose. He means to destroy you *first*—you must see that! And you've no idea what he might do to Mary Lambert—or the children. Do you honestly think they're safe from the likes of him?"

He went pale. "You don't believe he'd hurt his own children?"

"Oh, Andrew, I doubt this man even considers them his own. And with what he's done to that poor woman so far—and to you—I wouldn't put *anything* past him. Don't you see? Mary Lambert and those children are as much a threat to him as you are—even more so."

She hesitated, unwilling to cause him more pain but determined to make him see that he was in real jeopardy. "There's no telling what a man like Warburton might do to avoid the kind of scandal Mary could create for him," she said, softening her voice. "You've already seen that he's not going to stand by and let his reputation be ruined. Please, Andrew, if there's any way to stop him from ruining *you*, you have to let Frank Donovan handle this."

He got up—with some difficulty, Bethany noticed—and

stood studying her with a worried look. Finally, he nodded. "I suppose you're right."

Pain ripped at her when she saw the hopelessness, the humiliation in his eyes. He was *ashamed,* she realized. Ashamed of a past he'd thought locked away, ashamed of what its revelation would mean to his patients, his practice—but most of all for what it would mean to her.

She moved closer and grasped his hands in hers. "Oh, Andrew! Don't look at me that way. We're not going to let this happen. We're going to fight it, and we're going to win! Don't you *dare* think anything else."

"Bethany," he said, his voice hoarse. "This isn't your battle."

Bethany lifted her hands to his shoulders and held him fiercely. "It's just as much my battle as yours! I'm going to be your wife, remember? Besides, where's your faith, Andrew?"

He frowned.

"I've heard you tell more than one troubled soul that we don't fight our battles alone, that the Lord is at the forefront fighting *for* us. That we've only to stand firm and believe, and He'll give us the victory."

A somewhat sheepish expression settled over him, and he even managed a faint smile. "Do you believe everything I say?"

"Do *you?*" Bethany countered.

He shook his head. "Hardly." He paused, searching her features. "But I do believe God's promises. And it seems you just reminded me of one of them."

Bethany framed his face in her hands and brought his head down to hers. "Then see that you don't forget it," she said, kissing him gently on the cheek and then the lips.

He pulled in a ragged breath. "Well," he said, his smile a little steadier now, "at least all this has accomplished one thing I never thought I'd see."

Bethany arched an eyebrow.

"You agreeing with Frank Donovan," he explained.

"It's not likely to become a habit."

"No," he said, cupping her chin in his hand. "I'm sure it won't."

He moved as if to kiss her again, but Bethany put a finger to his lips. "We have patients waiting. And we've kept them waiting too long."

He glanced toward the door. "Patients? Really?"

"Really," she assured him, freeing herself from his arms. "You take one, and I'll take the other."

—

Frank Donovan didn't give a second glance to the squalor surrounding the Women's Clinic and Convalescence Center. He knew it well. The area never changed, unless it was to grow even more disreputable.

He parted the boozers littering the street corner and dodged the debris—mostly broken bottles and animal waste—as he headed toward the steps. Inside, he paid little heed to the dingy surroundings, also familiar to him. Instead he went immediately to the matron, who sat at a table piled high with papers, dirty dishes, and a suspicious-looking pan covered with a towel.

There was a stench in the place that reminded him of a hospital smell but with some unidentifiable odor added—something sweet and putrid and unwashed. The woman at the table looked up as he approached. She wore a plain gray dress and threadbare white apron, and Frank noted that her hands were dirty. But then, in a place like this, perhaps it was difficult to keep them clean.

"Sergeant." The matron's tone made it clear she remembered him from their last encounter, which had been anything but agreeable. On that occasion he'd brought in a girl not yet sixteen years of age who had been repeatedly raped by a drunken stepfather, a piece of garbage who'd also passed consumption to the girl.

This particular matron had fought with Frank, insisting they could not take a consumptive patient who would likely spread the disease throughout the center. In the end, Frank had threatened to have the afflicted girl cough in the woman's face if she didn't find her a bed where she could be secluded from most of the other patients and see that she received the proper medical attention.

Her hostile glare didn't faze him now, although she gave herself airs as if he would be wise to show her some respect. To avoid laughing at the pretentious old scold, he fixed his stare on the sizable mole by the corner of her mouth.

"Where would I find Mary Lambert?" he said.

Miss Savage looked down her nose—no easy feat, Frank noted, since it was a long way down—and snapped her reply. "This isn't a hospital. We don't observe visiting hours."

"I'm not a visitor, darlin'. I'm the law."

If looks could maim, no doubt he would have found himself missing all four limbs. Miss Savage—a fitting name if ever he'd heard one—fixed a stare on Frank that sawed its way through every bone in his skull until it drilled a hole into his brain. He'd have thought the woman would warm to his endearment, for surely she would have heard precious few.

"Where," he repeated, "would I be findin' Mary Lambert?"

"Down the hall," she snapped, not looking at him. "Last room on the right."

"Ah. My thanks, dear."

Frank could feel the blade still slashing away as he turned the corner and started down the hall.

He walked in without knocking and stopped just inside the room. Two sets of sagging beds faced each other on opposite sides of the room, indicating it was shared by four women. At the moment, only two occupants seemed to be present.

"Mary Lambert?" He addressed his words to the woman nearest the door. A somewhat blowzy sort, with wild black hair and knowing dark eyes—attractive enough if a man liked her kind—she looked him over and smiled. Frank smiled back, a firm believer in the old saw about catching more flies with honey than vinegar.

He was surprised when a soft reply came from the far side of the room.

"I'm Mary Lambert."

The woman curled in the chair by the window was small and fragile and looked much younger than she must be in reality, given Doc's account of the years she'd been Warburton's mistress. She had a cloud of fair hair tied back with a yellow ribbon and was swathed in a wrapper that looked to have belonged to someone twice her size.

She was not what he'd expected, to say the least.

He turned to her roommate. "Would you mind takin' a turn down the hall, lass? I need to be speakin' to Miss Lambert alone, you see." He made sure she understood he wasn't asking.

The woman got up, glanced from Mary Lambert back to Frank, then gave a lazy shrug and left the room.

Frank walked over to the window where Mary Lambert sat and took a closer look. She quickly uncurled herself and straightened, one hand gripping each arm of the chair—most likely, Frank speculated, to still their shaking.

She was slender, too slender by far, and had the fair, porce-

lain skin of a fine doll-baby. With her wide blue eyes and
dainty features, she appeared impossibly young—and unmis-
takably frightened.

For a moment or more, Frank felt at a loss—a condition
almost unknown to him. He had been prepared to either turn
on the Irish charm and sweet-talk a fallen woman into telling
him any and every tawdry little piece of information that
might prove helpful in putting an end to that snake
Warburton's shenanigans or, if need be, bully his way past her
defenses until he had all he needed.

He was sorely afraid that this strangely childlike creature
staring up at him with the fearful eyes was going to make either
contrivance next to impossible. He suddenly felt as brutish as a
wild boar. Even his size, which most often served as an advantage, now seemed to turn him into a great clumsy oaf, and he
felt the irrational urge to keep his distance for fear his very
shadow might somehow bruise the slight woman before him.

With some effort, he yanked himself back to his senses and
pulled up a chair across from her. "We need to talk, Mary
Lambert," he said, forcing a hard note into his tone. "My name
is Frank Donovan—*Sergeant* Donovan—and I'm a friend of
Dr. Carmichael's."

The apprehension in her eyes flickered and ebbed just a
little, but she watched him closely, saying nothing.

"I need you to tell me everything you know about Robert
Warburton," Frank said. He hated the way she seemed to crumple under the impact of his words, but she had flummoxed him
just enough that he didn't quite know what tack to take with her.

"Everything," he said, doing his best to ignore the pain that
had replaced the fear in her eyes.

"From what I understand," he added, "you would be
knowin' him better than anyone else."

EIGHTEEN

DECISIONS FOR RENNY

BEHOLD ME NOW,
AND MY FACE TO A WALL,
A-PLAYING MUSIC
UNTO EMPTY POCKETS.

ANTHONY RAFTERY (TRANSLATED BY DOUGLAS HYDE)

R enny Magee walked the floor in the bedroom she shared with little Emma and Nell Grace, treading lightly to avoid waking the other girls. This was the second sleepless night in a row for Renny. Soon the sun would be up, and she had her chores to do no matter how poorly she was feeling. Her eyes were hot and sandy, and every few minutes her stomach roiled as if she might be sick. Was this, then, what it was like to be "flattened"?

Flattened was Conn MacGovern's word, and he used it often. It seemed to mean that he was either dead tired or famished to the point of queasiness.

Renny didn't think she was famished, although she hadn't eaten much at all yesterday, or the day before either for that matter. She definitely had that queasy, faint feeling that used to strike her when she was still on the streets of Dublin trying to earn enough coins for a proper meal.

The reason for her upset had nothing to do with hunger, but everything to do with the MacGoverns. Last night she had posed the question to herself as to whether she should leave. Sure, and no one in the family wanted her around any longer, since more than likely each of them blamed her for the death of their son and brother.

After all, she would have never made it to America in the first place had she not used Aidan MacGovern's passage to get here. Hadn't she begged to come in his place when he announced he'd not be using it? And hadn't Conn MacGovern argued up one end and down the other with Vangie that they shouldn't waste their son's ticket on the likes of Renny Magee?

But Vangie had prevailed. It had been Vangie who made the final decision to allow Renny to board with them.

By now, no doubt, Vangie surely regretted that decision.

The thought of Vangie sharpened the sickness in Renny even more. Vangie had been near to dying for days, lying still as a stone, ignoring the new babe—not eating, not talking, but simply . . . existing.

Even when she'd roused a bit and finally begun to nurse the infant, she paid him little heed, as if she would do what she must to keep him alive but no more. She scarcely looked at the poor wee thing. Indeed, Vangie hardly noticed anyone or any- thing these days, other than to give a nod by way of reply or a dull word of instruction. Even Conn MacGovern had had no success in coaxing her back to some semblance of the way she had been before their eldest son's death.

When Vangie spoke to Renny these days, which was seldom enough, she didn't actually look at her, just said what needed doing as she stared across the room or down at her hands. She didn't seem angry so much as merely . . . absent.

Renny thought angry might have been easier to take.

She supposed she would have to leave soon. Every day she thought to do it. But then would come the question as to how she could leave Nell Grace with most of the work of running the household and taking care of the new babe.

And how could she leave her friend, Maylee, the only true friend she'd ever had? Maylee was fading more and more every day. Lately it seemed to Renny that she would simply continue to fade until there was nothing left of her, not even a shadow.

Maylee depended on her, Renny knew—her visits, the "treasures" from outdoors, the foolish old tales and ditties from Ireland with which Renny often regaled her. How could she turn her back on Maylee?

And how could she ever bear to leave Vangie? *Especially* Vangie, who had become, at least in Renny's imagination, the mother she'd never had.

A mother who didn't want her, who in truth must resent her something fierce.

But, oh, wouldn't it be a terrible grief to no longer be a part of Vangie's life—of the MacGoverns' lives?

Renny looked around the pretty room with its big windows letting in the first light of dawn, and the thought of leaving it to again go on the streets was like a knife to her heart. But wasn't it more painful to live in a household where she wasn't wanted than to live on her own in a city of strangers?

Abruptly, she stopped pacing and went to wash her face. She had her chores to do, and the rest of the family would be up before long.

A few minutes later, she left the house quietly—and unnoticed.

———

That afternoon, Renny found Maylee waiting for her. The younger girl looked a bit better today, less pallid and tired. She also looked excited. She was propped up on a huge mound of pillows with another plump cushion at her midsection. On this the kitten—Maylee had named it Cookie—was curled up in a ball, sleeping.

Renny grinned at her as she handed over the day's "treasure"—a small glass jar that held a few marbles contributed by the MacGovern twins and a scrap of pale rose material with a faint green stripe. Nell Grace had sent the latter, thinking it might be just the right size for Maylee's doll bed.

"Oh, Renny, marbles! I've never had marbles before. And this material—it's so pretty! Are you sure Nell Grace meant for me to keep it?"

Pleased by Maylee's response, Renny perched on the side of the bed. "It was her idea. And the boys have plenty more marbles."

The dozing kitten stirred, stretched, and yawned, her attention immediately fastening on the piece of material in Maylee's hands. She batted at it a few times, then lost interest and tried to poke her head down in the jar of marbles.

"No, Cookie," Maylee scolded. "You'll get stuck, you foolish kitty. Here," she said, handing the jar to Renny. "Set it on the window sill, would you, Renny? That way the marbles will catch the light."

When Renny returned to the bed, Maylee was looking at her with an odd expression, and again Renny thought she seemed excited about something.

"The *maestro* wants to talk to you!" Maylee blurted out. "You're to go down the hall to his study before you leave."

Renny's hands turned clammy. What had she done?

"Why does he want to talk to *me*?" she croaked.

"Don't worry, Renny! It's a surprise. You'll see!"

"You know what he wants, then?"

"Yes . . ."

Renny could see that Maylee was both eager and reluctant to tell.

"Well?" she prompted. "*What?*"

Still the other girl hesitated. "Well, I don't know if I'm supposed to tell you . . ."

"Sure, you are!" Renny eyed her warily. "Am I in trouble for something?"

"No! Why do you always think you've done something wrong, Renny?"

Renny gave a shrug. "I used to get in trouble now and then." She paused. "Before, when I was a lot younger."

"Well, you're not in trouble now."

"I expect I can't be sure of that, now can I, since you won't tell what this is about?"

"Oh, all right! It's something really, really good, Renny! The *maestro* is going to ask you to play your tin whistle in the Independence Day concert! In the park!"

Renny stared at her friend. "What concert? What park? What are you talking about anyway?"

"On the Fourth of July—America's Independence Day—the *maestro* and his orchestra are going to perform in Central Park. It's a special celebration to celebrate the country's one hundredth birthday! And the *maestro* wants you to take part in it. He wants you to play your tin whistle! Aren't you excited, Renny?"

Renny made a face. "You must be mad entirely. Or else

you're funnin' me. Conn MacGovern says the—*maestro*—is famous. Him and his orchestra both. Now just why would a man like that be wantin' anything to do with the likes of me?"

Maylee's expression turned sober. "Why are you always so hard on yourself, Renny?" she said.

"I'm *not* hard on myself. I'm just trying to figure out what you've been eating that's made you crackers."

Maylee shook her head. "You're forever making light of yourself. Sometimes I just can't figure you out, Renny Magee."

Renny tapped her head and grinned. "'Tis because I'm smarter than you, don't you see? Now, what brought on this foolery about the blind man and my tin whistle?"

Maylee frowned. "He has a name, Renny. Don't call him 'the blind man.' Most folks call him *Maestro* because he's a great musician."

"Oh, he's a great musician, is he?" Renny shot back, enjoying a chance to tease her friend. "You wouldn't be sweet on him, now would you? I'd watch out for Miss Susanna, if I were you. She won't like you taking a fancy to her sweetheart!"

"Oh, Renny, you're . . . incorrigible!"

Renny hadn't a thought as to what *incorrigible* meant, but she could tell that Maylee wasn't really upset with her.

"Are you going to be serious or not?" asked Maylee.

"Yes, ma'am. Please, ma'am, go ahead with your story."

"This will be a *very* important concert. The *maestro* and his orchestra will be performing some special new music he wrote in honor of the United States. There will probably be *thousands* of people there, according to Miss Susanna."

Renny studied her friend. Confusion and disbelief warred with a flare of excitement. Maylee *couldn't* know what she was talking about. Could she? Why, the blind man—the *maestro*—had never even heard her *play* the whistle.

She didn't realize she'd voiced the thought aloud until Maylee replied.

"He has *so* heard you, Renny. Plenty of times. When you visit me—and outdoors too."

Still skeptical, Renny didn't reply. The man was Conn MacGovern's employer, after all, and the MacGovern was *her* employer. That being the case, the *maestro* was the head of this whole place and the boss of them all. Why would he even give her a thought?

Still, she'd have to say that he was always kind enough when they chanced to meet—which was seldom indeed. He never treated her like most of the grownups back in Ireland had, as if she were no more than a troublesome dog on the street. To the contrary, he was politeness itself. He would give her a smile and a funny little bow and call her "Miss Renny," almost as if she were a lady.

Ha! That was because he couldn't see her. One glance would tell him Renny Magee weren't no lady! Though Vangie had done her best to tame her hair, it more often than not stuck out like a destroyed bird's nest. And although she had taken to wearing a skirt now and again—only to humor Vangie, of course—she wore a pair of boy's trousers under the skirt so she could climb a tree whenever she wanted or go hiking in the woods without scraping her legs.

Maylee's voice jarred her back to her surroundings. "Renny? You're not afraid of the *maestro*, are you?"

Renny straightened. "I'm afraid of no man," she stated. "And certainly not a blind man."

Maylee looked hurt, and Renny instantly wished she could take her words back. "I didn't mean anything," she muttered. "But I'm not afraid."

In truth, she wasn't afraid of him. It was just that she never quite knew how to act around the man or what to say. It was strange, even uncomfortable, knowing he couldn't see her, when she could see him.

"Well," she said, giving a small laugh, "perhaps you ought to tell the *maestro* what I look like. That would take care of this peculiar notion of his, I'll warrant."

"See," said Maylee, "you're doing it again."

"Doing what?"

"Making light of yourself. The *maestro* wouldn't care what you look like, even if you were ugly as an old witch—which you're not. He wants you for the music you make with your tin whistle, not for the way you look." She paused. "You don't even know how pretty you are, do you, Renny?"

Renny burst out laughing. "Now I *know* you're crackers! You're touched in the head for certain, girl!"

Maylee just shook her head. "You ought to appreciate what you have, Renny. You could always look like me, you know."

Renny swallowed, suddenly feeling awful. Poor Maylee, too thin by far, and with her almost bald scalp and peeling skin and old-age spots all over her hands and arms. There was no denying that she looked more like a little old lady than a girl of eleven years.

"You're pretty too," she lied without a qualm.

Maylee smiled at her. "No, I'm not. But I will be someday."

Renny cocked her head and looked at her.

"Some day I won't look like my own grandmother anymore. I'll have a perfect body, and I'll be strong and healthy. Like you."

It dawned on Renny then, what the other girl was getting at. "You're thinking about heaven," she said.

Maylee glanced toward the window, where the late afternoon sun had struck the glass jar of marbles with shafts of light that made them sparkle and flare. "Yes," she said softly. "I think about heaven a lot."

When she turned back, there was a look in her eyes that squeezed Renny's heart and yet made her wonder at the stillness her friend seemed to wear like a cloak.

"Sometimes," Maylee went on in the same quiet voice, "I can't wait to get to heaven, so I won't look like this or hurt anymore or be a bother to others. Some day I'll be out of all this."

She glanced down at her frail body. "Some day I'll be able to be myself, the way I really am inside, instead of what people *think* I am now, when they can only see the outside of me. I'll be able to run. I could even challenge you to a race—what do you think of that? Or maybe I'll even be able to fly." She smiled. "I think it would be the finest thing of all, to be able to fly. To just throw off this ugly old body and fly free."

Renny didn't know what to say. She simply stood, staring at the floor and trying hard not to think about the day Maylee was referring to. Because that day would mean her friend would be gone. Gone forever.

"Now, then, Renny Magee," Maylee broke into her thoughts, her tone now brisk and matter-of-fact. "You just march yourself down the hall and listen to what the *maestro* has to say. I promised I'd send you to him when you arrived, so you mustn't wait any longer. Besides," she added, "I'm very busy. I'm making you a present for Easter."

"You're making *me* a present?"

Maylee nodded. "Easter Sunday is next week, and I'm making something I think you'll like. It's not much, of course, since I can't go out to get what I need. But Miss Susanna is helping me." She paused. "I love Easter, don't you? I love hearing about the empty tomb, how Jesus escaped from being dead and came back to life, to live forever."

Renny liked the story about Jesus rising from the dead, too, but right now her mind was racing, already trying to think of a gift—something special—she could get for Maylee. Only when the other girl gave her a stern look and wagged a finger at her, ordering her once more to "go," did she start for the door.

More than an hour later, Renny practically flew down the hill between the Big House and the MacGovern cottage.

Maylee had been right! The *maestro* had asked her to play her tin whistle at the concert.

There would be two fiddles, he'd said. Two fiddles, an Irish drum—the *bodhran*—and herself, with her tin whistle. She would be playing *his* music—music he'd written himself. A "selection" he'd called it, with an Irish "motif," whatever that meant.

He and Miss Susanna would help her with the music, he'd told her. "Although I expect you'll pick it up quickly, gifted as you are," he'd said.

Gifted. A great musician like himself had called her "gifted!"

Faith, and her not knowing the first thing about the dark squiggles on the paper he'd showed her or the fancy words he'd used in that Eye-talian way he had of speaking.

And she was to be *paid*, he'd said! She would be paid to trill a tune or two with some fiddlers and a drum.

Renny was tempted to pinch herself to make sure it was real!

She was nearly wild with excitement, so much so that not until she reached the back door did the thought of the MacGoverns and their troubles come barreling in on her. But the minute she stepped into the kitchen and heard the babe wailing in the bedroom and saw Nell Grace all teary-eyed with wee Emma squirming in her arms, it all came rushing back.

She felt a sting of guilt for allowing herself such happiness when the people she loved more than everything in the world were burdened with so much trouble.

Only then did she remember that she probably wouldn't even *be* here for that foolish concert in July. More than likely, she would be gone by then.

And so, more than likely, would Maylee.

NINETEEN

A Mother's Love

If I were drowned in the deepest sea,
Mother o' mine, O mother o' mine!
I know whose tears would come down to me,
Mother o' mine, O mother o' mine!
If I were damned o' body and soul,
I know whose prayers would make me whole,
Mother o' mine, O mother o' mine!

RUDYARD KIPLING

Conn MacGovern had known few days without worry over the past twenty years. Lately, he had known not even one.

Pitchfork in hand, he straightened, catching the perspiration on his brow with his shirt sleeve. He stood leaning on the door of Amerigo's stall, breathing in the pungent odors of the stables and the horses, staring at nothing, worrying about everything.

Behind him, the big black stallion threw his glossy head over the door of the stall, snuffled Conn's neck inquisitively, then snorted and returned to his restless pacing. They got along well, the big horse and the big Irishman. In a sense, they'd rescued each other—Amerigo from the brutal treatment of his previous handlers, Conn from a life of jobless misery in the slums of New York. Their chance encounter at the harbor, when Conn had managed to calm the frantic stallion and earned himself a position on Michael Emmanuel's estate, had seemed like a new beginning, a harbinger of hope.

But in just a few months—half a year—it had all gone sour.

Conn's stomach clenched and burned with the sense of dread that had hounded him for days. What with the pitiful look of his newborn son, the long faces of his other children, and his wife's unrelenting sorrow, he felt himself engulfed by despair. Even Renny Magee seemed hard-pressed to force a true smile these days, a stark departure from her usual tomfoolery.

Scarcely an hour went by these days when Conn wasn't struck anew by the memory of how he had failed his wife throughout the years of their marriage—all the times when he couldn't put food on the table, when they'd lost their home because he couldn't find work and had no money for rent, when he couldn't prevent his children's illnesses because they couldn't afford the needed medicines. Those past failures, bitter as they were, seemed small in comparison to his failure now to help his Vangie in her time of need.

Always before, it had been she who managed to buoy him and the children, to rally their spirits and keep their hopes high. No matter how hard things were, Vangie's strong faith invariably had held desperation at bay for them all.

But now it was Vangie who was drowning in despair, and he seemed helpless entirely to save her. Nothing he said, nothing he did, made a difference. It was as if her grief at the loss of Aidan was gnawing a hole in her spirit, eating her up from within, where no healing could reach the wound.

Conn had tried everything he could think of, but most of

the time he had all he could do to keep from giving in to his own grief and sense of hopelessness. In front of the children, he did his best to hide his pain and keep a cheerful face. The children needed a strong father they could depend on, a father with a backbone, not a weak-kneed whiner as fearful as a child himself. But the truth was that without Vangie's unflagging faith and optimism, he knew himself to be pitifully weak, a man undone.

The stallion made one more circle of his roomy stall, tossed his head, and gave the walls a purposeful kick just to make the point that he could escape the stable if he wanted.

"Ah, my boy," Conn told him with a rueful smile, "we'll be havin' none of that. It's wantin' your own way so strong that gets you in trouble."

He leaned both elbows on the top of the stall and reflected, "Guess it's what gets us all in trouble."

There was no escaping the fact that their son's death was, at least in part, his own fault. If only he hadn't waited so long to write and make peace with the boy, Aidan might have made the crossing sooner, thereby avoiding the doomed ship that had cost him his life. Or, if only he hadn't been so hardheaded and, as Vangie often accused him, bent on asserting his will with the lad all the time, perhaps Aidan would have come across with the rest of the family and they wouldn't have been separated to begin with.

If only . . . if only . . .

Conn knew no good could come of thinking this way. It did nothing but deepen the despondency in which he already felt trapped. What he needed to do was act, take steps to make things better. There must be something that would rouse Vangie from the state she was in, something that would make her smile again, allow her to hope.

But what?

He had asked himself that very question over and over again throughout these oppressive days, but there was never a reply, nothing but a cold and heartless silence.

The thought occurred to him that perhaps he and the children had depended too much and too long on Vangie. And now that she needed *them* to be strong for *her*, they didn't know how to begin.

Perhaps for the time being the best they could do was to lean on each other. If they could be strong for one another, then perhaps some of that strength would eventually find its way to Vangie and she would see that this was her time to depend on *them*.

Sighing deeply, Conn MacGovern picked up his pitchfork and opened the door to the next stall. Even when he didn't know what to do, he always knew how to work.

—

Vangie MacGovern stared down at the small red face at her breast. His tiny fists were clenched as if in anger, and he jabbed at her and the air even as he nursed.

Weak as she was, she tried to summon some nudge of feeling, some vestige of tenderness and maternal affection for the wee, wrinkled babe in her arms. A vague memory stirred in her, a remembrance of how, with the other children, she used to love this time of warmth and closeness.

These days she felt nothing—nothing but the inertia and fatigue and . . . deadness . . . that had become second nature to her. What was meant to be—and once *was*—an act of love and nurturing was now nothing more than routine, a task to be tended to, a duty.

Even though she knew she might be inflicting harm on her own child, Vangie found it impossible to shake herself free of the numbness that held her captive. The Wise Women in the village of her childhood believed an infant could sense the rejection or the indifference of a mother and claimed that such a child wouldn't thrive, but instead would eventually grow ill and perhaps even die.

But somehow even the memory of those horrible tales couldn't stir her to more affection for this babe. It was as if the part of her that had once held the capacity to *mother* a child had died in the same cursed shipwreck that took the life of her eldest son.

A cold shudder racked the length of her body, and the babe jerked and wailed. Automatically, Vangie placed him back at her breast, where he suckled even more voraciously, as if he feared that any moment she might cast him away.

She studied the babe, guilt clawing at her soul like a deranged buzzard. Not merely the guilt occasioned by her lack of feeling for her newborn son, but a guilt prompted by her previous resentment of Conn for not trying to make peace with their *firstborn* son—a resentment so fierce she had delayed telling him she was with child again until she could no longer hide her condition. And there was also the ever-present suspicion that, by allowing her bitterness and unhappiness to show, she had driven her husband to finally write Aidan in an attempt to reconcile and coax him into make the crossing to America.

If she hadn't made her misery known to Conn, he might never have written to Aidan, and if he hadn't written . . .

She choked down the acid taste of her misery, her heart seizing with another twist of grief. Weakness swept over her and, trembling, she called for Nell Grace to come take the babe.

—

After walking the floor for over an hour with her fretful baby brother, Nell Grace sighed and carefully put him down in his cradle, waiting to make certain he wouldn't wake.

Even sleeping, he seemed restless and agitated, as if he could find no comfort, no real peace. His teeny mouth twitched, his little hands knotted and unknotted, and his legs jerked beneath the blanket with which she'd covered him. Already his few wisps of hair revealed the same red hue as his mother's, the fiery red that all of the MacGovern children had inherited. And he had the high, broad forehead of their da.

And of Aidan as well.

Nell Grace shook her head. She wouldn't think about her older brother right now. Aidan was lost to them. Baby Will—*William,* named by Da with no input from their mother—was here. He needed her attention, needed the attention of all of them.

What he needs is his mum.

The thought wrenched her heart. Her mother had no interest in the infant boy who lay sleeping so unfitfully in the same cradle Emma had used only three years before.

Her mother had no interest in anything *these days,* Nell Grace thought, swallowing down a rising gorge of resentment. Mum had taken to depending on *her* for everything, especially anything to do with the baby. It was left to Nell Grace to comfort him when he cried, which was most of the time, to change his didies and give him his baths—indeed, to see to his every need, except of course for his feeding.

It just wasn't right. Nell Grace loved the poor wee boy dearly, but he needed more than a big sister. He needed his mother. But his mother—well, she just couldn't be bothered.

Nell Grace knew it was wrong to think so harshly of her mother—the woman who only weeks ago had evoked nothing but feelings of affection and admiration. But she couldn't help it. Of late it was difficult, sometimes impossible, to realize that the frail, lethargic woman sleeping in the bed nearby, indifferent to her own newborn son, was the same woman who had once loved her children so fiercely, sacrificing her own needs and desires to fulfill their wants and needs.

Aidan's death had turned her once beautiful, fiery mother, so filled with a zest for life, into a listless, mourning shadow of herself. Nell Grace could almost see her fading, slipping away from them like a cloud of smoke, carried out to sea by the wind.

Something had to be done. There *must* be a way to bring her mother—her *real* mother—back to them.

Nell Grace touched one finger to her tiny brother's smooth cheek. His mouth pursed, but he didn't wake. Tears scalded her eyes as she watched him. He was so precious, so perfect, so sweet.

So tiny . . . so fragile . . . so needy.

Abruptly she straightened, stalked across the room to the piled-up laundry basket, and began folding clothes with far more energy than the job required. And thinking, hard. She had to do something. There must be something that would draw her mother back to reality, force her to see how much baby Will needed her.

How much they *all* needed her.

And then, as she was shaking out one of William's little didies, an idea slipped into her mind—so quick it surprised and unsettled her. The fabric hung limp in her hands as she turned the idea over in her head.

Could it work? It wouldn't be easy. It would depend almost entirely on Miss Susanna and Mrs. Dempsey—would they be willing to help? And Renny Magee would have to do her part. But Nell Grace sensed that Renny would do anything to help, anything at all.

The real question in Nell Grace's mind was whether *she* could carry it off. She was terribly soft where both her mother and baby Will were concerned. Could she really go through with such a thing?

There was only one way to find out. But first, she must talk to Miss Susanna.

In the meantime, she could only hope she knew her mum as well as she thought she did.

TWENTY

An Unexpected Summons

God of mercy! God of peace!
Make this mad confusion cease;
O'er the mental chaos move,
Through it speak the light of love.

William Drennan

A few minutes after seven that evening, Andrew opened the door of his flat to find Edward Fitch's driver standing there, hat in hand.

"It's Mrs. Guthrie, sir," the man told him. "Mr. Fitch apologizes for the lateness of the hour, but requests that, if possible, you come right away."

Andrew was surprised but didn't hesitate. Mrs. Guthrie's condition must have worsened significantly for Edward to send for him so late in the day.

He fretted all the way to the Fifth Avenue mansion, trying to think of something he could do for Fitch's mother-in-law that he hadn't already thought of. He had exhausted every medical avenue he knew, and she had often been in his prayers, but her condition had steadily worsened. At this point, he was at a loss as to how he could help her.

Despite this frustration, he felt a measure of relief that he'd been summoned. Given the rumors that were spreading in certain circles, he wouldn't have been surprised if Edward Fitch had joined a number of his other patients—*former* patients—in shunning him.

Another letter had appeared in the papers just two days ago—this time in the *Tribune* and even more vitriolic than the one in the *Herald*. Without actually naming Andrew, this second letter left no doubt as to the target of its accusations, describing him as a "physician from the British Isles" and again making reference to his "female associate." Although it had been written in such a way as to make it seem penned by a different hand, Andrew was convinced the same person was responsible for both letters.

Predictably, Andrew and Bethany's patient load had dwindled still more following the appearance of the second letter. Humiliated by the venomous letters, the reduced practice, and the cold shoulder he was receiving at the hospital, it was all Andrew could do not to give in to the depression that lurked continually at the edges of his spirit.

A part of him was enraged by the unfairness of it all. Warburton, if indeed it *was* Warburton behind this heinous campaign, seemed invincible in his efforts to destroy him, while Andrew felt virtually helpless to defend himself.

He couldn't deny the charges completely—not when his journals partially confirmed them. In order to make a rebuttal, he would have to admit that he *was* an addict at one time. And such an admission, for many, would do nothing but confirm the allegations. Among some of his colleagues and his patients, there would be no forgiveness, no quarter given—only the speculation that one was never free of such an addiction.

And in all honesty, he couldn't refute *that* charge either. Who knew better than he that, for an addict, there always loomed the danger of falling from grace?

Why had he ever been so foolish as to confront Robert Warburton? That singularly unpleasant visit had accomplished absolutely nothing for Mary Lambert and her children. It had incurred immeasurable trouble—and quite possibly total ruin—for himself. And Bethany, who had worked so hard and made so many sacrifices to practice her chosen profession, was in danger of being ruined as well.

She tried to appear untouched by the whole wretched business. But he had seen the pain in her expressive blue eyes, even when it was masked by anger. He would die before he'd hurt her. And yet she *was* being hurt, and hurt badly, by these malicious attacks. She didn't deserve what he had brought down upon her—any more than he deserved *her* and her love.

The idea of giving Bethany up for her own sake occurred to him daily, even though he couldn't bring himself to entertain the thought for more than a moment. If he were a stronger man, a better man, he would free her from her promise to marry him. Instead, he needed her more than ever.

He hated himself for wondering, but he couldn't help but question whether Bethany would altogether reject the idea of bringing their engagement to an end.

—

He found Natalie Guthrie noticeably weaker. The deterioration of both her physical health and her mental stability was so dramatic that Andrew, who thought he'd seen her at her worst, was shocked.

She was a forlorn figure, her shoulders hunched as she sat on a small chair near the fireplace, where, in spite of the mildness of the evening, a fire blazed. She looked up as her son-in-law left the room and Andrew walked the rest of the way in. Every vestige of the dignity and pride that once lined her elegant countenance had disappeared. Her skin was ashen and her hair had gone almost white. The combination gave her a bloodless, almost ghostly appearance.

He could tell she had been weeping, and the moment their eyes met, she began to weep again, a racking, punishing seizure of sobs that shook her entire body. Andrew quickly went to kneel in front of her, taking her hand to steady her, but saying nothing.

When she finally quieted, she motioned for him to pull up the chair from beside the bed. "Please sit with me for a while, Dr. Carmichael. There's something I must tell you."

Andrew seated himself and leaned forward a little, waiting.

"Today—" She looked at him, her eyes glazed with a hint of the familiar wildness he'd come to expect in her. "—today I decided to . . . end my life."

Alarmed, Andrew again reached for her hand, but she shook her head. "No, it's all right. I'm telling you this so you'll know how desperate I've been. Besides, as you can see, as with everything else I've attempted, I lost my nerve and couldn't do it."

She paused, gave a small sigh, then went on. "I was able to pray today," she said, wringing her lace handkerchief into a rope. "I haven't prayed for a long time, not really *prayed.* I've . . . 'said my prayers,' given lip service to the effort—that's all. For so long, the words have seemed meaningless, as if they simply bounced off the walls and fell back at me.

"But today—I don't know why, but today was different.

When I tried to pray, I . . . I simply fell apart. It was as if I were breaking into pieces. It was actually painful. Physically painful. I finally just . . . threw myself at God and begged Him to take me, to put me out of this unbearable misery. I did, doctor—I begged Him to let me die. I suppose that was a terrible sin, but I just felt I couldn't go on any longer."

Again she broke off and sat watching Andrew, her eyes now clear. She was obviously gauging his reaction to her words.

"Something . . . happened," she whispered. "I can't explain it—I don't understand it. But I tell you, doctor, that God spoke to me in that moment. He somehow—I don't know how else to say this—He broke through to me, through the cloud of sickness in my soul. He stayed my hand from harming myself. And He impressed upon my heart that I was to send for you."

A chill edged its way down Andrew's spine. That *something* had happened to Natalie Guthrie, he didn't doubt. And there was no doubting the fact that she meant to make him a part of it.

But why?

"I delayed, not wishing to bother you," she continued. "But the more I hesitated, the more desperate I felt. Somehow I knew I *must* confide in you."

Andrew swallowed, for the life of him unable to imagine what could be driving the woman—and a little reluctant to find out. Yet he couldn't doubt her earnestness. He knew that whatever had possessed Natalie Guthrie to summon him here this evening was of monumental importance to her.

She leaned closer, still studying him with a peculiarly intense expression.

"Tell me, Dr. Carmichael," she said, her words coming slowly now, her voice thin and strained. "Do you believe that a secret sin can drive one to the edge of madness?"

TWENTY-ONE

A HEALING TRUTH

THOU MUST BE TRUE THYSELF
IF THOU THE TRUTH WOULDST TEACH;
THY SOUL MUST OVERFLOW IF THOU
ANOTHER'S SOUL WOULDST REACH!

HORATIUS BONAR

Andrew sat staring at Natalie Guthrie, shaken by the blunt and entirely unexpected question that hung between them. He had to remind himself that the woman was obviously speaking of her own sin, not his.

He formulated his reply carefully. "Yes, I suppose I do believe that. It seems to me that sin is very much like acid."

She was still watching him closely. "Acid?"

"Yes. If sin remains unconfessed and unacknowledged, I think in time it—in a manner of speaking, of course—can burn a hole in one's spirit. And that, in turn, it can quite possibly lead to all manner of illnesses, including disorders of the mind."

Natalie Guthrie looked strangely satisfied by his reply. "Yes! Yes, that's it exactly! And I believe that's what has happened in my life, doctor! My sin has finally eaten a hole in my spirit, and perhaps in my mind. Oh, I knew you'd understand!"

She was growing quite agitated, and Andrew put a hand to hers to try to calm her. "Mrs. Guthrie, what is it? What do you want to tell me?"

"Oh, Dr. Carmichael! You have no idea of the dreadful thing I've lived with all these years. You can't imagine—"

She stopped, again wilting into the demoralized woman he'd seen upon entering the room. Andrew gave her a moment, and eventually he could see her making a determined effort to pull herself together.

"My daughter must never know," she said, searching Andrew's eyes. "Neither Caroline *nor* Edward can ever know what I am going to tell you."

Andrew gave a nod of assent. "You have my word that whatever you say to me will remain strictly between us."

She waited two or three seconds more, then glanced away, toward the other side of the room. "Caroline is . . . illegitimate," she said heavily. "My late husband was not her father. He never knew. Caroline doesn't know. I've never told a soul the truth until today."

Somehow, Andrew wasn't surprised. This wasn't the first time it had occurred to him that Natalie Guthrie's condition might be prompted not by a disease of the body, but by a sickness of the soul—a condition he understood all too well. He made no reply but simply waited in silence for her to continue.

Her voice grew a little stronger as she went on. "It doesn't really matter who her father was. I don't want to talk about him, not even to you. It's enough to say I was . . . infatuated. I was quite young, and he was an older man, very cosmopolitan.

I told myself he took advantage of my almost ludicrous naiveté. The truth is, I was flattered by his attention, and I'd been day-dreaming about romance, as girls of that age will sometimes do, and—well, it happened, that's all. Only once. But—" she shrugged. "Merritt, my late husband, had been courting me for more than a year, and when I first realized I was going to have a child, I agreed to marry him. I . . . also agreed to a very brief engagement."

The tears were falling again as she lowered her head. "I never told Merritt about the . . . the other man. If he suspected, he kept it entirely to himself. He was a good man, my Merritt," she said, her voice unsteady. "He really did love me, and in time I grew to love him. After a while, I couldn't bear to hurt him, and if he'd known the sordid truth about my . . . indiscretion, it *would* have hurt him. Terribly."

"So I've lived with the knowledge of my sin and with the harshest kind of self-reproach every day of my life since. Truly, doctor, especially in this past year, I have longed for death, just to be free of the guilt."

She covered her face with her hands, her shoulders shaking as she lapsed into another bout of weeping.

Andrew knew this was no time for platitudes, so he simply waited for her to regain her composure. And while he waited, he prayed for her.

When she finally dropped her hands away from her face to look at him, her features were contorted by exhaustion and grief, her eyes red and swollen from unrelieved weeping. But Andrew thought he detected a new clarity and even a kind of strength in her gaze.

"Mrs. Guthrie? I must ask you: why do you think it was so important that you tell *me* about this?"

She unknotted her wrinkled handkerchief and wiped her

eyes. "I'm not sure," she said. "I thought perhaps *you* might know."

Andrew shook his head, trying to digest what he'd heard and why he'd been . . . *selected,* if that were the case, to hear it.

"I believe I've finally been forgiven."

Her words fell quietly between them, like drops of rain on soft ground.

"I'm so glad, Mrs. Guthrie," Andrew said, greatly pleased but still puzzled.

She nodded. "I've asked forgiveness before, of course. But to tell you the truth, I never once believed God *had* forgiven me. In fact, I was convinced He *wouldn't* forgive me. I had no excuse for what I'd done, and I'd deceived my husband and my only child all those years. Why should God show me any mercy?"

"Why should God show any *one* of us mercy?" Andrew said. "But go on—please."

She leaned forward. "Something happened today, Doctor. I don't understand what it was or why it happened. But while I was praying this afternoon, something changed. It was as though God put His arms around me and *told* me all was well. And I was forgiven—I just *knew.* But I also knew that I had to . . . to confess to someone else. I had to tell *someone* the truth, the entire ugly, terrible truth. But I couldn't tell Caroline or Edward. I simply couldn't. And then your name came into my mind like a banner and wouldn't go away until I convinced Edward to send for you." She paused, then added, "And I think I know why."

Andrew smiled a little. "Then I must admit you are a ways ahead of me, Mrs. Guthrie. Why?"

"Because," she said, again worrying her handkerchief between her hands, "I know you're a very wise man, doctor—a godly man. I need your advice as to whether I must tell Caroline or if I may simply keep my silence."

Andrew ran a hand over his forehead. The woman was asking for wisdom he didn't have. How could he possibly answer such a question?

"Mrs. Guthrie, I don't see how anyone can decide that for you. You can only act on what you truly believe is best—for you, and for your daughter."

He almost added that she'd also need to be ready to bear the consequences if she *did* tell her daughter she was illegitimate, but he caught himself. Now wasn't the time for such a caution.

"But what do you *think*, doctor?" Before he could reply, she went on. "I have to admit I'm terrified by the very idea of admitting my sin—and my deceit of all these years—to my daughter," said Mrs. Guthrie, her voice trembling. "I don't know if I can actually bring myself to hurt her in such a terrible way, and I can't see how such news could benefit her. But I suppose I'm also being selfish. I can't imagine how I could possibly endure—the loss of her love."

This was definitely not his province. Natalie Guthrie was an intelligent woman. She would have to think this through for herself, and Andrew didn't envy her dilemma. But the Lord had brought her to this place. Surely He would also guide her to make the right decision about what, if anything, to tell her daughter.

Suddenly, he remembered the night he told Bethany about his opium addiction—how frightened he'd been that he would lose her once she knew about his past.

But he *didn't* lose her.

"I can't tell you what to do, Mrs. Guthrie," he finally said. "I'm not nearly as wise as you seem to think. But let me try to reassure you of one thing. Sometimes we badly underestimate the people we love. I don't know your daughter very well, but I *have* seen the love and devotion she feels for you. Please understand, I'm not suggesting that you necessarily *need* to tell her the circumstances of her birth—that's for you and the Lord to decide. What I *am* saying is that if you reach the point where you believe you *must* tell her, then try to have enough faith in her—and in her love for you—not to expect the worst. Naturally, it will be a tremendous shock. But I truly believe that love is almost always strong enough to bear the truth."

He reached to free one hand from the handkerchief she was wringing. "It's fair to say that the truth can hurt," he admitted. "But it's just as important to remember that the truth can also *heal.*"

In that instant, Andrew sensed something trying to work its way to the surface of his own mind, but it disappeared as quickly as it had come. He gave her hand a gentle squeeze, then stood. "I'll stop in to see how you're doing tomorrow. In fact, I'll be sure to do just that, because somehow I don't expect you'll need me much in the future."

A hesitant smile slowly broke across her face, and she got to her feet. "Even if you're right about that, Doctor," she said, her voice still somewhat tremulous, "please don't ever think you need a reason to stop by and see us. You will always be welcome in this house."

As he started down the hallway, Andrew was surprised to realize just how much her words had meant to him. It had been quite a long time, he thought, since he'd felt really welcome anywhere.

With *that* thought, he recognized the beginnings of an unwelcome burst of self-pity and shook it off before it could tighten its grip.

—

Downstairs, he spent a few minutes with Edward Fitch, trying as best he could to explain the change in his mother-in-law's condition without revealing anything Natalie Guthrie had told him in confidence.

"You honestly believe she's going to recover?" Fitch asked hopefully.

"I don't think there's any question," said Andrew.

"Was this—was it all in her mind, Andrew? Some kind of hysteria?"

Andrew thought for a moment before replying. "No. Not entirely. Mrs. Guthrie has also been suffering from exhaustion and anemia—mostly because she hasn't been eating or sleeping as she should. She's had a difficult time of it, so her body's resources have been fairly depleted. But I believe you'll see a marked improvement over the next few weeks. Just be patient with her."

The other man studied him closely. "You're not going to tell me what that 'difficult time' was all about, are you?"

"Can we just accept the fact that Mrs. Guthrie has turned a corner and leave it at that?"

"How very cryptic of you, Andrew."

Andrew managed a smile, but it quickly fled at Fitch's next words.

"I'm deeply grateful to you for your help—and for your patience with us. Especially since I'm aware that you've been going through your own, ah, difficult time."

Andrew had no intention of getting into his personal problems with Edward Fitch, but the other wasn't to be put off.

"Gratitude aside, I just want to say that the calumny presently being attempted on you and your reputation isn't going to work. I can't imagine anyone who knows you believing a word of it."

Moved by the attorney's show of trust, Andrew said awkwardly, "Thank you, Edward. I appreciate that. But—"

"All the same," Fitch interrupted, "I'd strongly suggest that you make a public statement and defend yourself, even bring suit against the perpetrator of this outrage." He cracked a sly smile. "And I just happen to know where you can find yourself a good attorney, should you decide to take such action."

Caught off guard by the suggestion, Andrew stumbled over his reply. "Why—I hadn't even considered such a thing. Besides, the truth is—"

Fitch made a dismissing gesture with his hand. "You owe me no explanation, Andrew. All I need to know is that you are most definitely not guilty of what this lunatic is accusing you of. If you ever had such a problem—well, that's past history, and quite frankly I couldn't care less. But again, I hope you'll at least consider a public defense of some sort. You're an excellent physician, and you're a good man. But you're in a position where doing nothing could conceivably cost you your reputation and your career. If there's anything you need to divulge about your past, I'd urge you not to be afraid to do so. Whatever it is, it couldn't be worse than the garbage these scandalmongers are dishing up."

Fitch paused, then added, "The truth can be a formidable weapon against these kinds of tactics, you know. And don't forget the words of our Lord—that the truth will make us free. The Gospel of John, chapter eight, as I believe you know."

Surprised, Andrew looked at him. "You're a believer?"

Fitch burst out with a laugh. "Don't look so shocked! Even lawyers can be saved!"

Embarrassed, Andrew tried to cover his gaffe, but Edward

Fitch wouldn't have it. "It's all right, Andrew! I'm used to getting that look when I step onto my soapbox. But nevertheless, I hope you'll consider what I said. Now, I know you need to get home to your supper. I believe Thomas is waiting to drive you back. And, Andrew?"

Andrew waited.

"Thank you. On behalf of Caroline and her mother—and myself—*thank you.*"

Andrew thought he might have a little more spring to his step as he left the Fitch residence and started for the carriage. Despite the troubles that had been wearing so heavily upon him for days now, he was acutely aware he'd been doubly and richly blessed in the course of just one evening.

He was also aware that he had some very serious praying and reflecting to do about all the discussion that had taken place tonight regarding *truth*. More than once he'd felt that familiar nudge that signaled that the Holy Spirit was trying to get his attention.

And somehow he couldn't quite shake the feeling that Natalie Guthrie's unexpected summons this evening had been as much for *his* sake as her own.

TWENTY-TWO

A Job for Nell Grace

THERE IS ALWAYS HOPE

FOR ALL WHO WILL DARE AND SUFFER.

JAMES CLARENCE MANGAN

Caterina was one step away from being completely out of control.

"I'm going to the circus—the circus—the circus—"

"Caterina! Either you take five deep breaths," Susanna cautioned, "and stand perfectly still until I finish your braids, or else I'm calling your papa in here to settle you."

Had she *ever* seen the child this unruly?

Only at Christmastime, she decided, and the day of her grandfather's arrival. Well, there was also the day of her *own* arrival, Susanna remembered. But surely all children didn't turn into such monkeys over a circus, did they?

As she attempted to secure her niece's right braid for the third time, Susanna realized that most children probably *did.*

"There," she said, giving the stubborn braid a final tug. "You are ready to go."

That was the cue Caterina needed to begin chanting and bobbing up and down again. Susanna turned her around by both shoulders, unable to suppress a smile at the girl's high spirits as she held her firmly in place.

Papa Emmanuel and Rosa Navaro were treating Caterina to a day in the city, which would include the child's first visit to P. T. Barnum's "Greatest Show on Earth." She had been practically wild for over a week now, ever since she'd learned of the outing. Indeed, Susanna had announced to Michael more than once that, in future, any plans that might lead to excitability were to be kept secret until the very hour of the big event.

Caterina threw her arms around Susanna's neck and pulled her forward for yet another hug. "I *love* you, Aunt Susanna! Is it time to go yet?"

Susanna tugged the child's other braid, laughing at the little minx and her exhausting energy. "I *do* hope so!" she teased. "Otherwise, I'm going back to bed and hide under the covers."

Caterina kissed her on the cheek and then, with surprising strength, tugged at Susanna until she got to her feet. "Let's go downstairs and see if Grandpapa is ready!" she urged. "I hope he knows we can't be late for the circus!"

Downstairs, to Susanna's huge relief, they found Papa Emmanuel ready and waiting. Michael and Paul had come to the door to see them off, and when Caterina saw her father she practically leaped into his arms.

"Papa! Don't you wish you were coming with us?"

Michael hoisted her a little higher and smiled at her excitement. "Of course, I do. But cousin Paul and I have much work to do before our concert next week, so we must stay at home." He kissed her soundly on the cheek, then set her to her feet.

"You are going to have a wonderful day, Cati. Nothing is more fun than the circus. You're a very fortunate little girl, to have a grandpapa who takes you to such special events."

Susanna was surprised to see Caterina suddenly grow solemn. "I wish Maylee could come with us, Papa. I feel so bad for her, having to stay in her room all the time now. She can't even come to the table with us anymore."

Her niece's words brought an ache to Susanna's throat, and she noticed the flurry of pain that crossed Michael's features. He stooped to his daughter's level and pulled her into his embrace. "I know. But Maylee wouldn't want you to be sad on her account. You go with Grandpapa now and enjoy yourself. Perhaps you will say a prayer for Maylee on the way to the ferry. And, Cati?"

"Yes, Papa?"

"You make me very proud, to know that you remember someone less fortunate even when you are so happy. I know Jesus is pleased too."

Caterina hugged him once again before turning to her grandfather and taking his hand. By the time they stepped out onto the porch, she was singing again.

Both Michael and Paul turned to go back down the hall, but Susanna stopped them. "Michael, wait. I know you're busy, but I need to ask you about something."

When Paul made as if to leave them alone, Susanna said, "No, that's all right, Paul. Please stay. I'll only take a moment."

She explained then that Nell Grace MacGovern had been to the house early that morning, asking if there might be work for her to do through the day.

"Here?" Paul said, his eyes wide. "At the house?"

Susanna curbed a smile. Paul was so badly smitten with the MacGovern girl he could scarcely speak her name without stammering.

"Yes. For a few hours a day."

"But isn't she very young?" said Michael.

"Not too young to work. And she implied that she needed the extra money."

Michael frowned. "The MacGoverns need more money? I'll raise MacGovern's wages. I should do so anyway. The man deserves it."

"Wait, Michael," said Paul, putting a hand to his cousin's arm. "Perhaps Nell—perhaps Miss MacGovern is wanting to earn money of her own. She's not a child, after all."

"So I am told," Michael said dryly.

"Well, just so you know," Susanna put in, "Moira could certainly use the help. And so could I, " she added.

"What about Mrs. MacGovern?" Michael said. "Is she well enough now to do without the girl's help?"

"I asked Nell Grace that very question. She told me that Renny Magee is willing to take on extra responsibility so that Vangie won't need to overdo."

"There!" Paul said. "It will all work out, no? Don't you think it's a good idea, Michael? Since Susanna and Moira are in favor of it?"

Susanna looked at Michael and saw the slight twitch at one corner of his mouth. "Obviously, *you* are in favor of the idea, Pauli," Michael said. "All right, then, it's fine with me. You decide on her wages, Susanna." He stopped. "Does Moira know about this?"

"Yes, and she actually seems pleased," Susanna replied. "Moira is slowing down, Michael. I really do think she needs the extra help."

He nodded. "Good, then. And, Pauli?"

Susanna knew he was feigning the stern expression he suddenly adopted.

"You be very careful around this girl. She is quite young—"

"She is a young woman," Paul offered.

"—as I said, she is *quite* young, and I suspect Conn MacGovern is not one to tolerate a man playing light with his daughter."

Paul's face flamed. "You know I would never do that! Not with any woman! And especially not Nell Grace—Miss MacGovern."

"I rather imagine that in the case of Conn MacGovern and his daughter, Pauli, you must avoid even the *appearance* of dallying. I have the distinct impression that he is most protective of his family."

Paul sighed. "*Sì*, Michael. You do not have to warn me of this. I know the man." He brightened. "But surely there can be no harm in my speaking with his daughter from time to time? And now I must leave you. I have much to prepare for our day's work."

Susanna watched him as he turned and went down the hall. "He's practically skipping," she said to Michael.

"Love will make a fool of the best of men," Michael offered just before kissing her on the cheek and following his cousin.

—

"I'm sorry, Mum, but I have to do this. We need the money."

Nell Grace MacGovern had steeled herself for an argument from her mother. She'd known this wouldn't be easy, especially since she was already dodging volley after volley of guilt. But *something* had to be done, and she could think of nothing else.

"We don't need the money so badly that you should hire

yourself out as a servant! And how am I to get along while you're up at the Big House all the time?"

"You'll be fine, Mum. And I won't be there all the time. Only a few hours a day. Da says he can check on you often, and Renny is going to assume more chores. She's already doing a great deal as it is, you know. She's a good worker, Renny is. And the twins will help as well."

"The twins will be at school most of the day," her mother pointed out, her tone bitter. "And Renny's not one to handle the babe. She says she doesn't feel easy with such a . . . *responsibility.*"

Nell Grace knotted her hands behind her back, bracing herself as she said, "Well, but you're doing so much better, now, aren't you, Mum? You don't need Renny or me as much as you did. This will work out just fine, you'll see." She paused. "It's important that I do this, Mum."

"Important to who? That cousin of Mr. Emmanuel's? He's the *real* reason you're going to work up there, isn't he?"

Nell Grace felt the heat rise to her face. "No, he is *not* the reason!"

It was the truth, she told herself. She knew Paul Santi was sweet on her, and she liked him well enough. Maybe a lot more than well enough. Every time she was around him, she took on the strangest feelings, and her brain seemed to turn to pudding.

But she wasn't doing this because of Paul Santi. She was doing it for her mum—and for baby Will. She knew it might not be the best idea in the world, but it was her *only* idea for the time being, and she was going to try it.

Her mother was silent, and Nell Grace thought perhaps this wouldn't be as difficult as she'd feared. She was wrong.

"I'm going to talk to your da about this, Nell Grace. I don't think for a moment he'll go along with your foolishness."

"I've already talked to Da. He said it's all right."

Something flared in her mother's eyes—something Nell Grace had not anticipated. She realized then that what she was seeing was fear. Her mother was actually afraid.

But afraid of what?

"I can't—I can't take care of the baby by myself," her mother argued, not looking at her. "I'm not strong enough yet, Nell Grace. I can't—manage alone."

"You won't be alone, Mum. Besides, didn't the doctor say that the more you do from day to day, the sooner you'll get your strength back?"

"He doesn't know everything. What does a man know about having a baby? The birth was so hard . . . and after losing Aidan . . ."

Her mother's words drifted off, unfinished. She made a weak gesture with her hand and slumped back in the chair.

She was actually whining.

Vangie MacGovern whining—Nell Grace could scarcely believe it. Her mother had always been *death* on whining. The MacGovern children simply were not allowed to whimper or complain. If they did, they'd be taken to task as soon as word reached Mum's ears.

More to the point, the whining was working, and Nell Grace could feel herself about to relent. Any minute now she'd give in and say she was sorry and she wouldn't go to work at the Big House after all.

No! She wouldn't give in. She couldn't. If there was a chance at all of helping her mother and her wee baby brother, she had to take it. No matter how difficult Mum made it, she must stand up to her.

"Well, Mum, we'll work it out, I'm sure," she said before her resolve failed her entirely. "I start tomorrow, so I'll spend this afternoon tidying the house and cooking something ahead."

Before her mother could protest further, Nell Grace hurried out of the room and went in search of Renny Magee.

—

"Are you clear, then, Renny? About what you're to do—and what you're *not* to do?"

"Aye," said Renny. She was clear about it all, she thought, except why exactly she was doing it—or not doing it, whichever the case might be.

"Tell me again," said Nell Grace. "Just to make certain we haven't forgotten anything."

Renny dug at the floor with one foot. "I'm to keep the house clean and tidy and keep the kettle on at all times."

"And set the table as well, Renny. Don't forget that. But I'll be home in time to make supper in the evening. And I'll fix extra to tide you over for the midday meal next day."

Renny nodded. Nell Grace ought to know by now she wasn't no eejit. She could remember a few simple chores in the girl's absence, now couldn't she?

"And what else, Renny?"

"I'll be feedin' the chickens and emptyin' the slops and carryin' anything heavy in or out, should your da or the twins not be here to do it." She grinned. "And make sure to keep the creepy-crawlies away."

Nell Grace allowed herself a smile. Her mum's fear of bugs was a constant source of amusement to Renny Magee, who found it hard to believe that such a strong woman could quail and quake at the sight of spider or a cockroach. Renny had long ago appointed herself in charge of bug-busting in the MacGovern household and had dispatched many a creature to its reward—or captured it in a bottle and taken it up the hill to show Maylee. Nell Grace, being none too fond of crawling things herself, was happy for Renny to take care of such chores entirely.

"Very good," she told her. "Now tell me, what are you *not* to do?"

Renny shot her a dubious look. "I'm *not* to take care of wee William. Even if Vangie should ask me to."

"That's right. And that's the most important thing of all, Renny, as I explained. Do you understand?"

"Aye. But what if Vangie *insists?*"

"You just keep telling her you can't. Tell her you're afraid, that you don't know *how* to care for a baby and you simply can't do it. And look . . . frightened if she tries to coax you."

Renny frowned. This was the part that had her worried.

"Renny," said Nell Grace. "I know you care deeply for Mum."

Renny looked up, reluctant to have her deepest feelings known even by Nell Grace.

"I know you care about Mum, Renny," she said again, "but don't you see? That's why we're doing this. It's to help her. She's unhappy, Renny. She's miserable. It's not like her to ignore a babe—*any* babe, not just her own. More than anything else, she's a *mother*. A *good* mother. The way she is now—it's not natural for her! She's just not herself, don't you see? I know losing Aidan broke her heart. But she can't go on ignoring baby Will. He *needs* her."

Nell Grace stopped and took Renny by the shoulders. "I know I'm asking a lot of you, Renny. I'm putting more work on you—"

"I don't mind the work, Nell Grace."

"I know you don't. And I know you hate saying no to Mum. But if this works, it won't be for long. And then we can all get back to normal." She paused. "So, you'll do it then, just as we agreed?"

Renny found it almost as hard to say no to Nell Grace as she did to Vangie. Especially when the girl insisted they were doing this to *help* Vangie.

She nodded. "I'll do my best."

"Thank you, Renny! And, by the way—"

Renny had turned to go, but stopped, waiting.

"Pray, Renny," Nell Grace said, her gaze as intent and solemn as Renny had ever seen it. "Pray really, really hard. For Mum. And for baby Will. For all of us."

Renny gave a nod. Nell Grace needn't worry about that part of things. She'd be praying, all right. Amongst everything else, she'd be praying that Nell Grace knew what she was doing.

For heaven help them all if she didn't.

TWENTY-THREE

CHOICES

THE TISSUE OF THE LIFE TO BE
WE WEAVE WITH COLORS ALL OUR OWN,
AND IN THE FIELD OF DESTINY
WE REAP AS WE HAVE SOWN.

JOHN GREENLEAF WHITTIER

Susanna was doing her best to keep the house quiet for the day.

With Papa Emmanuel and Caterina away, she thought it should be relatively easy to give Michael and Paul several uninterrupted hours in which to work. She knew Michael was hoping to spend most of the afternoon on his *American Anthem* suite, once he and Paul ironed out a few items in the upcoming concert program. Later, she would go in and do whatever she could to help, although at this point he kept insisting he wanted to keep the finishing touches a surprise to her.

She was in the drawing room, trying to mend a pull in one

of the sofa's antimacassars when she heard a crash in the music room and went running. She met Paul midway down the hall. His face was flushed, his eyeglasses riding low on his nose, the collar of his shirt slightly askew.

The moment he saw her, he threw both arms in the air in a gesture of futility.

"Paul? What's wrong? What was that noise?"

"*That,*" he said with marked emphasis, "was the sound of my genius cousin—and your usually good-natured betrothed—making a profound statement of dissatisfaction with his own work." He stopped. "In other words, he barely missed my foot with one of those river rock paperweights from the mantel."

She stared at him. "Michael threw a paperweight at you?"

He waved a hand. "No, no, not at me! He was aiming at the floor, I believe. My foot just happened to get in the way."

"Good heavens! Why was he throwing a paperweight?"

Paul shrugged. "The music is fighting him, he says." He glanced around, then turned back and lowered his voice. "Between you and me, Susanna, I think it is Uncle Riccardo fighting him."

"What do you mean?"

"I don't think Michael is concentrating so well these days. Uncle Riccardo keeps shooting these little darts at him, you know?"

Susanna shook her head. "I *don't* know. What are you talking about?"

Again he glanced behind him to make sure Michael hadn't come out of the music room. "He sometimes says things that disparage Michael's music. He insinuates that Michael should be doing more . . . important work."

Anger swept over Susanna like a fever. For an instant she

felt like throwing one of those paperweights herself. "And this is affecting Michael's composing?"

Paul lifted his shoulders. "*Something* is. He tries not to show his irritation with Uncle Riccardo, but I believe these remarks are hurtful—and discouraging to him. He's, ah, stuck, he says, in the last movement. He says it's going nowhere." He stopped, looking at Susanna as if considering whether he should say what he was thinking.

Apparently, he decided to risk it. "I've never before known Michael to be . . . temperamental." Unexpectedly, he grinned at her. "He's behaving like a *musician.*"

Susanna was unable to manage a return smile. "Is there anything I can do?" she said. "Or perhaps *you* could speak with Michael's father?"

He looked at her over the rim of his glasses, eyes wide. "It is not my place, Susanna. And besides, it takes more than talk to change Uncle Riccardo's opinion once he sets his mind to a thing."

That didn't surprise Susanna. In the brief time Michael's father had been with them, she had already learned that he could be frustratingly stubborn.

She sighed, wondering how such a likable man—and she *did* like Riccardo Emmanuel—could also be so aggravating.

"Well, I'll at least go and talk with Michael."

"Keep your eye on the paperweight," Paul said dryly.

—

She found Michael slumped on the piano bench, one hand thumping idly on the keyboard. His hair was wild, his mouth set in a hard line. He looked for all the world like a great black bear with a thorn in its paw.

In front of the fireplace, Gus the wolfhound, looking somewhat wary and at loose ends without Caterina to tend to, sat watching his owner. At Susanna's entrance, his tail began to whop in a circle, but he remained where he was.

Michael gave no indication that he heard her enter, which wasn't like him at all. Usually he responded to her presence the moment she walked into a room.

Susanna came up behind him and put a hand to his shoulder. "Michael?"

After a slight hesitation, his only response was to reach back and cover her hand with his.

"I heard a terrible crash. Paul said you dropped a paper-weight." She glanced around and spied the large piece of polished rock still on the floor.

"*Sì.*"

His tone was as petulant as his expression.

"Is there anything I can do?"

He shook his head, then sighed and straightened a little. "No. But I should go and apologize to Pauli. He probably thinks I'm upset with *him.*"

"What *are* you upset with?"

"Myself," he said flatly.

She squeezed his shoulder. "The music isn't going well?"

"The music," he said somewhat caustically, "is not going at all. It's a dead thing, like an animal shot and skinned."

Susanna cringed at the analogy even as she fought to suppress a smile at his flair for the dramatic.

"Your music is absolutely brilliant, Michael," she said calmly. "Don't you even think of belittling it. Now, why don't you tell me what's really wrong?"

Again he shook his head. "I'm getting nowhere. I knew the last movement would take much time, but this is ridiculous! And it's not even because of the music itself. It's because I've simply . . . stopped. I can't seem to get past the point where I am now."

Struggling to find just the right words, Susanna clasped his shoulders with both hands. "I've heard what you're doing, you know. Right up to this . . . stopping place. And it's *wonderful,* Michael! Truly, it's an incredible work. Surely you haven't lost your passion for it?"

When he didn't answer, Susanna gripped his heavy shoulders a little more tightly. "Michael?"

He startled her by shooting to his feet and whipping around to face her, practically flinging her hands off his shoulders. "It's not so simple, Susanna! It's—I don't know *what* it is! What I *do* know is that at this rate, I'll never have it ready for the Centennial concert."

"That's still months away—"

"And I'm still months away from completion," he countered.

He turned his back on her and paced over to the fireplace. Hurt, Susanna stayed where she was. She had never seen him like this. It was a good thing that Riccardo Emmanuel was out of the house. Had he been here, there was no telling what she might have said to him.

"Well, then," she said uncertainly, "I suppose I should leave you alone."

Before she could go, however, he turned back to her. "Susanna, I'm sorry," he said, raking a hand through his hair. "I didn't mean to take my frustration out on you. Don't go. Please."

Susanna watched him, still keeping her distance. "Michael, this has something to do with your father, doesn't it?"

A muscle near his eye jerked. "Of course not."

"I think it does. What has he been saying to you, about your music?"

For a moment she thought he wasn't going to answer. He

stood with one arm propped on the mantel as if he couldn't decide what, if anything, to tell her.

Finally, though, he pushed away and came to stand closer to her. "You already know what he wants for me."

Irritation flared in Susanna again. "Yes, he wants you to return to the opera. But that's not what *you* want." She paused. "Is it?"

He started to speak, then stopped, giving a slight shake of his head. "No, you know it's not. But . . . what if he's right and I'm wrong, *cara?* What if I *am,* as he seems to believe, wasting my gift?"

Susanna studied him, then tugged at his hands and led him to the sofa, coaxing him to sit with her. "Michael, don't you see what's happening? Your father is trying to influence you. He's attempting to change your mind about what direction your music should take. And I can't help but wonder if it might be working."

He frowned. "Don't be upset with him, Susanna. He genuinely believes I'm wrong. He means only to help me."

"But he's *not* helping you," Susanna pointed out. "In fact, he's *hurting* you. I've no doubt that your father means well, Michael. He loves you dearly, and he believes wholeheartedly in your gift—your voice and your potential. But it isn't right, what he's doing. He's confusing you. I think he's actually making you question your decision to leave the opera. How can you let him do that?"

She paused. "After everything you went through to make that decision, how could you be anything but convinced it was the right one, the choice God wanted you to make?"

Silence, in which Susanna sensed he didn't know what to say.

"Think about this, Michael. Had you ever at any time, before your father came to visit, questioned your decision?"

His response took some time in coming. But the shake of his head was firm and final. "No."

Susanna squeezed his hands. "Then it seems to me there's only one reason for your questioning it now. Oh, Michael, I know it must be incredibly difficult to stand up to your father when you know he wants only what's best for you! Papa Emmanuel genuinely believes that you might be squandering a God-given gift. And your former success in the opera world would even seem to confirm—to *him,* at least—that he's right. But how many times have I heard you say that one's success in a chosen field doesn't necessarily mean God's blessing is on that choice—or the success?"

He raised his face. "*Sì.* From my own experience, I know that to be true."

Susanna didn't move, said nothing, and simply waited.

He turned his head as if to ease the tension in his neck. "So, then, you're saying that I'm allowing my father to divert me from what I know in my heart is right?"

Susanna felt his hands tighten on hers. "I'm saying that you made your choice once, and I believe it's *still* your choice. Michael . . . darling . . . it couldn't be clearer. You must choose to please either your earthly father . . . or your *heavenly* Father."

With that, she felt she had said enough. She leaned toward him and very gently kissed him on the cheek. "I'll leave you alone. I want to speak with Nell Grace before she leaves and see how her first day in the house went for her—especially how she and Moira got on together."

Even as she was still speaking, the wolfhound came to rest his head in Michael's lap. The two were still sitting there, both quiet and seemingly contemplative, when Susanna left the room.

AN UNEASY SEARCH

ALL DAY LONG, IN UNREST,
TO AND FRO, DO I MOVE.
OWEN ROE MAC WARD (TRANSLATED BY JAMES CLARENCE MANGAN)

The rain was already picking up again when Frank Donovan walked into the Women's Clinic and Convalescence Center for the third time in a week.

Try as he would, he couldn't altogether ignore the snide voice—a voice remarkably like his own—that had taken to questioning the motivation behind these frequent visits. Then he reminded himself that the good name and even the very future of his closest friend might be riding on what he could learn from Mary Lambert.

The very sight of Miss Savage—"the Matron from the Pit," as he'd come to think of her—immediately soured his stomach and his mood. Even so, he wasn't going to miss a chance to get under her skin as much as she got under his.

"Ah, Miss Savage," he said cheerily, doffing his rain-drenched hat and putting on the Irish, "Wasn't I hopin' you'd be here?"

He knew from the instant the smirk appeared that she was going to give him trouble. Normally, she reserved her fiercest glare for him. Not today. She was definitely smirking, all right, and it was the kind of knowing, mean-spirited smirk the woman might wear to the execution of an archenemy.

Someone like himself.

In an attempt to thwart whatever the harridan might have up her sleeve, Frank shot her a smile of his own, guaranteed to melt her resistance.

In return, he received a thoroughly venomous scowl.

There would be no melting of the Iron Matron today.

All right, then—back to business. "I'll just be speakin' with Miss Lambert," he said, starting down the hall.

"Not today, you won't," she said, stopping him on the first step.

Surprised—for he'd already determined that the woman was a coward at heart and would quickly retreat in the face of an actual challenge—Frank slowly removed his hat, tucked it under his arm, and leaned forward, bracing one hand on the table at which she sat.

"Is that so? And why would that be, Miss Savage?"

There was the smirk again. "Because she isn't here."

She leaned back and crossed her arms over her bony bosom, watching him with a kind of gleeful malice.

Caught off guard, Frank straightened. "What do you mean, she isn't here?"

"*Miss* Lambert had already exceeded the time allotted for treatment. She was checked out this morning."

"By whose orders?"

Her eyes glinted. "Mine, of course. I *am* the head matron. Or weren't you aware of that—*Sergeant?*"

The wicked old fishwife was clearly indulging in some sort of unholy amusement at his expense. Frank wanted to go across the table and snatch her by her wattled throat. Instead, he checked his temper and favored her with a tight-lipped smile.

"So, then, where would I be findin' Miss Lambert?"

Her eyebrows shot up in a look of mock innocence. "Well, how would I know that? The clinic's responsibility for a patient ends when she walks out the door."

Despite Frank's resolve not to let the woman provoke him, she was doing an admirable job of just that. "You set her out in the rain, not knowin' if she has a place to go?" he said, his tone hard with an edge of warning.

"As I told you, Sergeant, we can hardly be responsible for every addict we treat after they leave the premises. Now if you'll excuse me, I have other patients who require attention."

She made a show of gathering up some charts, and now Frank *did* go across the table. He slammed his hat down, sending her charts flying in all directions and, bracing both hands on the scarred wooden top, he leaned forward until he was in her face, close enough to smell her stale breath.

"You don't want to aggravate me, Miss Savage," he bit out with deliberate menace. "Really, you don't. If you have a thought as to where Mary Lambert might have gone, it would be in your best interests to tell me and not make me ask again."

At least he had the satisfaction of seeing her shrink from him. To her credit, however, she recovered quickly. "I told you. I have absolutely no way of knowing where the woman might have gone. Now I suggest you leave, Sergeant, or else—"

"Or else what?" Frank countered, digging his fingers into the desk to keep from shaking the old witch. "You'll call the police?"

He could feel the rage boiling up in him but knew he'd accomplish nothing by exploding, so he contented himself with taking a swipe at the row of tins and bottles on the table and knocking them to the floor with a terrible clamor. Then he straightened, pointed a finger at the furious matron, and issued a warning: "You'd best hope I find Mary Lambert, *Miss* Savage! She's at the heart of a criminal investigation. And if I *don't* find her and find her soon, I'm coming back here to haul your sorry self straight to the Tombs for obstructing that investigation."

As he went tearing out the door and down the steps into the rain-slick streets, it crossed Frank's mind that he hadn't a hope of doing any such thing. He could hardly lock up a clinic matron for discharging a patient—though he doubted Miss Savage knew that.

Besides, he had no intention of carrying out his threat.

He *would* find Mary Lambert, and he would find her today.

—

The thought of that poor woman walking the streets of New York—homeless, defenseless, in a sorely weakened condition, and in this weather—rode Frank's back like a devilish buzzard. He practically pounced on every slight figure with fair hair until each turned around with a look of wanting to slap his face or else take off running.

He didn't dare question himself too closely as to why one small woman with an opium habit should be important enough for him to lose a full day's work in an effort to find her. True, she was crucial to his efforts to rescue Doc from that barrage of vile attacks and clear his good name in the process. But was that the only reason for his dogged search?

Some carefully guarded place deep inside him was trying to force itself open and entice him to search among the secrets hidden there, along with the possibilities and forgotten dreams. But Frank Donovan had long ago learned to keep that place securely bolted even against himself. Once again he deliberately closed his mind to it—refusing to think, refusing to question, as he continued to roam the teeming streets of the city.

All day he walked in the rain, pressing his way through the crush of other pedestrians and vehicle traffic, finally taking to his department's mount, the dun-colored Attila, in an increasingly desperate search for Mary Lambert.

If an occasional uneasy thought nagged him about the reason for his tireless pursuit, he reminded himself it would take more than a frail, flaxen-haired woman to bring down the walls of that well-guarded chamber in his heart.

DREAD REMEMBRANCE

SAD ARE OUR HOPES,

FOR THEY WERE SWEET IN SOWING

BUT TARES, SELF-SOWN,

HAVE OVERTOPP'D THE WHEAT.

AUBREY THOMAS DE VERE

The rain was steady now. It would soon be dark, and Mary Lambert still had nowhere to go.

Many hours had passed since she had been dismissed from the Women's Clinic. Morning had turned to afternoon, and afternoon to evening. The rain poured down in cold sheets and Mary fervently wished she had a coat. When Miss Savage discharged her this morning, she'd said Mary wasn't wearing a coat when she was admitted, and since it was April, she wouldn't be needing one anyway.

It might be April, but Mary was cold. Cold all the way to the bone.

Her dress was sopping wet and clung heavily to her body. Her hair hung in sodden ropes. It was a miserable evening, and she glanced longingly into the shop windows that displayed their various wares in the warm radiance of gaslight and candle glow. She wasn't exactly lost, but she was frightened and trying not to show her fear lest some of the bounders roaming the Bowery try to take advantage.

Her first thought when she was released was to go and find her children. Robert and Lily and Kate. She longed to see their faces, tell them how sorry she was. But although Dr. Carmichael had told her where they were staying, in the fog of withdrawal from the opium, she had forgotten what he said. So she had gone to the old flat on Mulberry Street, knowing her hopes were foolish but still compelled to see for herself that her children were no longer there.

Not only were her babies gone, but so was everyone else she had known in the neighborhood. She should have expected as much. Renters came and went in waves in the tenement districts.

After that, she'd set out to find the doctor's office. Surely he would help her. He was a kind man, and Dr. Cole was such a fine lady. Good people—and Mary hadn't known many good people during the time she'd lived in New York.

The trouble was, she couldn't remember which street the doctor's office was on, if indeed he had told her at all. So she'd wandered aimlessly for awhile, feeling weak and numb and increasingly ill. Despite all the misery she'd gone through to shake her opium habit, she knew that if she had any money at all she would go looking for the evil stuff.

But she had no money. She had nothing. Growing desperate now, she stopped a middle-aged man who wore the clothing of a laborer and appeared a decent-enough sort. He eyed her somewhat curiously, but his voice was kind when he directed her to Dr. Carmichael's practice.

The moment she spied Elizabeth Street, she began to run, the water squishing out over the tops of her shoes as she went. At the sight of the shingle announcing the doctors' offices, she slowed, then flung herself against the door at the side of the building—only to find it locked. She went around to the front and peered through the window, but there was no light, no sign that anyone was inside.

At that point, Mary could bear no more. She went back to the side door and inched herself under the narrow overhang of the tin roof. Exhausted and weak to the point of collapse, she slid down onto the stoop and began to weep.

What a miserable failure she was. She had failed everyone who ever loved her. She had failed her children most of all. Oh, what she had done to them!

She had failed her parents as well. They had begged her not to leave their home in Ohio. But, oh, she *would* come to New York, for she was going to be a great stage actress. That dream had faded in a cloud of smoke before her first year in the city had passed. She was "too small," they said, "too childlike," and her voice wasn't "right."

She'd been left to support herself by washing dishes in a Bowery tavern during the afternoons and checking coats and hats in a "gentlemen's club" at night. The trouble was that many of the "gentlemen" picking up their outerwear after a night of drinking and gambling were interested in picking *her* up as well. She'd been dismissed from that place after slapping a horse-faced young dandy with bold hands and a filthy mouth who was intent on dragging her into the coat room.

That was when she'd gone to the mission house seeking assistance. And that was where she'd met Robert Warburton.

—

She'd been so naïve all those years ago. Even after a year in the city, she still thought a properly dressed gentleman with a *Reverend* before his name, a man with a kind smile and a "God bless you!" for each unfortunate in the food line, could be trusted.

Robert was volunteering that day, helping to serve meals alongside some of the women from his congregation's benevolence committee. He seemed to take a personal interest in everyone he served, coming around to the tables, introducing himself, and visiting with each one individually.

He was a plain man, not the sort to fancy himself irresistible to women, and he had an amiable, almost an avuncular manner that set her at ease from the first meeting. His concern for Mary appeared to be sincere and immediate, and when he appeared the next afternoon at the tavern where she washed dishes she was genuinely glad to see him. Then when he offered her employment as assistant manager of an apartment building he claimed to own—a position that included free rent and furnishings—she nearly fell at his feet and wept.

If it struck her as curious that a man of the cloth would own an entire apartment building—much less *more* than one—she didn't bother to question it too deeply. After inquiring among a few of the regulars at the mission, she soon learned that Warburton's congregation was one of the largest and most prosperous in the city. It was said that his wife was also an heiress, a very wealthy woman in her own right.

Even when he began to drop by the apartment just to check on "the building" and see how she was faring, Mary suspected nothing improper. He was a clergyman, after all, and she was one of his employees. It never occurred to her to question whether his other employees were treated as well as she.

As time went on, he began bringing her gifts, small things, at first—a tin of sweetmeats, a canister of coffee, a loaf of bread from the nearby German bakery. Later, when the visits became more frequent and the gifts more lavish, he dismissed her protests with the explanation that, not having children of his own, he took great pleasure in "fussing over" his younger employees.

Over time, Mary actually grew fond of him—not in a romantic sense, but as she might have developed affection for an older friend or relative. She looked forward to his visits with an eagerness that had nothing to do with the gifts he brought or any sort of interest in a clandestine relationship, but much to do with her need for human companionship. She was lonely, and he was kind to her, and she was willing to overlook the questionable propriety of his visits for the simple pleasure of his presence.

Then came an evening when she was feeling particularly isolated and downhearted. Robert came around later than usual, bearing a small velvet box in which rested a delicate gold and pearl locket, the loveliest piece of jewelry Mary had ever seen. As she knew she must, she refused to accept it—and continued to refuse until, crestfallen, he appeared to wipe some suspicious dampness from his eyes. At that moment she softened, and he declared his affection for her, slipping the locket around her neck and begging her to listen as he explained, haltingly at first, the true state of his marriage. A wife who was no helpmate, a sickly older woman whom he respected and would never embarrass or humiliate, but whom he could not bring himself to love.

Mary realized later that the whole tale was taken straight from the pages of the most lurid dime novel, a story that countless men before him had no doubt used to win over an innocent. But she was young and admittedly foolish, and he had become more important to her than she'd realized.

That was the night she became his mistress.

Robert continued to be good to her as time passed. Indeed, when they were together, no husband could have been more devoted.

She knew all along that he wouldn't marry her, of course. He'd made that perfectly clear from the beginning of their affair. He was a widely known, influential member of the clergy, a respected community leader, and an esteemed author and speaker. He told her clearly that he would never do anything to hurt his wife or disappoint or disillusion his "flock." The Lord was depending on him to further His kingdom, and no hint of scandal must be allowed to touch him or his expanding ministry.

Mary understood. For the most part, she was glad of his attention and company. He brought her books and newspapers, told her she was beautiful and talented, made sure she had what she needed. The security of knowing he cared for her outweighed the nagging shame of being a kept woman.

Gradually, however, things began to change. He didn't come to the flat as often, and when he did come, he seldom brought a gift. He also began to exhibit certain behavior during their intimate times together that disturbed her slightly. For the most part, however, she managed to dismiss her disappointment and uneasiness.

Besides, she was expecting a child.

Not long after their son was born, Robert moved them to a larger flat. For a time, he seemed to lose interest in the physical side of their relationship. He spent an afternoon or an evening with them once a week or so, but seemed content merely to have dinner, play with the baby for a while, and then leave.

Most often he appeared to be tired and preoccupied. But because Mary knew how involved and busy he was—and because she had no real choice—she never complained.

For over a year they existed this way, more as companionable friends than as lovers. Then everything changed, and the undercurrents of perversion she'd sensed earlier in their relationship came to the surface. Little by little, his demands turned aberrant—or at least what Mary sensed to be aberrant. She was ignorant for the most part about such things, but despite her naiveté, she knew that much of what Robert Warburton required of her was unnatural. Unnatural and degrading . . . and painful.

In a matter of months, he had involved her in practices that made her lose all respect for him and even begin to hate him. She learned things about him she would have never dreamed of—horrid things that both astonished and sickened her.

She begun to plot and scheme about getting away from him, taking little Robert and escaping to a place where they couldn't be found. She had no money—he kept close watch on the meager "household funds" he allowed her. She was desperate to leave, but with no independent income and little Robert just past two, there was little hope of escape. She was trapped, at least for the time being.

She decided to stay and make the best of it, at least until her son was older. But the months turned into years, and eventually she found herself with child again—and again, for within months of giving birth to Lily, she discovered that Kate was on the way.

The only thing that kept her from completely going to pieces at this point was her fear for her children—and the fact that at least when she was pregnant, Robert left her alone. It was as if he was repulsed by her condition. The respite from his deviant physical practices was such a relief that she dreaded the day when the child would be born.

As it happened, the baby came early. Another little girl. Kate was a sickly infant from the beginning. She couldn't seem to nurse properly, and she suffered so badly from colic that at times Mary thought she would go mad with the infant's incessant screaming.

This time, when Robert began to demand "his rights" again, Mary fought him and refused any further physical intimacy. She also made the incredibly foolish mistake of threatening to make his wife and even his church congregation aware of what she knew about him.

It was the worst thing she could have done. Robert was not a tall man, but he was thickset and brawny, and he found it nothing more than an inconvenience to force himself on the much smaller Mary, especially as weak and ill as she was at the time.

The physical pain of that encounter was so fierce that Mary thought she would surely die of it. Robert actually seemed remorseful that night, and before leaving he coaxed her into trying some "medicine" he'd brought with him. Knowing how "delicate" she was and how difficult it seemed to be for her to contend with his "admittedly strong passions," he explained that he had procured something for her that would not only ease her "discomfort," but would also counteract those "terrible black moods" from which she seemed to suffer more and more.

That was the night Mary first discovered opium.

That was the night she sold her soul to hell.

TWENTY-SIX

UNDONE BY A FALLEN WOMAN

A PITY BEYOND ALL TELLING
IS HID IN THE HEART OF LOVE.

W. B. YEATS

Frank found Mary Lambert huddled under the overhang at Doc's office.

His eyes never left her as he dismounted Attila and tethered him. She was soaked through and shivering with every breath, for she didn't have so much as a sweater around her thin shoulders.

And she was crying. Crying like a lost child.

Frank was unprepared entirely for the effect the woman had on him. The sight of her hit him like a blow to the stomach, shocking him out of his resolve to stay detached and throwing every bolt that held in place his deepest feelings. He would never have admitted it to a living soul, but the force of his reaction almost frightened him.

He knelt beside her, rainwater streaming off his hat and face, and for an instant he had the oddest feeling that he was weeping with her.

He shook his head to dispel the foolish notion, then put a gentle hand to her shoulder.

"Mary," he said, his voice raw with the swelling in his throat. "It's all right now, Mary."

Her head came up, her eyes wide and frightened as she flinched and shrank from him.

The idea that she was afraid of him turned in Frank like a jagged blade. "Don't be afraid, Mary. I mean only to help you."

She was all in a tremble, shaking fiercely and hugging her arms to herself as if to keep from falling apart.

Frank shrugged out of his raincoat and pulled it around her. It was heavy with rainwater, but it would at least keep the worst of the wind off her.

She tried to say something but was shaking so hard the words wouldn't come.

"We need to get you inside. Doc's door is locked, is it?"

She nodded.

"Well, I know where he keeps the key."

Frank straightened and went to the door, running his hand over the lintel until he found the extra key to the office. He unlocked the door, then helped Mary to her feet and took her inside, tossing his hat behind him on the floor of the entryway.

After settling her on a chair near the iron stove in the waiting room, he went to start a fire, working it and punching it up until he had a good, vigorous blaze going.

One glance back at Mary, wrapped in his wet coat and still shaking, sent him in search of a towel and a blanket. He found both in the linen closet between the examining rooms and, after easing his wet coat from around her shoulders, did his best to dry her hair before wrapping her snugly in the blanket.

This would help some, but it wasn't enough to keep her from getting the pneumonia. She needed a thorough change of clothes and something warm to drink.

The entire time he was working with her, she said nothing, but merely watched him through those deep-set, sorrowful eyes. Finally, he stood back and tried to think. He didn't know quite what to do with her. He could keep her here for awhile, but sooner or later he'd have to report in, or the captain would set him to cleaning up horse droppings in the Bowery for the next week. She needed somewhere to go, somewhere she could stay.

For now, he sat down in the chair next to her. "Is the fire helping?" he said.

She nodded. Frank reached for her hands, and she jerked at his touch until he shook his head, saying, "You're too cold, Mary. I mean only to warm you."

She relented, and Frank managed to keep his expression impassive as he took in the smallness of her hands, the fragility of her bones. He could have crushed them with his own big paws with no effort at all. No wonder she was afraid of him.

He looked up to find her watching him, and when their eyes met she didn't glance away but continued to search his gaze. Her eyes were filled with questions, and Frank realized then she wasn't accustomed to having someone fuss over her or take care of her. The realization caused his heart to wrench, and he was surprised at the strength of his desire to protect her.

She glanced away, but not before he saw that she was weeping again, large tears that tracked slowly down her face. This silent evidence of the depth of her despair nearly undid Frank. Overcome by a fierce desire to gather her into his arms and provide a fortress of protection for her, he shuddered.

He had to stop this. The woman who was turning his mind to mush was an opium addict. A kept woman, a woman who had allowed herself to be used by the same man who meant to destroy Andrew Carmichael. And Frank's one purpose where she was concerned was to elicit any information she could give him about Robert Warburton.

Never in all the years he'd been on the force had Frank Donovan allowed personal feelings to interfere with his work. And he wasn't about to start now.

But he couldn't ignore the rasp he heard in her breathing or the bluish tinge to her lips or the hard shaking that still wracked her small frame. He couldn't question—or bully—a sick, shivering woman, could he?

There was no help for it at present. He had to do what he could for her until she was up to another round of questions. So he disregarded the instinct hammering at him that he should release her hands *now* and go sit across the room from her. Indeed, he was still warming her hands between his own when Doc and Bethany Cole walked in.

—

They stopped just inside the doorway and stood staring with bewilderment and disbelief.

Frank had no doubt that the last thing the two doctors expected to find was himself and the miserable-looking Mary Lambert sitting by the fire in their office waiting room.

He realized then that he was still holding Mary's hands, and he dropped them as if her skin had suddenly scalded his own.

"Frank?" Doc said, looking altogether baffled.

Frank stood. "Doc," he said, then inclined his head to Bethany Cole. "Dr. Cole."

Doc had already come across the room and was now standing

over Mary, taking in her wretched appearance. "Mary? What's happened? What are you doing here?"

She sat staring at him but made no reply, instead looking to Frank.

"The clinic turned her out," Frank said. "Sent her packin' in the rain, with no coat and nowhere else to go."

"*What?*" Dr. Cole now came to stand on the other side of Mary. "Oh, Mary, you're absolutely drenched!"

"Do you think you could find something dry for her to put on, Dr. Cole?" said Frank. "She's chilled bad."

Doc took over then. "Bethany, please take her in back and get her as dry as you can. I'll go upstairs and find a clean night-shirt for her."

"Can I do anything, Doc?" Frank asked, watching Bethany Cole help Mary from the waiting room.

Doc turned and eyed him with a dark look. "You can tell me what's going on! I'll be surprised if the woman doesn't have pneumonia. And look at you—you're as soaked as she is! Where have you been, Frank?" He paused. "Tell me you're not still harassing Mary about this Warburton matter."

Frank ignored the bit about his "harassing" Mary. "Well, it's like this, Doc. As I said, that terror of a woman at the clinic— Miss Savage is her name, and a fitting one it is—set your Mary Lambert out today with nothing but the clothes on her back. And since I figured she had no business wanderin' about in the rain, I've spent a good part of the day trying to find her. And where I found her was *here*—sittin' out there by your door, as drenched as a sewer rat and pretty much undone."

He saw his friend wince. "This is my fault. I knew they wouldn't keep her much longer, and I've been so—involved with my own affairs I neglected to find another place for her. This is my fault," he repeated.

"Seems to me it's the fault of the clinic, Doc," Frank pointed out. "And I'd say you've had enough to handle lately that you can't be expected to remember everything. Will she be all right, do you think?"

"Well, I need to examine her before I can answer that. But you can see for yourself that her condition is anything but good."

Frank nodded. "I'll just wait out here while you check her over."

Doc looked at him as if he'd lost his wits entirely. "You surely don't mean to bother her yet tonight? I'll not hear of it."

Frank hitched his thumbs in his belt loops and met Doc's look straight on. "Beggin' your pardon, Doc, but it's not up to you to tell me when I can question her."

"Now see here, Frank. Mary Lambert is my patient, and I *will* tell you when you can see her. Besides," he added, "you don't intend to just talk with her. You mean to ply a sick woman with questions about something she had nothing to do with."

"I mean to question Warburton's sick *mistress*," Frank growled. "Now I'll wait just as long as I need to. But I *will* wait." He paused and let out a long breath. "Look, Doc, this woman has already told me plenty about the good *Reverend*. But I know in my gut she's holdin' back more than what she's told me—and I intend to get it all. I'm convinced this woman is the best chance we've got of stopping Warburton and his dirty tricks."

He stopped, then put a hand to the other man's shoulder. "In case you haven't noticed, Doc," he said, lowering his voice, "things are getting worse for you by the day. I don't see too many patients in your office anymore, and I hear plenty of talk around the streets that isn't exactly favorable to your reputation, if you take my point. And so you see why I need to know everything Mary Lambert knows about Warburton. If I'm right, I can fix him so he won't be doin' you any more damage."

Frank could see the other man fighting with the urge to tell him to get out—and he also knew the instant Doc's common sense won the battle.

"All right," Doc said, clenching his swollen knuckles into fists. "If I decide that Mary's up to speaking with you, you can talk with her. Briefly. But if she's simply too weak—or, worse, yet, if I find evidence of pneumonia—you're leaving, Frank. I mean it. I won't let you badger her if she's as ill as I think she might be."

Frank had no intention of "badgering" the frail Mary Lambert. All his better instincts clamored for him to protect her, not mistreat her. But he merely grinned and said, "I get the picture, Doc. For the time being, you're the boss."

Doc made a small sound of disgust, and on the way out the door muttered something about a "hardheaded Irishman."

"Sour-tempered Scot," Frank fired at his back.

Doc kept on going, as if he hadn't heard, but Frank knew he had.

—

More than an hour later, Doc having given his reluctant consent, Frank again found himself in the role of Mary Lambert's merciless interrogator. He had all he could do not to back off entirely from the woman. He found the whole process loathsome, and the longer he went at her with his questions, the more he disgusted himself. But he sensed that he finally had her where he wanted her, ready to spill everything she knew about that snake, Warburton, and so he would continue his unrelenting drive for the truth.

After examining Mary, Doc had taken her upstairs to the sofa in his apartment, where he'd wrapped her snugly in blankets. A fire was crackling and hissing in the grate. Indeed, the room was so warm that Frank longed to stick his head out the window and cool himself off in the rain.

The woman was weeping again, and Frank thought he would strangle on the sight of her misery and humiliation. Instead, he bent over her, swallowing down his own shame and self-disgust as he repeated his last question, the one that had triggered this fresh bout of tears.

"You told me he was a terrible man, Mary, but you haven't told me why. I need to know more than that. There's an entire host of terrible men walking about town, but without evidence as to what they've done, there's no stopping their mischief. What is it about a man of the cloth that would make you say such a thing?"

She stared up at him, the blankets tucked all the way up to her chin, looking more like a girl than a grown woman.

He yanked himself back to reality by remembering where she had been and what she had done. Mary Lambert was no innocent child.

"Mary?" he prompted her.

She squeezed her eyes shut. "He's *not* a man of the cloth," she said in little more than a whisper.

Frank didn't move. "What?"

Mary opened her eyes and looked at him. Frank bent lower.

"I said he isn't really a man of the cloth. He . . . a long time ago, he was a kind of . . . salesman. Then, later he took up with a . . . with one of those . . . tent healers. The ones that travel around the country holding revivals. Robert used to laugh about it, how he got his preacher training in the back of a wagon and the front of a tent."

Frank straightened, his mind racing. "He's a charlatan, then? A confidence trickster," he said quietly, more to himself than to Mary.

She nodded.

Frank felt like he imagined a man might feel who'd been holding his breath under water and suddenly came up for a lifesaving gulp of air.

"You're sure of this?"

Again she nodded. "He seemed . . . proud of the fact. He swore me to secrecy, of course, warned me not to tell even the children. But I believe he liked to think he'd pulled off something clever."

"All these years," Frank said, his mind scrambling to take in what he'd just heard.

He stood looking down at Mary Lambert, who had turned her face away from him. "How could he pull it off as slick as he did? The man is *famous*—practically a saint in this town. How'd he fool so many for so long?"

She shook her head. "To hear him tell it, it wasn't all that difficult. And I told you, he'd been a salesman. He has . . . a way with people. He could make you believe anything he wanted you to . . ."

Her voice broke, and Frank felt a pang of sympathy. This might be good news for him, but Robert Warburton had been nothing but *bad* news for her.

She drew in a breath. "Robert's a smart man. Educated. He used to read the newspapers, and he could read the entire paper in the time it would take me to read one page. And he remembers everything." She paused, her voice quaking when she repeated, "He's very smart."

The bitterness in her voice caught Frank's attention. Looking at the woman on the sofa, her eyes again glazed with tears, her body so slight as to almost disappear inside the blankets, Frank saw something more than the humiliation of a woman taken in and used by a consummate deceiver. Something more dreadful had happened to her than falling victim to a corrupt man and an addictive narcotic. It was as if something had snuffed the *light* from Mary Lambert, had battered her and bruised her until there was nothing left in her except shadows. She was . . . fading. Draining away.

"What else, Mary?" he said, dropping down to his knees beside the couch.

"Nothing," she said quickly. Too quickly.

Frank touched her hair. Something like pity, but stronger, more personal, gripped him, and he had to fight the impulse to gather her to himself and try to dispel her shadows with his own life force.

Deliberately, he softened his voice. "Mary," he said. "You must tell me."

She turned to look at him. "You said before . . . you said that Robert is making bad trouble for Dr. Carmichael."

Frank nodded. "I know he is, but I have to prove it. If there's anything else you can tell me—anything—I need to know what it is, Mary."

She closed her eyes. "I *can't*." Her voice was hoarse.

"Please, Mary. Doc—Dr. Carmichael has been good to you, hasn't he?"

She nodded, the tears now spilling from her eyes.

"He's a good man, Mary," said Frank, reaching to stroke her hair away from her face. "You know that. He's . . . more a man of God than most preachers, I'm thinking. I'm proud to call him my friend. And Warburton is close to ruining him."

He told her everything that had happened, from the vandalism of Doc's office to the letters in the papers, the rumors,

the scandal, the outright shunning of Doc by some of his colleagues and many of his patients.

Her expression was stricken. "No." The word caught like a sob.

"Oh, I mean to stop him, Mary. I *will* stop him. And I *can*
with your help. But you have to tell me everything. Everything
you know about him. Anything I can use."

"I *can't*." She sounded as if she were choking on the words.
"I *can't!*"

She looked up. Frank followed the direction of her gaze to
the doorway, where Doc and Dr. Cole had come to stand like
silent sentinels.

Mary looked at them for a long time, then turned back to
Frank. "I can't tell *you*," she said. "But . . . I'll tell Dr. Cole."

Frank held her gaze, then slowly nodded and got to his feet
and crossed the room. "She has something she won't tell me,"
he said to Bethany Cole, who glanced toward Mary. "She says
she *can't* tell me. But she'll tell you."

Dr. Cole looked at him, then back at Mary. She seemed
uncertain, hesitant.

Frank put a hand to her arm. "Whatever she means to tell
you, it's almost sure to be . . . ugly. But I have to know what it
is. No matter what she tells you, you'll have to tell *me*. For
Doc's sake."

Bethany Cole searched his eyes, and for the first time since
he'd met the woman, Frank saw something besides dislike or
irritation at him. Finally she nodded, and Frank dropped his
hand away from her arm. She started toward the couch, then
turned back.

"Andrew," she said evenly, "you and Sergeant Donovan will
have to leave the room now. I want to speak with Mary."

TWENTY-SEVEN

THE MANY FACES
OF STRENGTH

THERE IS NO HEALING

FOR ONE WHO HAS KNOWN NO PAIN.

THERE IS NO DARKNESS

FOR ONE WHO CHOOSES TO IN THE LIGHT REMAIN.

ANONYMOUS

More than an hour later, Andrew Carmichael was still sitting in the kitchen of his flat with Frank Donovan.

Darkness had drawn in on the night, and a kerosene lamp flickered on the table between them. Frank was clearly growing more and more impatient with the waiting. He would sit for awhile, then get up and pace the room. Andrew had lost count of how many cups of tea they'd consumed between them.

When Bethany appeared in the doorway, her appearance triggered an urgency in Andrew to go to her, lest she faint. He did get to his feet, as did Frank, but something in her expression warned him not to approach her.

She looked . . . ill. Tendrils of her fair hair had escaped the confines of the neat little knot at the back of her neck. Her porcelain skin had turned ashen, and her eyes deeply shadowed, with an almost startled expression. But even more stark was the mask of pain she wore.

"Bethany?" Andrew suddenly wished he had tried to stop her from talking with Mary Lambert. Whatever she had heard had left her . . . different. Changed.

Clearly shaken, she seemed not to hear him. She leaned heavily against the doorframe, staring into the room but obviously not seeing them.

"Dr. Cole? What did she tell you?" Frank's voice, stronger and not so cautious as Andrew's, seemed to snap her out of her peculiar state. Slowly she raised her head, lifted her shoulders, and walked the rest of the way into the room.

She faced them both at the table. Andrew hoped he would never again see such a look of anguish on her face as he saw in that moment. Her hands trembled when she gripped the back of the chair, and when she spoke, her lips trembled too.

She looked from one to the other, her countenance still taut with distress. "I'm so ashamed," she said, shocking Andrew and, from his expression, Frank, as well.

Andrew reached to cover her hand with his, but she pulled away from him and shook her head. Although hurt and confused by her appearance and her behavior, he stood very still, sensing her need for quiet.

"I judged her, you know." Her voice was unsteady, yet there was no sign of wavering. "The first time I saw her, when we went to that awful tenement building and found her and her children in such wretched circumstances, I was so angry with her. I thought she must be a terrible woman, to degrade herself and allow her children to live in such squalor."

"Bethany, don't—" Andrew tried to interrupt, but she raised a hand to silence him.

"No, let me finish. I want to say this before I tell you anything else." She seemed to gain strength as she went on. "I judged her to be a weak and selfish woman. A woman with no morality, no self-respect."

She moistened her lips, then swallowed, as if she were finding it extremely difficult to get the words out. "I was wrong. Although Mary Lambert may have been naïve and too trusting for her own good, she *wanted* out of her situation. But she believed herself to be trapped—by the three pregnancies and later the addiction—and Warburton threatened her and the children if she should try to leave him." She paused. "I've only now come to realize that, in her own way, Mary Lambert is a very strong woman."

She stopped to pull in a deep, ragged breath. "At least she survived, and that makes her stronger than I. I would never have survived what she's lived through."

She locked eyes first with Andrew, then with Frank, and the pain in her expression reflected the hideous nature of what she had heard from Mary Lambert.

"I . . . wanted you to know that before I tell you anything more. You mustn't make the same mistake that I did. You mustn't judge her. She doesn't deserve that."

There was still horror in her eyes, but her features softened when she turned to Andrew. "I can't talk to you about this, Andrew. Please understand. You and I, we're—" She shook her head. "I . . . couldn't bear to tell you the things she described to me. But Sergeant Donovan—" She glanced at Frank. "—he's a policeman. I'm a doctor. And he needs to know . . . what Warburton really is."

She touched Andrew's hand, her gaze meeting his in a look

of appeal. "Perhaps you could check on Mary while I speak to the sergeant?"

At first he didn't understand, and he was about to object, but something in her eyes told Andrew not to press. Apparently, Frank sensed the same thing, because he was quick to chime in. "Why don't you do what Dr. Cole suggested, Doc? You stay with Mary for now and let us talk."

Andrew didn't like it. If what Bethany had to tell was so horrible she couldn't repeat it to him, how could she tell Frank—a man she scarcely knew and didn't even like?

He knew if he voiced what he was thinking, he would risk sounding peevish. As it happened, Frank offered an answer before Andrew could ask the question.

"There's no shockin' a copper, Doc. What I haven't heard most likely hasn't happened. But there's some things a woman shouldn't have to discuss with the man she's going to marry, and I'm thinkin' what Dr. Cole has to say may just fall into that category. So you go on now and tend to Mary while Dr. Cole and myself have a chat."

Andrew glanced back at Bethany, and when she nodded he took his cup of tea and started for the bedroom.

—

Frank Donovan sat drumming his fingers on the kitchen table, staring at the flickering flame of the oil lamp. He was aware that Bethany Cole, seated across from him, was avoiding his gaze, and it wasn't difficult to understand why. She might be a doctor, but she was also a lady. As a physician, she'd doubtless encountered a number of situations that would have horrified other women. But that didn't mean she found it easy to confront the sort of ugliness she had just related to him.

He cringed to think that Mary Lambert had lived with this

sort of ugliness for years. The very thought kindled a hot flash of anger.

With more than two decades under his belt as a policeman, Frank had known surprisingly few individuals he would have categorized as altogether evil. There had been some, of course, but even they had rarely evoked in him the dark bloodlust that ran through him now, the kind that makes one man feel as if he might murder another.

At the moment he was trying to figure whether the urge to hurt Robert Warburton, to destroy him, was due entirely to the unqualified evil the man seemed to personify. Or was it more because Warburton had inflicted that evil on Mary Lambert?

An equal dose of both, most likely. But whatever the reason, it in no way lessened the fury building in him that made him want to grind Warburton under the heel of his boot like the vermin he was.

The man was a plague, more vile than he'd even thought.

"So he's a pervert as well as a charlatan," he muttered, speaking aloud what he was thinking.

"What will you do?"

Bethany Cole's strained voice yanked him back to his surroundings. He looked at her, and saw, not as he usually did, a woman physician—and a testy one at that—but a woman. A woman who was tired and still badly shaken from sharing the confidence of Mary Lambert.

"Nothing near what I'd like to do," Frank bit out. "And he's just snake enough to get away with it all."

"That can't happen! The man is a monster! You're going to arrest him, aren't you?" Outrage had stained her pale skin an angry crimson.

"Oh, I'll go after him, all right. But don't be surprised if he never sees the inside of a cell. In fact, I expect he'll be gone like a shot as soon as word leaks out."

"What do you mean?"

Frank leaned forward a little on his elbows. "What brings down a man like Warburton is a public scandal. Once it gets out that he's not and never has been what he's passed himself off to be—well, that'll be the beginnin' of the end for him, don't you see? His fancy church will throw him out on his ear, and all the speeches and the book writing will come to a halt, so there'll be no more funds coming in. Now, if Mary's right, it's Warburton's wife who holds the purse strings. So just how likely is it that she'll be spending much of it on him once she knows what he's been up to all this time?"

"I think she does know. Or at least knows in part. It was his wife who first came to Andrew and asked him to make a call on Mary Lambert. Andrew recognized her the day he went to Warburton's house."

Frank lifted both eyebrows. "Is that a fact now? Then that means she must be a decent enough sort. All the more likely that she'll send him packing."

Rather enjoying the scenario he was painting for Bethany Cole, Frank went on. "New York will wash its hands of him, and he'll simply pull out some night when no one's about to see him go. And no one will care."

"That's too easy for him!"

"I agree with you, Dr. Cole, but I know how things are done in this city. And though I'd like nothing better than to walk him to the hangin' tree myself, I'm about as sure as I can be that he'll disappear before I have the chance." He drew in a long breath. "He'll more than likely just pull up stakes here and start all over again somewhere else."

"But if you arrest him—"

"His fancy lawyer will have him out before the sun goes down. So far as we know, he hasn't murdered anyone, and there's no clear evidence of fraud or theft—at least not the kind you can prove, the kind that will put a fella behind bars. No, listen to me now. As much as I'd enjoy cleaning the city streets with his bare hide, I'm more interested in undoing the damage that's been done to Doc. That's what I intend to take care of before anything else."

Bethany frowned. "But how? Warburton has all but ruined Andrew with these fiendish attacks. What can you do?"

Frank stood. "I'll have to work on that, Dr. Cole. But don't you worry—I'll think of something."

He braced his hands on the table and leaned toward her. "Something I want to know first. What can you and Doc do to help Mary Lambert?"

She looked surprised. "Why . . . I'm not sure." She paused, studying him with an intensity that made Frank squirm a little. The woman had a way of looking right through a man.

In spite of the sadness engraved upon her face, a slow smile began to tug at the corners of her dainty little mouth. She looked as if she'd just realized something of great interest. "Don't you worry, Sergeant," she said archly, mimicking his words to her. "We'll think of something."

"Well," he said gruffly, "if there's a question of money for any special care she might be needin', you've only to ask. I've a bit put by."

Her smile grew even wider, and, tired as Frank knew she must be, for an instant her eyes took on a peculiar shine. "That's very generous of you, Sergeant—Frank. Andrew will be pleased to know you want to help."

Eager to escape that curious look, Frank started for the door. "Tell Doc I had to go," he said. "I'll stop by tomorrow."

TWENTY-EIGHT

KEEPING THE PEACE

MY CROWN IS IN MY HEART, NOT ON MY HEAD;
NOT DECK'D WITH DIAMONDS AND INDIAN STONES,
NOR TO BE SEEN: MY CROWN IS CALL'D CONTENT;
A CROWN IT IS THAT SELDOM KINGS ENJOY.
WILLIAM SHAKESPEARE

On the Wednesday before Easter, chaos reigned at Bantry Hill. Michael was working in a frenzy on his *American Anthem* suite in addition to preparing for two concerts before the Independence Day event. His calls for help were frequent but erratic, and he seemed to expect Susanna and Paul to anticipate each request. He was usually more reasonable than this, but, as Susanna was learning, he *was* by nature a musician, and as such tended to isolate himself in his own world when the pressures of his work engulfed him. Until, that is, he needed some-thing—when he had a way of bursting forth from *his* world and rocking the axes of *other* worlds. Of course, when he was actively composing, he really did require assistance—and these days, he seemed to be composing most of the time.

Then there was Caterina, who was in a fret, insisting that her dress for Easter Sunday needed the hem let out and the shoulders eased. Susanna found this hard to believe since the dress had been finished only six weeks before. When she tried it on her niece again, however, she realized Caterina was right. The child had grown just enough that the garment *was* too short and needed more give in the shoulders. There was nothing to do but alter the dress before Sunday.

Moira Dempsey and Nell Grace, who seemed of one mind these days, especially in regard to the extra cleaning and preparations required by the Easter season and the approach of spring, were dashing about from one task to another, attacking each with great energy. Susanna could not have been more grateful for the addition of the MacGovern girl to the household staff, for Moira seemed to have taken a liking to her and was happy to share the work. The negative was that there seemed to always be someone dusting or polishing or cleaning *something* in any room Susanna happened to enter. There was simply no way of getting out from underfoot wherever she went.

Papa Emmanuel tried, in his own way, to be of help, but he had his own method of doing things—and unfortunately his way never seemed to coincide with Moira's way. Consequently, he spent much time following individual family members or staff about the house, offering his unsolicited suggestions—and sometimes his criticisms—regarding their activities. To Susanna's dismay, the two people he most closely adhered to were Moira and Michael.

Riccardo Emmanuel and the Dempseys had known each other forever, of course. Michael and his parents had often spent

KEEPING THE PEACE   225

weeks with his mother's family in Ireland, and the Dempseys had been friends and neighbors of his grandparents. Although they had not seen each other for several years, one would have thought that Papa Emmanuel and Moira had never been apart, so familiar were their habits to each other and so personal and heated—and frequent—their disagreements.

In the midst of all this pandemonium, too, ran a somber undercurrent: Maylee's obvious decline. While everyone else in the house was running about in a constant flurry, Maylee lay abed almost all the time now, watching through her window as winter ended its last dance to make way for spring. Dr. Carmichael had cautioned them all during his last visit that these were almost certainly Maylee's final days.

Given this painful reality, when Susanna was tempted to grumble about the extra work and confusion, she tried to stop and give thanks that she and the rest of the family had been blessed with the strength and the good health to carry out their daily busyness. At the same time, in light of what the ailing child in the front bedroom had to endure, she found the household skirmishes and everyday irritations increasingly difficult to tolerate.

More and more, she understood why Michael had such a deep need for peace in his home and in his life . . . and why he so often went out of his way to thank her for whatever she managed to do to *keep* the peace at Bantry Hill. What he didn't know was how often she had to pray for patience with those who sometimes seemed intent on disrupting that peace.

—

Papa Emmanuel could easily be heard throughout most of the first floor when he raised his voice. For that matter, so could Moira Dempsey when, as Michael put it, "her Irish was up."

That being the case, Susanna didn't feel *too* guilty when she happened to overhear the argument taking place in the kitchen that afternoon. In truth, she was tempted simply to walk in on the fracas and hope that her intrusion would put a stop to their bickering, which of late seemed to be an almost daily event. But when one heard one's name being bandied about by raised voices, it was awfully difficult not to listen.

So she stopped just outside the door long enough to hear Riccardo Emmanuel pronounce her "too young," and "possibly too far removed from the music world to understand Michael's genius," and to know "what was best for him in his career."

Susanna bit her tongue, fully expecting Moira to agree with Michael's father. It hadn't taken her long to realize that she wouldn't have been Moira's choice for Michael. Nor had she forgotten another conversation she'd overheard some time back—goodness, she'd been eavesdropping *then*, too; she really mustn't allow this to become a habit. During *that* exchange, Liam Dempsey had been defending her to his wife, while Moira insisted that 'Even if she means well, she's too young. A girl like that is not going to tie herself down with a blind man and a child for long!'"

All the more reason she was caught completely off guard by Moira's next words. "Aye, she's young, but she understands more than you think. I say she's been good for the lad. You haven't been here long enough to notice the difference she's made in him."

Riccardo made the sound he typically uttered when he disagreed or was put out with someone. Susanna likened it to an audible breath with a nasty edge. "*Sì*, she is a pleasing girl," he said, "and perhaps she too has the gift of music—my son tells me this. But I think she is not so wise—or she would want him to return to his first love, the opera. She should want him to accept Conti's offer for *Lucia*."

Susanna's eyes widened at Moira's retort. She could almost see the housekeeper waving a kitchen utensil at Michael's father as she took him to task. "He had that world, now didn't he? And what good did it do him is what I'd like to know? Why can't you get it through that thick Eye-talian head of yours that the lad was sick of all that? Didn't he give it up? And it seems to me that should be *his* business! Sure, it's not *yours!*"

Susanna took a sharp breath. Michael's father would never stand for such disrespect.

As she'd expected, his rebuttal was harsh with anger as his accent grew stronger. "I am his father! My son's welfare—it *is* my business! And who are you, you Irish . . . busybody, that you should talk to me in such a way?"

Silence. Susanna waited, her nails digging almost painfully into the palms of her hands.

"Well, this Irish busybody has spent a good deal more time with your son than *you* have these past years," Moira shot back. "I saw what he went through when he lost his eyesight—you didn't. And I saw how that *other* one—that *Deirdre*—nearly unmanned him with her wanton ways and her drunkenness and her mean-spirited devilment. You didn't. And I've seen how much happier the man is now. Miss Susanna might be young, but she's good for him. And what's more, she'd be the first to encourage him if she thought he wanted to go back to that other world, that *opera*. But she's smart enough to know that has to be his choice, not hers."

Moira stopped, then added in a tone as cold and hard as a gravestone, "And it's for certain not *your* choice, Riccardo Emmanuel. You best stop tormenting that girl—and stop interfering in your son's life!"

The sound that came rumbling up from Papa Emmanuel's throat sounded almost dangerous. Susanna decided she'd heard enough. Besides, she fully expected Michael's father to come charging out of the kitchen like an enraged bull at any moment. With no further delay, she gathered up her skirts and hurried off.

Halfway down the hall, however, she caught herself smiling. The very idea—Moira Dempsey *defending* her! She would never have dreamed such a thing could happen.

—

Michael's morning had gone reasonably well so far. There had been few interruptions in his work, and his session with Renny Magee had been pure pleasure.

The girl was extraordinarily gifted in a number of areas, not the least of which was her perfect pitch and an innate, precise sense of rhythm that was impossible to teach. She had only to hear a tune once, and she could duplicate it almost note for note on that tin whistle of hers. Michael was already planning to try her on a flute and then a piccolo; he wouldn't be at all surprised if she didn't take to both like an eagle to flight.

His one failure with her seemed to be the ability to cheer the girl's heart. She and Maylee had become so close, such extraordinary friends, that Renny was grieving the other child's deteriorating condition. He had hoped that the music would in itself work to brighten Renny's spirits, but although she breezed through the music like a professional and did every-thing as she was told, Michael sensed that her heart wasn't altogether in her performance.

He, too, grew saddened when he thought about Maylee. He had grown quite fond of the girl. He admired her courage, her optimism, her faith, and her indefatigable sense of humor. The child could find at least a touch of lightness in almost anything, including her own condition.

He was still thinking about Maylee when his father walked into the room. It was almost as easy to identify Papa's entrance as it was Susanna's. Riccardo Emmanuel didn't so much enter a room as *sweep* into it. Surprisingly light on his feet for a man of his size, he never moved slowly. Every step seemed propelled by the man's enviable energy.

"Papa," Michael greeted him.

"Ah, at least my son concedes the fact I am his father."

Michael groaned, but silently. His father's tone as much as his words pointed to a fit of pique. No doubt he and Moira had been at it again.

"That—*woman,*" his father declared, "is *una minaccia!*"

A menace. So he *had* been arguing with Moira.

"I don't understand why you put up with her!"

"If you're referring to Moira, Papa, you know very well why. She and Liam are family to me. As they were to Grandmama and Grandpapa. I can't think what I'd do without them."

His father uttered a sound of disgust. "I never did understand your grandparents'—and your mother's—affection for the woman."

"You've been arguing again?"

"Ha! There is no arguing with that one. She is always right. I am always wrong. She is—" Michael could almost see him tapping his head. "—the great sage!"

"Papa—"

"Never mind, never mind, is not important. I have an idea and would like you to consider it."

"Of course. What kind of an idea?"

"I think we should invite *Signor* Conti to supper one

evening soon. After all, he has paid you high compliments, and it seems we should at least be gracious to acknowledge his interest in you."

A sharp pain stabbed at Michael's right temple. He pressed a hand against it, clenching his other fist. He would *not* let his father anger him or put him out of sorts—not this morning. But the headache had already begun.

"I think not, Papa. At least not anytime soon. Things are far too hectic as it is right now."

"But I think perhaps you misunderstand me. I know what you've said about not returning to the opera, and it is, of course, your decision. I mean only to be courteous to the man. Giocomo Conti is most important in the music world, yes?"

"*Sì*, he's a very important man, Papa. But I must remind you that I have no intention of performing in his *Lucia*—or in any other opera ever again."

"Michael—"

Michael heard the frustration in his father's voice and knew he was in for yet another debate about his decision to stop singing. He pulled in a long breath, bracing himself. At the same time, the pain in his head intensified.

"*Figlio mio*, why are you being so stubborn about this?"

"Why am *I* being so stubborn?" To give himself time to cool his irritation, Michael got up from the piano bench and walked to the mantel, keeping his back to his father for the time being.

"I am suggesting only a friendly meal, Michael. Nothing more."

Michael turned around, not speaking until he was sure he could do so without being argumentative. He loved his father too much to wound him or insult him, but lately Papa was trying his patience to the limit.

"Papa, don't dissemble with me. I think you're hoping that

if I share a meal and a little friendly conversation with *Signor* Conti, I'll agree to perform again."

His father tried to interrupt, but Michael warned him off. "No, let me finish, please. If I'm right, if that's your intention, it would be a complete waste of his time—and ours—to invite him here. Please, Papa, hear what I am saying. There is nothing you can do to change my mind. *Nothing.*"

Somehow he must convince his father to accept the fact for once and for all that he was finished—for good—with the world of opera. Papa's incessant harping on the subject was driving him to the end of his patience, and he knew Susanna was exceedingly tired of it as well.

"Michael, you are not being reasonable, I think—"

"Papa!" Michael cringed at his tone—when had he ever raised his voice to his father before today?—but what with the headache and Papa's obstinacy, he was finding it nearly impossible to curb his impatience. With great effort, he lowered his voice, but he was still rigid with frustration. "Papa, I love you, and I respect you—more than any man I know. But I must demand the same thing from you. I need you to accept the decisions I make regarding my own career—and any other area of my life. You must believe me. If I had any doubt in my heart—*any* doubt—that I made a mistake by leaving the opera and turning to composition and conducting, I would admit it. And I would carefully consider your opinion. But I have no doubt."

He stopped long enough to think. "I am a man, Papa, not a boy. I haven't been a boy for a very long time. You must begin seeing me as a man—your son, yes—but a man. And as a man, I believe that God has called me to this . . . place in my music—where I am today. You have no right to interfere with God's will for me, Papa. And with all respect, I must say to you that you are attempting to do just that."

He heard a sharp intake of air from his father, but he could not, he must not, relent. "Papa, don't you see? I had that other world once. I had it all—the crowds, the celebrity, the money, the . . . excitement. And I found it worthless. It gave me no peace, no joy—only emptiness. It turned me into a man I didn't even like, a man I couldn't respect."

Michael paused, struggling to find the words that would pierce his father's intransigence. "I don't regret for a moment leaving that world, and you must stop trying to make me want it again. I want you to be proud of me, Papa, to be proud of my music, what I am doing *now*. But I can't be what *you* want. I have to be what I am."

The throbbing in his head had built to a crescendo. Again he pressed his hand against his temple, trying to ease the pain. "There's one more thing, Papa. I need to say this. You have been critical of Susanna, and that too must end. This is the woman I love, the woman I have chosen to spend my life with. Susanna is a wonderful person. She has brought peace and love into my world, and I had almost given up hope I would ever find either. She loves me, and she loves Caterina— and Caterina loves her as well. And she will love you, too, Papa, if you let her. I'm asking you, for my sake, to please . . . accept Susanna as she is. Stop looking for her failings. Instead, get to know her. If you do, I believe you will find much that you approve of, much to love. But even if you don't, I cannot allow you to be disrespectful of her—you must see that. It must end."

The silence was unnerving, especially since Michael couldn't see his father's face or interpret his response. For a moment he thought he might have left the room. But, no. Michael heard a slight movement, then the sound of his father's voice, uncommonly hoarse and broken.

"Oh, my Michael . . . you cannot think I'm *not* proud of you? Surely not! *Figlio mio,* but of course I am proud of you! No man ever had such a son—such a fine son! You are my greatest pride, my deepest joy, in all the world! I would be proud of the man you are even if you could not—what do they say in the English?—carry a tune. You are my *son!*"

Caught completely unaware, Michael suddenly felt himself embraced—vigorously embraced, and held so tightly as to make him lose his breath. His father's hands were on his head, his face, his shoulders, and when Michael skimmed a hand over the other's face, he felt the dampness of his father's tears.

"Forgive me, Michael! I am a terrible man!" A dramatic explosion of Italian followed these words, along with another hard embrace, and Michael suddenly found himself comforting his father.

"Papa, no, you are not—"

Their reconciliation was abruptly interrupted by a growling, barking wolfhound who bounded into the music room and threw himself at Michael's father. Apparently Gus had heard the commotion and, believing his master to be in danger, had rushed to perform a heroic rescue.

Now Michael had to turn his efforts to convincing the great hound that he was in no jeopardy. It took both of them, Michael and his father, to calm the dog and assure him the ruckus had been friendly and nonthreatening. Soon the wolfhound was waltzing back and forth on his hind legs between the two of them, and Michael and his father were laughing like two mischievous boys at play.

Susanna picked that moment to come hurrying into the room to see what all the noise was about. Almost instantly, Michael found himself deserted as the wolfhound and his father went to Susanna.

Her cry of surprise told Michael that it was her turn to receive the attentions of Gus the wolfhound, along with one of Papa's bear hugs.

And her laughter told him she didn't mind in the least.

TWENTY-NINE

LETTERS

TWO ARE BETTER THAN ONE.

ECCLESIASTES 4:9

Frank Donovan took a friend with him when he called on Robert Warburton.

Well, not *his* friend exactly—but a friend of Doc Carmichael's. A friend who wanted to help.

Doc had been reluctant to mention Edward Fitch's offer to help. But once he did, Frank had decided the prominent attorney might be just the ticket for getting rid of that snake. Not only could Fitch fill Frank in on the finer points of the law; his reputation was bound to carry weight with a social climber like Warburton.

So dressed in his best uniform, his badge polished, his gun

on full display, and Edward Fitch at his side, Frank paid a visit to the *Reverend* Warburton.

A dignified-looking black man opened the door. When he hesitated to announce them, Edward Fitch pulled a calling card from his pocket and put a foot in the door. "Just tell your employer we need to speak with him on a most important police matter. We'll wait until he's free."

Warburton was a surprise to Frank, to say the least. Though he hadn't exactly expected the man to have horns and breathe brimstone, he wasn't looking for him to be as unimpressive in appearance as he was. He was short—a fact Frank appreciated, having found he could intimidate some blokes just by glaring down on them. The man also had a bad complexion and eyes that reminded Frank of a pig.

Clearly, he meant to keep them standing in the fancy hallway, but Frank thought he might change his mind when he heard the nature of their business. This wasn't a fella who'd want his wife listening in on what Frank and Fitch had to say.

"How can I help you . . . gentlemen?" Warburton asked.

"You might want to talk with us in private—*Reverend.*" Frank made absolutely no effort to conceal the contempt in his tone.

Warburton's gaze flicked over him, then Fitch. He lifted his eyebrows and smiled. "Goodness, what does a clergyman do to rate a call from a policeman *and* an attorney?"

He thought he was slick, Frank decided. Well, they would just see *how* slick.

"For starters, he commits fraud and defamation," Frank replied in a voice just as oily as Warburton's. "Oh, and then there's also the matter of breakin' and enterin' and vandalism of private property."

He stopped, smiling grimly at the other man's red-faced look of outrage.

"You want to talk privately *now*, Reverend?"

"In here," Warburton said, his tone sharp. He marched in front of them and opened the doors on a room Frank assumed to be a study, though quite a swanky one for a "preacher."

Warburton went to the other side of his mahogany desk and sat down. He offered no indication that Frank and Edward Fitch should do likewise, but when Frank plopped down in one of two chairs across from him, Fitch followed suit. As previously agreed, Edward Fitch took up the conversation by citing the crimes Warburton could be charged with.

It didn't take long for the man on the other side of the desk to jump to his feet, his face livid. "This is the most ridiculous thing I've ever heard! It's ludicrous! Why would you even think of accusing me of such—atrocities? Don't you know who I am?"

Edward Fitch rubbed a finger across his upper lip, staring at Warburton. "We know exactly who you are, and you're no more clergyman than I am. You're a two-bit salesman with a clever tongue and a fast pitch. You learned whatever you might know about religion in a traveling tent show."

He paused, and Warburton tried to jump in, but Fitch stopped him with a snap of his fingers.

"We also know about Mary Lambert and your illegitimate children," Fitch went on. "Oh, and I'd rather not go into detail about this, but we've come up with a fairly clear idea of your sexual perversions. You really are a disgusting man."

Frank thought he might have enjoyed this if he didn't have to *look* at Warburton. But he couldn't seem to stop thinking about that snake touching Mary Lambert, putting his hands on her. The idea that a loathsome piece of rubbish like Warburton had humiliated her—and *hurt* her—made him itch to get the man's throat between his hands.

He gave himself a mental shake. Fitch was the best one to

handle this. He knew the finer points of the law, and he could outtalk Warburton without batting an eye.

In fact, he had him squirming like a worm on a hook already, although the man was doing his best to wiggle free.

"I won't hear another word of this," Warburton sputtered. "I don't know this . . . *Mary Lambert* person. And all this nonsense about vandalism and such—I don't know what you're talking about! You simply cannot come in here and insult with me with this filth."

Frank could no longer hold his tongue. "Ah, but we *are* here, and if it's filth you want to talk about, let's us have a talk about what you did to Mary Lambert."

Fitch reached over and put a hand to Frank's arm. Frank straightened a bit and closed his mouth.

"Sergeant Donovan here is prepared to take you with us as we leave," Fitch said, his tone casual. "You'll be charged and held, you understand, until you can hire yourself an attorney."

Then he stopped and locked eyes with Warburton. "But whoever you hire won't be able to help you very much if we produce a witness who can substantiate most of the charges brought against you. The breaking and entering might be a bit shaky, although I imagine it won't be all that difficult to locate the thugs you hired for the job."

Warburton twisted his mouth into an ugly scowl. "If you're so sure of yourselves, why haven't you arrested me already?"

Again Fitch smiled. "Is that what you really want? We'll be glad to oblige if you do."

Now it was Frank's turn. He got to his feet and pulled himself up to his full height. "A couple of things you need to know—*Reverend.* Doc Carmichael is a good friend of mine—my closest friend, as a matter of fact. And Doc is a real good man. I mean a *good* man, not that you'd know much about the breed."

Frank shook his head. "But me—I'm not a good man at all. In fact, I can be a very nasty fella altogether, and I'd just as soon make mutton out of your face as anything I can think of right about now. I just plain don't *like* you. And if I thought you were going to be locked up, out of my reach for any length of time, I'm afraid I'd have to at least settle my differences with you before they threw you in the cell. But Mr. Fitch here, he thinks there's a better way to maybe save your skin and work things out for all concerned. If you're interested, you might want to hear him out."

Warburton settled a killing glare on Frank. "Why *should* I be interested?"

Frank lowered himself back to the chair as Edward Fitch took over. "It might keep you out of jail, for one thing. Oh, by the way, I don't think I've explained that, like Sergeant Donovan, I'm also a good friend of Dr. Carmichael. He once saved my life. So you can imagine that I'm grateful. That's why I'm here."

Fitch dusted a speck of lint off his suit coat before going on. "Here's what I think might help your situation. You'll make a complete, detailed statement of your involvement in the vandalism of the doctor's office. You'll confess to the outrageous letters that have been appearing in the newspaper defaming Dr. Carmichael—you'll send a copy of that admission to those same newspapers, by the way."

"I didn't write those letters!" Carmichael burst out.

"If you didn't," Edward Fitch shot back, "you know who did. But you'll confess to them, all the same—and retract the accusations. Then you'll admit to your abuse of Mary Lambert and make arrangements to pay for the support of your illegitimate children—say, through a trust fund. I can assist you with that matter this very afternoon."

Warburton looked as if he might keel over from a massive stroke at any moment. Edward Fitch, however, was not quite finished. He made a clucking sound with his teeth, then said, "You know, Warburton, you very likely could have saved yourself a great deal of trouble by simply agreeing to what Andrew Carmichael asked of you in the first place. If you had consented to pay for the support of your own children, more than likely no investigation would have ever taken place. I must say, that was quite foolish on your part."

By now, Frank was growing impatient with all this gentlemen's blather. "So what's it goin' to be, Warburton? A cell or a retraction?"

Warburton ignored him, directing his reply to Edward Fitch instead. Frank decided that he must like lawyers better than cops.

"If I do this, I'll lose everything," Warburton whined. "I'll have to leave town, my ministry—"

"Your *ministry?*" Frank burst out. He couldn't help himself. The man was either a fool or a lunatic.

Warburton leveled a look of pure hatred on him, but Fitch redirected the man's attention. "Well, you're right about losing everything, of course. And as you might have realized, that's exactly what we want and expect."

Warburton sat leaning on his elbows, his fingers laced in front of his face. "You'll guarantee I can . . . leave . . . if I do what you ask? There will be no jail time?"

Fitch sat forward a little. "You can leave. About the jail time—well, that depends on what you get yourself into wherever you land next, now doesn't it?"

The man's shoulders finally sagged, as did his features. "All right. I'll do it. Not because I'm guilty, you understand, but I can see you're resolved to frame me."

"Whatever you say," Fitch said, "Now, I don't believe either Sergeant Donovan or I are in any particular hurry. We'll wait for you to write your . . . information. We'll need two signed copies, by the way. But take your time."

Warburton obviously knew he'd lost. Fishing some stationery from his desk drawer and a pen from its holder, he began to write. Frank sat watching, knowing Fitch had been right about the probability of Warburton's getting off. A sharp lawyer in New York City could get a man acquitted of just about anything, including murder. But he didn't like letting this slime get away with what he had done.

On the other hand, perhaps losing his reputation, his fortune, his fancy house—maybe even his rich wife—might be more punishment for a man like Warburton than a jail cell would ever be.

Frank fervently hoped so.

In his study, Andrew Carmichael prepared to write a letter of his own. He had known for some time now that he had to do this. The way the word *truth* kept insinuating itself into his life and his thoughts was no coincidence, he was certain.

He had seen the way lies had nearly destroyed Natalie Guthrie. And deceit—along with some abnormal appetites— had turned Robert Warburton into a veritable monster.

But that wasn't all. On a daily basis now, every Scripture Andrew turned to, every book he read, seemed to emblazon the word *truth* on his conscience and in his heart. How much clearer did God have to make it?

The Lord was relentlessly pressing the need for this letter upon him, and he dared not delay any longer. For Bethany's sake, he dreaded its almost inevitable consequences. To spare her the shame and humiliation, though she would certainly object, he would try to convince her to break their engagement.

That prospect hurt most of all. Andrew thought he could lose everything he had without half the pain that losing Bethany would bring him. But if he kept Bethany and continued to live in the shadows of a sordid past, wouldn't their relationship eventually suffer from it? No, he *had* to tell the truth, no matter the cost.

He saw now that the damage to him and his reputation wasn't entirely due to the rumors or the accusatory letters. It came from half-truths and his unwillingness either to deny the accusations—which of course he couldn't do—or else bare his soul and admit there was indeed some truth in the letters and the rumors. He needed to tell the whole story and trust the Lord for what would happen next—though he was fairly certain he already knew.

With a heavy heart but a convicted conscience, Andrew Carmichael locked his study door, sat down at his desk, and began to write.

———

Bethany knocked lightly on the closed door to Andrew's study, but there was no response. She waited another moment before trying again, thinking he might be in conference with a patient. When there was no answer to her second attempt, she spoke his name.

"I'm busy right now, Bethany. I'll be out later."

His voice sounded weak and tight, as if he were either ill or under a great deal of strain.

"Are you all right, Andrew?"

In the same peculiar tone, he replied, "Yes, of course. I just need some time alone, please."

Disturbed and a little hurt, she hesitated, then finally walked to the waiting room door and ushered an elderly woman, one of their two waiting patients, into the examining room. By the time she'd completed the examination and that of the next patient, a young woman from Russia who spoke only a few words of English, Bethany expected to find the door to Andrew's study open.

But it wasn't. By now she was growing uneasy. Andrew had never shut himself off from her this way, not for so long a time and certainly not without an explanation. After everything that had happened over the past few days, she didn't know what to think. Andrew had been so . . . different lately. And despite her earlier resolve, she couldn't keep the doubts from her mind.

She hated herself for doing so, but she went to check the pharmacy cabinet in his examining room. Before she could unlock it to see if anything was amiss, however, she pressed her face between her hands and ordered herself to stop.

She deliberated only a few more seconds before again going to the closed door of his study and knocking firmly. "Andrew? Please, may I come in?"

After a long hesitation, he replied in a voice so quiet she had to strain to hear. "Not just yet. I've something I need to finish."

Now she was frightened. In spite of the disgust she felt for what she was about to do, Bethany went back to the examining room and unlocked the cabinet that held their supply of narcotics and other drugs. There didn't seem to be anything missing. But *something* was obviously going on in Andrew's office—something he didn't want her to know about.

She stood in the hall, staring at the closed door. Then, her decision made, she tossed off her apron and left the building.

—

Frank Donovan had returned to the station house with one of Warburton's signed confessions in hand. The knowledge that the lying trickster would be out of town before the week ended was little comfort, but he knew he had to let it go. At least this guaranteed that no silver-tongued attorney would get the serpent off scot-free.

And maybe, just maybe, once she realized Warburton was out of her life for good, Mary Lambert would be able to heal and begin a new life. He was considering asking Miss Fanny Crosby to call on her. The woman made him uneasy with her constant urgings to "accept the Lord," but Frank somehow knew Miss Fanny would do everything she could to help Mary. It was known all about the city that the little blind woman was more than a famous writer of hymns. She was also a good one to call if you needed help.

Come to think of it, maybe he'd best pay a little more attention himself to what Miss Fanny had to say. It couldn't hurt. He'd been so mired of late in the disgusting goings-on of the likes of Robert Warburton and some of the other filthy rabble he encountered on his job that he was beginning to feel a bit soiled himself. And it wouldn't be making any sort of commitment just to listen, after all.

He was leaning back against the counter, reading through the confession for the fifth time, when Bethany Cole walked in.

"Well, now," he said, straightening and doffing his hat. "I'd ask what a lovely lady like yourself is doin' in a place like this, if I didn't know that you often venture into *worse* places, Lady Doc. To what do I owe the pleasure?"

He took a closer look at her and saw that she was in no mood for his teasing.

—

When Bethany saw Frank Donovan leaning against the counter in the crowded police station, his usual smirk in place, she had to remind herself of everything the big Irish policeman was doing to help Andrew. Even so, at the moment she had no patience for his sarcasm.

"I think I might need your help," she said.

Donovan stood watching her, twirling his hat on the tip of one finger. "You'll understand if I seem a bit surprised to hear that, Dr. Cole. By the way, the Warburton business has been taken care of. Doc's going to be all right. But what is it that brings you here?"

"It's Andrew," Bethany said, so tense she was sure her nails must be drawing blood from her clenched hands.

He stilled, his expression instantly changing to one of concern. "Something's happened to Doc?"

"I don't know," Bethany said, fighting to keep the tremor from her voice. "I need you to come with me. I'm afraid there's something wrong. Will you come? I'll explain on the way."

Donovan's dark eyes probed hers as he pushed away from the counter. "Is Doc all right?"

Bethany looked at him, fighting to hold off the fear closing in on her. "No. I mean, I don't know."

Donovan caught her arm and shouldered their way through a group of officers gathered by the door. "Over here," he said, propelling her toward a police wagon directly across the street.

—

Andrew stared in confusion as Bethany and Frank Donovan came bursting through the door of the waiting room and stood looking at him.

"Bethany?" She had the most peculiar look.

"Frank?" His friend, too, appeared somewhat bewildered.

"Andrew, are you all right?" said Bethany.

"Of course, I'm all right," he answered her. "Why?"

"You sure, Doc?" Frank put in before Bethany could reply.

"What's going on with you two? You look as if you've seen a ghost. Do I look that bad?"

He watched as Frank took a deep breath. "You look a bit peaked, to tell you truth, Doc."

"Well, I might be a little tired, that's all," said Andrew. "What are you doing here, Frank? Aren't you on duty?"

"Oh, aye. I am. But—" Frank stopped, darting a glance at Bethany, who was still studying Andrew.

"Are you quite sure nothing's wrong, Andrew?" she said.

He frowned, then decided to go ahead and tell them about the letter he'd just posted.

Frank looked as if he might be sick, and Bethany turned pale.

"Doc," Frank said, "there was no need to do that. We've got a full retraction from Warburton. The papers will print it, I'll make sure of that. You needn't have written a word!"

Bethany said nothing, but simply stood watching.

"I had to, Frank," said Andrew. "I couldn't defend myself as things were. Part of those letters to the editor were true. You know that. I *was* an addict."

"Even so, Doc, nobody ever had to know, not with Warburton owning up to what he did. And he'll be gone—out of your life—in a day or two." Frank actually looked woeful when he repeated, "Nobody would have had to know, Doc."

"*I* knew," Andrew said. "And I'm asking both of you to try to understand. I couldn't live with myself any longer. I've concealed this part of my past for years. I've let it eat at me too long as it is. I think it would eventually have poisoned me."

He turned to Bethany. "I'm so sorry, Bethany. I know this is going to make things harder for you, but I simply had to do it."

To his amazement, a slow smile broke over her face.

"What?" he said.

She shook her head. "I'm just so—proud of you."

Andrew stared at her. So did Frank Donovan.

"*Proud* of me?" Andrew said.

"Oh, yes," she replied, still smiling. "Very proud. It took real courage to write that letter."

Frank looked from one to the other. "It wasn't necessary," he insisted sourly.

Bethany turned to him. "I think it was, Frank. For Andrew, it was crucial."

"So you *do* understand," said Andrew.

She nodded and stretched to kiss him on the cheek. "I understand. And I think you're the bravest, most honest man I've ever known."

"Too honest for his own good, I'm thinkin'," groused Frank Donovan.

"Oh, stop it, Frank!" said Andrew. "You big phony. You don't fool me anymore. You're not half as tough as you want everyone to think. At heart, you're just like me."

Frank Donovan couldn't have looked more surprised if Andrew had stuck him. The look of total incredulity on his face actually made Bethany—and then Andrew—laugh.

"Well," Bethany said, "I don't know if I'd go *that* far."

Frank's ruddy face had turned a deeper shade than usual. He put on his hat, then took it off again. "If you think you had to do it, Doc," he finally said, "I suppose that's good enough for me." He hesitated, then said, "When are you two getting married anyway?"

They both spoke at once.

"Soon," said Andrew.

"Next week," said Bethany.

"Time to go," said Frank Donovan as he hurried out the door, banging his shoulder against the wall in his rush.

Andrew turned to Bethany. "Next *week?*"

She nodded. "Absolutely."

Andrew took her by the shoulders and allowed himself to be drawn into her gaze. "Next week," he said. "Absolutely."

THIRTY

WHEN GOD HAPPENS

THROUGH MANY DANGERS, TOILS, AND SNARES,

I HAVE ALREADY COME;

'TIS GRACE HATH BROUGHT ME SAFE THUS FAR,

AND GRACE WILL LEAD ME HOME.

JOHN NEWTON

No, Mum! I *can't* stay home today. I already explained all this to you. I promised Mrs. Dempsey and Miss Susanna I'd for certain work today, tomorrow, and Saturday. There's extra to be done for the family because of Easter."

Vangie MacGovern threw up her hands in resignation—and no small measure of frustration—at her daughter's reply. "What about *your* family? Or don't we matter all, now that you've got yourself such a fine job up at the Big House?"

She was irked by the way Nell Grace stood looking at her, hands on her hips, her mouth pursed in impatience.

"Am I not giving you enough of my wages, Mum? You know very well I'm not doing this for myself!"

Not waiting for Vangie to answer, she grabbed her sewing bag off the kitchen table and left the house, letting the door swing shut behind her with a thud.

Vangie tried to ignore the sense of shame that stole over her in the wake of their argument. In all fairness, Nell Grace had been more than generous with the money she earned. The girl hadn't a selfish bone in her body, and that was the truth. She helped fix breakfast for the children before she left for the hill in the morning, and after working a full day, she would come home to start supper for the rest of them, help the twins with their homework, bathe Emma, and do whatever was needed until bedtime.

But the girl was no help at all with the baby. And that was the source of Vangie's resentment, although she wouldn't have admitted it to anyone but herself. It seemed that everyone in the family was usually too busy to help with the babe, leaving almost the entire responsibility to her.

Something at the edge of her thoughts whispered that she *was* the baby's mother, after all. What did she expect? And what was wrong with her anyway, that after all this time she still hadn't the energy—or the desire—to care for her own child?

She told herself it was the fatigue, the continual exhaustion that had gripped her like a vise ever since she'd given birth.

And ever since she'd learned of Aidan's death.

Some mornings she actually got out of bed with the full intention of doing better, telling herself that today she would get back to being the kind of wife and mother she had once been. She vowed she would clean the house and cook Conn a nice noonday meal and spend more time with the babe and little Emma. Perhaps she would even fix herself up a bit, put on a pretty dress that Conn favored.

And in truth, she should have been able to do just that. She was stronger now. She could feel her health coming back. But by midmorning, after nursing the baby and putting him back to bed, her good intentions would disappear. The weariness and feelings of infirmity would send her back to her chair by the window, where she would sit and watch Emma play for the next few hours until Conn came in. Then she would get up and fix him and Emma a bite to eat, tend to the babe again and, after Conn was gone, put both little ones down for a nap. And then she would sleep—that is, when the baby *allowed* her to sleep.

The trouble was, the wee mite was restless and slept only fitfully. Lately he'd been colicky, and Vangie sometimes caught herself pressing her hands over her ears, unable to bear his feeble but piercing cries another moment. She would even shriek at him to be quiet, but the sound of her raised voice only made him scream that much louder. Yesterday he'd scarcely slept at all, and every time he cried, Vangie had also dissolved into a fit of weeping that left her limp as a scrub rag, her nerves completely raw, by suppertime.

Even then, Nell Grace made no attempt to take over the wee one's care. She busied herself in the kitchen after their meal, leaving the babe to Vangie.

As for Renny, *she* was worthless entirely where the babe was concerned. How a girl almost grown could be afraid of a tiny babe was beyond understanding, but that was definitely the case with Renny Magee. She simply wouldn't hold him at all unless she was forced into it, much less change a didy or give him a bath.

Lately, Vangie had grown so desperate that she sometimes caught herself intoning a monotonous prayer, over and over again like a chant, a plea that the Lord would help her see the babe with love rather than as a kind of . . . parasite, which was how she sometimes viewed him. Then her blood would chill as she realized what an unnatural thing this was, having to plead for the capacity to love her own child.

And then there was Conn. The man had been more patient with her than any woman deserved. But if she sometimes felt ashamed of the way she was hurting him—deserting him, in truth—she also felt helpless to do anything about it. She hated the pain in his eyes when he looked at her, so most of the time she simply turned away from him, refusing to look.

The awareness of what she was turning into made Vangie retreat even more deeply into herself. At times she felt as if she were buried, hidden away from everyone she knew. Indeed, the deadness of spirit with which she'd lived since losing Aidan seemed to be spreading over her like some dark creature of the sea, its tentacles choking off every part of her.

There were even moments when Vangie caught herself listening for her heartbeat to stop.

And moments when she thought she would welcome the silence.

—

Nell Grace felt as if she were drowning in the torrent of feelings that rushed over her as she climbed the hill toward the Big House. Never had she felt such a mixture of desperation and anger and helplessness.

Her grand plan wasn't working, that much was obvious, and she was beginning to feel like a fool for ever believing it would. Her mother might be going through the routine of caring for baby Will, but anyone could see that's all it was to her—a routine. If she had any feelings for the poor wee babe at all, she seemed intent on not showing them, especially to *him*.

What else could Nell Grace do? She couldn't *force* Mum to love the baby. No one could do that. Except perhaps the Lord.

But in spite of all her asking—and she *had* asked, countless times—He didn't seem to be listening.

She was beginning to get really angry with her mother, who shouldn't have made Aidan her whole life, after all. She had five other children, including herself, who needed a mother's attention and affection. And Da—well, he was about as helpless as a man could be in the face of what was happening. Every time she tried to talk to him about Mum, he would mumble something about her not being completely over William's birth yet or her not having all her strength back or how much better she would be once winter was gone and she could get outside and work in her garden. Nothing but excuses, and so far as Nell Grace could see, none of them reliable.

But Da had always been a bit soft where Mum was concerned.

No, Dad was a *lot* soft where Mum was concerned, and in truth, would she want him to be any other way? Besides, she knew he felt as helpless as she did, and that must be terrible for a man when he loved his wife as much as Da obviously loved Mum.

She looked up to see Paul Santi standing in the backyard of the Big House, watching her. He removed his eyeglasses, smiled and waved at her, and Nell Grace's heart lifted. They talked almost every day now, not for more than five or ten minutes, but she was learning to like him ever so much. He was the nicest young man. So polite and thoughtful and funny.

Da, of course, would take none of these things into account once he learned that she was interested in an Italian gentleman. She could almost hear him calling Paul just that, in that way he had of drawing out the words that made it sound as if he were saying something bad: "that *Eye-talian* fella."

Well, Da would just have to learn that she wasn't going to be ordered around anymore like a schoolgirl. She would soon be eighteen years old, the age of a woman, not a child. She had a job. She was an adult. She liked Paul Santi—and he liked her, she could tell. She thought he liked her a lot. And if she was old enough to work full-time for Mr. Emmanuel, help keep house and stand in for her mother with baby Will—not to mention raising the other children at least a part of the time— then she was old enough to talk to the young man of her choice, whether he happened to be Irish or *Eye-talian.*

So full of her imaginings about a coming conflict between her father and Paul Santi was she that, for a moment at least, she nearly forgot her sadness and discouragement about her mother and baby Will. When she remembered, she said yet another prayer for the both of them, then quickened her steps to meet Paul at the gate.

—

By midafternoon, after Conn had gone back to work and Emma had settled for her nap, Vangie felt the old, familiar lethargy begin to seep through her. The sky, earlier bright with sunshine, had darkened now, with clouds quickly moving in. The encroaching gloom seemed to reflect her mood.

She had heard nothing from the baby for over an hour. Although she was grateful for the quiet, she supposed she ought to go and check on him.

She found him lying quietly in the crib Conn had originally made for Emma. He wasn't sleeping after all, but wide awake, lying quietly and staring at the foot of the crib. Vangie watched him for a moment, and for the first time she seemed to really *see* his thinness, the nearly translucent quality of his pale skin, the red-gold highlights in the puff of downy hair that covered his head. *So delicate, so frail . . .*

Her other babies, the ones who had lived, had been sturdy

little things with rosy cheeks and plump limbs and round tummies. Aidan, especially, had been unusually large and robust. "All boy," she remembered Conn saying, pride evident in his tone and in his eyes.

The memory of her firstborn hit her like a hammer blow. Her eyes filled, and she was about to turn and leave the room when her attention was caught by the baby's faint gurgle and the way his attention seemed to be locked on his own feet.

She followed his gaze. There, inching its way toward one tiny foot, was the largest, most terrifying spider she'd ever seen. It was black and covered with fur and obscenely ugly.

Vangie cried out, and the baby snapped his head to look at her. He wailed, kicking his feet and flailing his fists. Vangie grabbed him, whisked him up under one arm, and frantically called for Renny Magee.

She had always been terrified of spiders. Even the small ones. She could imagine unknown horrors at the very sight of one. Indeed, she would shriek for Conn or Renny at the sight of a dark blot on the wall that turned out to be nothing more than a smudge. But this—this *thing* was the worst she had ever encountered.

And it had been in her baby's crib—it had threatened her child.

Renny was not to be found. Then Vangie remembered the girl had gone up to the Big House to visit her ailing friend. And Conn was down at the stables well out of earshot. Vangie paced the floor, holding the babe securely against her as she frantically tried to think what to do. Finally, drawing a determined breath, she hurried to fetch the broom from the kitchen pantry.

When she came back, the ugly thing was still squatting in the crib as if looking for new prey. Plopping wee William in his basket by the window, she swept the horrible creature through the rails of the crib onto the floor, where she proceeded to beat it with the flat of the broom as hard as she could until it finally gave up its struggle and shriveled into a lifeless blot on the floor.

Still shaking, she stared down at her grisly work with a peculiar sense of triumph, then set the broom aside and retrieved the babe from his basket.

She looked down at the baby boy cuddled against her shoulder. He was watching her with wide eyes but no sign of fear. Indeed, his expression was curious, as if this might be some sort of game devised for his entertainment.

Vangie carried him into the bedroom. Not until she collapsed on the rocking chair by the window did she begin to weep—softly at first, then harder. All the guilt and the anguish of the past weeks came rushing in on her like an avalanche, dislodging the wall she had set around her heart.

She saw it all now, saw what she had done, what she had allowed to happen—and it was a bitter awareness entirely. She had been so unfair to Nell Grace—to all of them. She had forsaken her own responsibilities as a mother and hardened her heart not only to the wee boy in her arms, but to her other children . . . and her husband, her faithful, long-suffering Conn. She had absented herself from the ones who loved her best. Because of her grief for the one lost, she had grieved the ones who needed her most.

Had it not been for the baby in her arms, Vangie thought she might have broken in half with the weight of her selfishness, her sin. She leaned her head back against the chair and squeezed her eyes shut and wept. *"Oh God, oh Lord God, forgive me!"*

Only then did the babe begin his own surge of wailing. Realizing that she'd startled him, Vangie quickly gathered him closer and began to soothe him, pressing her cheek against his as she patted his back and rubbed his silken head.

"Shush now, sweet William," she crooned softly. "You're safe now. Mother's here. Don't cry. Mother's here."

After a moment, he stopped. With her own tears still tracking down her face, Vangie turned him onto her lap, on his back, so she could study him. His soft white nightdress was too big for his teensy body, but he *was* growing some, she noticed. He had long fingers and long toes for such a wee thing, and she saw now that his ears stuck out just as the twins' had when they were born.

"Never you mind about those ears," she told him. "You'll grow into them soon enough."

She continued to look him over, each tiny part of him a discovery. "Why, he's perfect," she murmured, running a finger over the tops of his toes. So tiny, but perfect indeed. He quirked his fair, red-gold eyebrows as he examined Vangie's face, and what appeared to be a smile in the making appeared, tugging at the corners of his mouth.

Vangie's tears fell over him, and he lifted a wee fist to touch the dampness on his cheeks. She lifted him then and buried her face in the softness of his flannel-covered body and then, just as she had with her other babes, she inhaled the warm sweetness of him, breathing deeply of the promise and the glory a new babe had always held for her.

A few minutes later, little Emma came shuffling into the room, rubbing her eyes. She had obviously slept right through all the excitement but now intended to claim her place with her mother and baby brother. Thumb in mouth, she crossed over to the rocking chair and climbed up beside them.

—

That was how Nell Grace and Renny Magee found them when they came home later that afternoon—Vangie, baby

Will, and wee Emma all cuddled together asleep in the rocking chair by the bedroom window.

Nell Grace stood watching her mother with her baby brother, her little sister huddled close to them. After a long moment, she brushed a tear away, then turned to look at Renny.

Renny met her gaze, and Nell Grace smiled at her. "Mum will be all right now, Renny," she said.

"Aye," Renny said, her voice hushed, her own eyes damp. "So it would seem." She turned to again look at Vangie and the baby. "I wonder what happened."

Nell Grace, too, returned her attention to the scene by the window. "God," she said to Renny Magee. "I'm thinking God happened."

—

Late that night, with the moonlight streaming through their bedroom window, Conn MacGovern lay drinking in the sight of his wife and the infant in her arms, both sleeping soundly.

There could be no more beautiful sight in the world, he thought, swallowing hard against the swelling in his throat. Vangie, her riot of dark red hair fanned out over the white bed-sheet, the wee boy tucked against his mother's heart.

Contentment. Peace. Beauty.

All the lovely words he could think of, the words that spoke of God's blessing and a man's joy, went drifting through his mind. He was growing drowsy, yet was reluctant to sleep. He could be a happy man just lying here the rest of the night, watching the woman he had loved for more than twenty years and the tiny, newest evidence of that love.

Here, tonight, in this room that looked out on the place the Lord had brought them to, was everything a man could ever want, ever need. Oh, they'd been through their valleys, that was true. They had known hunger and homelessness and sickness and the loss of loved ones—*oh, Aidan, my son!* They had met with disdain and contempt and outright hatred in some places of this country they now called home. He supposed they'd experienced just about every hurt, every heartache, every loss, that human beings could know.

But in the midst of it all, they had also known grace. God's grace. That's what had brought them this far. And as he watched his sleeping wife and child, and as the years of their lives played through his memories and his thoughts like a continuous river of dreams, Conn MacGovern knew that in the years to come they would know that grace again. And again.

And again.

THIRTY-ONE

BEYOND THESE WALLS

WHEN MY SPIRIT, CLOTHED IMMORTAL,
WINGS ITS FLIGHT TO REALMS OF DAY,
THIS MY SONG THROUGH ENDLESS AGES:
JESUS LED ME ALL THE WAY.

FANNY CROSBY

Maylee died on Easter Sunday evening.

Miss Susanna had sent for Renny Magee late in the afternoon, so Renny was there when Maylee drifted quietly off to sleep and didn't wake up.

Up until then, she read to her from Maylee's favorite book, the Holy Bible, pausing once to remind her friend that the only reason she was able to read *anything* was because Maylee had taught her. She didn't know if Maylee heard her or not, but she felt the need to thank her one more time.

She also played her tin whistle, because Maylee always urged her to do so during their visits. She played Maylee's favorite hymn, one written just recently by Miss Fanny Crosby, a friend of the *maestro* and a frequent visitor to Bantry Hill. Renny knew she would never play or listen to that hymn again without hearing Maylee's pure, high voice singing the words as she almost always did when Renny played it:

All the way my Savior leads me;
Oh, the fullness of His love!
Perfect rest to me is promised
In my Father's house above:
When my spirit, clothed immortal,
Wings its flight to realms of day,
This my song through endless ages:
Jesus led me all the way.

Before she left, Renny looked back one last time at the room where she had spent so many hours with her friend. Cookie, Maylee's kitten, was peeping out at her from underneath the bed—Miss Susanna had promised she would take good care of her. The jar of marbles Renny had given Maylee still sat on the window sill, but their sparkle was gone without the sun to cast its light on them. The Easter present she'd given Maylee, a paperweight she'd made of multicolored, carefully polished tiles—now rested on the bedside table. Maylee's eyes had been heavy when Renny helped her open the package, but she had smiled at the sight of all the colors.

Renny managed not to weep until after she left the Big House. Even when Miss Susanna led her from the room after Maylee died, and even when both she and the *maestro* gave Renny a hug and told her what a good friend she had been to Maylee, she remained dry-eyed.

She was able to hold back her tears because she knew Maylee would have scolded her for weeping. She would have reminded Renny that she had been eager for this day for some time now and welcomed it when it came.

Outside the house, as she started home, Renny wondered if Maylee was flying now. The younger girl had always been keen on the idea of flying and talked about it often, especially when she talked about heaven.

Renny had never thought much about heaven one way or the other until she became friends with Maylee. Even though she had given her heart to Jesus several months before, heaven just didn't occupy much space in her thoughts. In truth, it was a subject that seemed to be reserved for old people.

But Maylee wasn't old, not really, even though her disease had made her look and feel old. Even though she was only eleven—almost twelve, as Maylee liked to say—she didn't mind talking about heaven at all. In fact, she *liked* to talk about it. She was always wondering if she really would "wing her flight" to get there.

"Even though I'll have a new and perfect body, I hope I'm not confined to just walking around all the time," she'd said to Renny during one of their conversations about heaven. "I hope I'll be able to just fly around with the angels and go everywhere and see all the wonderful things they see. I get so tired of never being able to go anywhere or see anything but walls."

The memory made Renny choke on a sob, and she stopped where she was, plopping down on the side of the hill toward home. No longer able to contain her grief, she finally let the tears flow. She wept until she thought her heart had been wrung dry and there could be no more sorrow in her.

Nell Grace found her there and eased down beside her. After a moment she put her arm around Renny's shoulders. And as the twilight crept in on the hillside and the stars began to fire the evening sky, the two girls sat and quietly wept together.

THIRTY-TWO

HOMECOMING

A HOUSE IS BUILT OF LOGS AND STONE,
OF TILES AND POSTS AND PIERS;
A HOME IS BUILT OF LOVING DEEDS
THAT STAND A THOUSAND YEARS.

VICTOR HUGO

T wo weeks after Easter, Renny Magee was finishing up the ironing—a task she actively detested and rarely undertook voluntarily. Today, however, she had offered to do at least a part of it in order to help out Nell Grace, who was working all day at the Big House.

As she ironed, she was watching over baby Will and Emma so Vangie could finish hanging the freshly laundered curtains in the twins' bedroom. The monotony of heating the iron and pressing the clothes gave her too much time to think, and since she'd mostly been thinking about Maylee, her mood had become increasingly somber.

Although the day was golden bright and warmer than any weather they'd had so far this spring, to Renny everything seemed faded and dull with the ache of Maylee's absence. Sometimes on days like this she still caught herself anticipating her afternoon visit with her friend. Then she would remember that there would be no visit with Maylee ever again, and the raw place deep inside her would burn with pain.

On this afternoon, too, there was something else on her mind, something that carried with it its own pall of gloom. With Maylee gone and Vangie back to her old self, there was really no need for Renny to stay on with the MacGoverns now. She had already stayed past the time she'd committed to work for them, delaying her departure as long as she could out of sheer reluctance to leave.

As crowded as things were in the small MacGovern house, more than likely they would be relieved to see her go. What with her having used their Aidan's passage to come across and then him later lost at sea, she couldn't fault them for any hard feelings toward her, though if such resentment existed among them, she'd seen no sign of it.

Even so, they no longer seemed to need her help as much as before, and there was really nothing to hold her here any longer. Nothing except her feelings for them all. And they wouldn't be knowing about *that*—or caring, even if they did.

Renny glanced at Emma, who was trying to get her wee brother's attention by shaking a baby rattle in his face. The baby, however, seemed more interested in what Renny was doing as she set the iron on its heel atop the stove.

He was a cute little fella, with those funny ears and the thatch of strawberry-blond hair on top of his head. It was a relief to see Vangie now so wrapped up in the new baby that she hesitated to let anyone else tend to him. Once Renny had overcome her initial nervousness, she'd discovered she actually enjoyed holding him now and again. And when he clutched at her shirt front with his wee fingers and studied her up close, as if he found her highly fascinating—well, she liked it well enough, she had to admit. On occasion she even fantasized about what it would be like to have a baby brother of her own, not that there was any chance of *that* ever coming to pass.

For another moment, Renny stood watching a squirrel scurry down the oak tree outside the kitchen window. Then she turned, gathered wee William up in his basket, and took Emma by the hand.

"Let's go change your baby brother's didy," she said, wrinkling her nose at the little girl to coax a smile. "Everyone will be in for supper soon, and we can't have him disgracing himself, now can we?"

—

It seemed to Renny that Conn MacGovern and Vangie were acting strangely over supper tonight. For that matter, Nell Grace also appeared to have something on her mind. There was much glancing back and forth across the table—long, meaningful looks accompanied by a smile or even a giggle now and then— and the twins were more rambunctious than usual. Their da had to quiet their whisperings and foolishness more than once.

When Renny scraped her chair back from the table after the meal and asked to be excused, she was caught unawares entirely by Conn MacGovern's reply. "Not just yet, lass. We've been wanting to talk with you, and now would seem as good a time as any."

Something shattered inside Renny. So it had come, then. They were going to ask her to leave before she could make the decision herself. She ought to have expected it. She should have been steeled for it. But she wasn't. She had all she could do to keep from blubbering like a wee tyke as she scooted her chair back up to the table and glanced around at the faces that were now all turned toward her, watching her.

Conn MacGovern cleared his throat—always a sure sign that he had a serious topic on his mind. Renny sat up a little straighter, forcing herself to look him straight in the eye.

"No doubt you'll recall that when we agreed to bring you across with us, we had an agreement," he began.

Renny nodded, and he went on. "You were to earn the price of your passage by working for us no less than six months after we arrived. Do you recall that?"

"Aye," said Renny, her mouth so dry she could scarcely get the word out.

"Well, then, as I'm sure you're aware, you've fulfilled your commitment and then some."

Again, Renny nodded. *Say it. Just say it, won't you? Let's have it over with.* She wanted to run from the room screaming. She wanted to be alone so they wouldn't see her pain. She wanted to shut her ears entirely and pretend this wasn't happening . . .

"Well, we've been thinking, lass, that although your work has been exemplary—"

Conn MacGovern did love his big words, Renny thought bitterly, squeezing her arms around her middle to keep the pain from stealing her breath.

"—and in truth we have no complaints, none at all, with the arrangement as it is—"

"Oh, for goodness' sake, Conn!"

Renny darted a look at Vangie, who was wiping her hands on her apron and frowning at her husband. She turned to Renny, her frown giving way to a smile. "What the man is trying to say, Renny—though why he's having so much trouble getting it out,

I can't think—is that we've talked with Mr. Emmanuel, who knows about these things. And he's agreed to help us go through the proper channels—if you're willing, that is—to adopt you."

Renny gaped at her, then at Conn MacGovern, who was grinning like a fox. To her dismay and utter humiliation, she felt her face begin to crumple. She blinked furiously, knotting her hands beneath the table so their shaking couldn't be seen.

"Adopt me?" she croaked, sniffing a bit to keep her nose from dripping.

"Yes, Renny," Vangie said quietly, still smiling. "We'd like it very much if you were to be our daughter. How would you feel about that?"

How would she *feel* about it? She would feel as though the angels were dancing on her shoulders—that's how she'd feel!

"You—you don't want me to leave, then?"

"*Leave?*" Conn MacGovern and Vangie and Nell Grace all voiced the word in unison. It was Vangie who answered her first.

"Oh, Renny! Of course, we don't want you to leave! You're one of the family!"

"You're like a sister to me, Renny," said Nell Grace. Emma clapped her hands and squealed, "Sister! Renny *my* sister too!" The twins nodded their agreement. Then Johnny poked James and James punched his arm in retaliation—and Vangie shot them one of her looks.

Renny turned then to Conn MacGovern, who, slightly red-faced, glanced around the table at his family, then lifted his tumbler of water high, inclining his head toward her. "We all agree that you're as much a part of our family as is any one of us, lass, and we wouldn't like to think of your leaving. We'll do whatever it takes to make it official for you to be our daughter, Vangie's and mine—and sister to the rest of these rascals."

He paused, his expression gentling as he locked eyes with

Renny. "So, what say you, Renny Magee?" he said softly. "Will you have us?"

There had been a time when Renny would have countered with a cheeky, impudent reply as a way of masking any trace of sentiment or her true feelings. But at this particular moment, she could think of *nothing* to say. It seemed that every broken thing in her was coming together and being made whole . . . that every cold, lonely place inside her that had never known the security of acceptance or the warmth of affection suddenly seemed aglow . . . that every wound, every empty space, in her heart of hearts began to heal and fill to overflowing.

She took a swipe at her eyes to blot the dampness, then lifted her face to Conn MacGovern. "Aye," she said, her voice hoarse but strong. "And it's proud I am to be asked. There's nothing I'd rather be than a MacGovern."

"Well said," proclaimed the head of the family.

—

The letter arrived the next day. The twins brought in the post, tossing the few pieces of mail on the table and immediately running back outside. Vangie called after them, as she always did, to stay clear of the creek.

She went to the table and thumbed through the mail. Her eyes came to rest on the envelope at the bottom, and she pulled it free for closer inspection. In that instant her pulse set up a roar in her ears that sounded like thunder, and her heart threatened to explode inside her chest.

Too stunned to cry out, she could only stand and stare at the writing on the envelope. Aidan's handwriting—but how? Had there been a terrible mistake? Was he alive after all?

Excitement flooded her. The questions came arrowing in on her like jagged bolts of lightning. Finally she managed to get to the kitchen door and then to the porch, where she began to scream for Conn.

—

At the sound of Vangie's screams, Conn MacGovern ran as fast as he could toward the house. Something must have happened to one of the children, something bad. The baby was hurt . . . or wee Emma . . . or Vangie herself.

Oh, merciful Lord, what now, what now?

The instant he reached the porch, Vangie threw herself against him. She had a letter in her hand and was waving it in the air, shrieking something about Aidan, but Conn could make no sense of what she was trying to tell him.

He managed to get her inside to the kitchen, where he helped her onto a chair.

"You open it, Conn," she said, thrusting the letter in his face. "I can't."

"Vangie, what—"

He took the letter from her, then saw for himself why she was raving. It was Aidan's handwriting on the envelope.

Hope flared in Conn as he ripped the letter open. After all this time, could it be? Was it possible?

His eyes went to the top of the page, where the date was written—and his hopes collapsed and died.

"It was—he must have written it just before he left," he said, his voice shaking, his hand trembling as he reached to touch her.

Vangie moaned as her own hopes came crashing down.

She reached for the letter, but he stopped her. "Wait." He scanned down the page, and his heart slammed in shock, then began to race as he read on.

"Read it to me, Conn," Vangie said, her voice little more than a whisper.

Conn had reached the end of the letter. His throat was so swollen he didn't know if he *could* read it to her. His emotions rioted, pain warring with a growing wonder, even a bittersweet kind of joy.

"Conn—"

He scraped a chair up close to hers and faced her. "Our Aidan wrote this just before he left Ireland," he explained. "Probably posted it on his way to the harbor. All right, love, here's what he says." And he began to read:

Dear Da and Mother,

I know this will come as an enormous shock to the two of you, and I'm sorry for that. I planned to tell you myself when I arrived in America, but then I got to thinking perhaps I ought to write and tell you now, just in the unlikely event that something might happen to me during the crossing. Once you read this, I am sure you'll understand why I would rather be telling you these things in person. On the other hand, I don't want to take any chances on something happening to me and you not knowing about this.

What I'm trying to say, and I might just as well say it, is that I am a married man. I wed my Riona O'Donnell nearly four months past—you'll remember Riona from her family's booth at the Summerfest, sure. We have just learned she is carrying my child. Although we've known each other a long time as friends, we were surprised to finally realize we wanted to be more to each other.

And that's a part of the reason for my delay in coming, you see. I was trying to raise the money for our passage. As it turned out, I'll be coming alone, for we simply couldn't manage the funds we'd need for both of us to make the crossing. We also feared that the crossing might be too difficult in her delicate condition, after all, so she must stay with her family in Enniskerry.

I plan to find a position right away and save everything I earn

to bring Riona and our child across as soon as possible. I don't know
how well you'll remember Riona, but I do know you'll both love her.
She is beautiful and courageous, like Mother, and has an unshakable
faith, also like Mother. I'd give anything if she were coming with
me—I can't think how I'm going to bear being without her, I love
her so. But I will be working hard, and I will have you and the rest
of the family to keep me company until I can send for her, so that
will help to get me through, I'm sure.

I beg you both to forgive me for putting this in a letter, but I also
beg you to be happy for me. There's one thing I must ask of you. If
something should happen and I don't make it to America, please,
out of your love for me, please contact Riona and bring her and our
child to you and give them a home. I want you to know my beloved
and her to know you. And I want my child raised as a part of the
grand family I belong to.

I love you all, and I can't wait to see you.
Until we're together again.

Your devoted son,
Aidan MacGovern

By the time Conn had finished reading the letter, he and
Vangie were both sobbing.

"Do you think he knew?" Vangie said. "Do you think he
might have had a . . . a warning or the like?"

Conn thought about it, then shook his head. "Don't you
hear the happiness in him, love? He was full of joy when he
wrote this letter, not the kind of joy a man would know if he
were afraid of dying. He was just being right smart, taking
precautions, you see."

"I suppose you're right," Vangie said, lifting the hem of her
apron to dry her eyes. "Oh, Conn, think of it—our Aidan

married to Riona O'Donnell—and with a child. Our *son* has a child."

A child he'll never see, Conn thought, the taste of sorrow almost choking him.

But then something else struck him. He looked at Vangie and saw her watching him. "You know what we have to do, of course?" he said.

Slowly, she nodded. "We must find Aidan's wife . . . Riona . . . and bring her here. Of course, if she's too far along with the child, she may have to wait until after it's born. But we *must* bring her to us. It's what Aidan wanted."

Conn put aside the letter and took both her hands in his. "And isn't it what we want as well, love? To have our son's wife here—and his child—where we can give them a proper life and look after them?"

Her eyes still glistening with tears, Vangie squeezed his hands. "Oh, yes, Conn! It will be almost like having Aidan with us." She paused. "Conn, have you realized? We'll have *two* babies in the house! We're going to be grandparents!"

He stared at her, then got to his feet, tugging her along with him and gathering her into his arms. "Aye, so we are, love. But I must tell you, Evangeline Mary Catherine MacGovern, that you don't look like any grandmother *I've* ever seen."

She lifted her head and smiled through her tears at him. "We're going to be all right now, aren't we, Conn?"

He cupped her chin with his hand and kissed her gently on the forehead. "We are definitely going to be all right, love. And not just for now. With God and our family, we will always be all right."

Happy Birthday, America!

LET MUSIC SWELL THE BREEZE,

AND RING FROM ALL THE TREES

SWEET FREEDOM'S SONG.

SAMUEL F. SMITH

July 4, 1876

For this one occasion, Susanna was pleased to be a member of the audience instead of a part of the performance.

Tonight she wanted to see not the backs of the orchestra members, but the faces gathered in community. She wanted to feel the thrill, the surge of excitement that she knew would energize the crowd at any moment.

That excitement had already begun to permeate the vast gathering of spectators waiting for Michael and the orchestra to appear. Indeed, Susanna had never seen such heightened anticipation among so many. She could actually feel the expectation stirring throughout the park, as if all there sensed that something that had never happened before was about to take place.

Susanna could scarcely control her own eagerness. After all these months of working with Michael and assisting him in a dozen different ways with the music—playing parts, sorting through page after page of notation, or at times simply supplying an opinion—she had yet to hear the entire suite orchestrated and in full.

The *American Anthem* had taken its toll on Michael. Some days she had almost feared he would have to give it up altogether, so frustrated was he with its progress and drained of his own physical energy. He had gone without sleep, even lost weight. But something had kept him going.

No, not *something*, she amended. *Someone.*

She believed that with all her heart

Michael himself was convinced that this was not just another score, not merely another work to be performed, but a kind of divine commission. And Susanna had heard enough to be just as strongly convicted that what she was about to hear was the offering of a man anointed by God's Spirit, a vision fulfilled by His guidance and grace.

As a child, Michael had been given only a glimpse of what he would one day undertake as a musician. As a man, he had finally realized that vision, but only after overcoming obstacles that might have felled one less driven, less dedicated to the Lord of his life.

Central Park seemed ready to welcome the event. In the early dusk, lanterns glowed like fiery stars throughout the entire area, even on the hillside rising above the park itself. A special bandstand had been erected to accommodate the full orchestra, and here, too, lanterns cast their twinkling lights among the red, white, and blue bunting and countless flowers woven through the trellises framing the platform. Gas lamps highlighted the American flag raised just beyond the bandstand. In the distance, the elegant Bow Bridge had been decorated as well.

Earlier in the day, families had gathered in the area for picnics and games, speeches, and other Centennial events. But now adults and children alike had come together to wait in smaller, more intimate groups, their voices lowered, their laughter subdued.

Suddenly, the drone of a bagpipe was heard. A piper in full regalia marched slowly across the field, approaching the bandstand with great dignity and solemnity as he intoned the melody to a work Susanna recognized as a part of Michael's *Anthem.*

A riotous burst of applause followed, and the audience of thousands rose to their feet as Michael and the members of the orchestra approached from the other side of the bandstand and began to file up the steps to the platform.

Michael stood waiting until every musician was in place, then turned to the audience. He was greeted by wave after wave of applause and raucous whistles. Somewhere a child shouted "God bless America!" and Michael's face broke into an unrestrained smile.

He finally had to lift his arms to quiet the crowds. A hush fell over the audience, still standing, the silence a kind of tribute. They were keenly aware that, although they could gaze upon him with respect, he could not see them, and that his blindness was only one of the many difficulties he had faced and overcome.

Caught up in an overwhelming range of emotions, Susanna began to weep before Michael voiced even his first words.

She could sense *his* emotion in his thickening Italian accent as he finally spoke. "I would like first to say, 'Happy Birthday, America.'"

The crowd erupted into more applause as children blew whistles and one of the trumpets in the orchestra blasted a brief fanfare.

Again Michael had to quiet the crowd before going on. "During the time I worked with the music we will play for you tonight, I was aware, painfully so at times, that there was always some vital element that eluded me. At times I feared I would never discover what was missing, and I knew that without it, the music would be less than it was meant to be."

He stopped, as if to consider his next words. "Finally, when I least expected it, God revealed to me that I was too, ah, *intent* on making everything perfect, making everything fit just so, as musicians are wont to do. I began to understand then that I must do with the music what we are meant to do as Americans. I was to celebrate the many voices of America, the differences that make our nation what it is."

He opened his arms in an encompassing gesture. "We are different kinds of people, we Americans. We come from different countries. We share different beliefs, different traditions, different dreams, and different music. But one thing we share in common. We are all God's children, all blessed by His love and His grace. For truly God has bestowed grace to this nation and its people, so that with all our differences, we might yet exist in unity. May we never cease to be mindful that we will exist as a great nation only as we are faithful to our great God."

Had Central Park ever been as silent as it was in that moment? Susanna wondered, her heart so swollen with love and pride she thought she couldn't contain her feelings for another instant.

"So please, as we first sing America's song, our national anthem, and then as the orchestra offers you my own *American Anthem,* join with us and let us celebrate the birthday of the greatest nation in the world."

After the most rousing rendition of "The Star-Spangled Banner" Susanna had ever heard, the crowds made themselves comfortable, some sitting on chairs, some on benches, most on blankets covering the ground.

Paul Santi, dapper and dignified in his dark suit, rose from his concertmaster's chair to supervise the discordant process of tuning. Susanna felt the crowd's expectation go up another notch as they waited through this necessary preliminary.

Then Michael tapped his baton, and the celebration began.

Susanna glanced around at those nearest to her. Caterina, her face rapt with attention and love for her father. Papa Emmanuel, who had pulled from his pocket a huge handkerchief and was wiping his eyes with it. And the elegant Rosa Navaro who, Susanna noticed for the first time, seemed to have her arm tucked snugly inside Papa's arm.

Moira and Liam Dempsey were there as well, and Miss Fanny Crosby, seated on a blanket, was smiling as always. The newlyweds, Andrew and Bethany Carmichael, sat close together on a quilt, their faces aglow with love and deep contentment. Close by, his eyes continually sweeping over the crowd, stood the gruff Irish policeman Susanna had met during her first few weeks in America—Sergeant Donovan, she recalled. And he was not alone. A small, fair-haired woman held tightly to his hand, and three children Susanna had never seen—a gangly boy and two younger girls—clustered around them. Susanna made a mental note to ask Bethany who they were.

The MacGoverns sat together on the lawn nearby—all of them, even the baby. Baby William sat in Nell Grace's lap, his round blue eyes taking in everything around him. But then, seeing his mother, he stretched out his little arms, and Vangie reached to gather him close. Nell Grace, her eyes fixed on the violin section of the orchestra, barely seemed to notice. Then Conn MacGovern leaned over to whisper to his wife, and the smile that Vangie gave him warmed Susanna's heart.

It seemed right, somehow, to gather here with family and friends, loved ones and neighbors—plus a few thousand of the folks who filled this remarkable and varied land. Her land, too—the new home that had given her so much. Thankful to share this experience with all of them, Susanna settled back to enjoy the *American Anthem*.

She wasn't in the least surprised that the suite was a work of genius. She had already accepted the fact that the man she loved, the man she would marry in just a few weeks, possessed a gift of which others could only stand in awe. But she *was* surprised at the length to which Michael had gone to incorporate into the music the many voices of which he'd spoken. She knew about the Negro choir he'd engaged. He had told her about the piper and the elderly Italian street vendor with his accordion. And she was eagerly anticipating Paul Santi's brief but haunting violin solo based on an old Tuscan theme—a little gift from Michael to his father. But, adamant that he would at least withhold *some* surprises from her, Michael had not divulged the appearance of the children's choir from the Cathedral or the Swedish vocalist or the Irish stepdancers or the Spanish guitarist.

There was no describing the music. Mere words couldn't possibly begin to define or describe the magnitude of what Michael, with God's guidance, had accomplished. *Overwhelming* was the only word that came to mind, and it was a poor substitute for what Susanna was feeling.

Partly because of her own Irishness but more because of her fondness for the girl, one of the brightest highlights of the evening for Susanna was when Renny Magee swept out from

behind the orchestra onto the platform, her tin whistle spilling
out Irish tunes like silver coins tumbling down a waterfall, her
feet flying as she dazzled the crowds.

As the music slowed and grew softer, the girl stooped to
exchange her tin whistle for something else. Susanna was close
enough to see the tears tracking down Renny's face as she
scurried down the steps from the platform and ran into the
crowd. As she ran, she released a multicolored kite, fashioned
in the shape of a butterfly, into the air, where it rose high and
sailed free on the summer breeze.

Few here tonight would know that Maylee, with Susanna's
help, had begun the kite as an Easter gift for Renny. Maylee
had died before she could complete the gift for her friend, but
Susanna had gone ahead and finished it, holding it back just
for this occasion. Only this morning, she'd presented the kite to
Renny in memory of Maylee, who had often spoken of flying
free of her poor, frail body, and also to commemorate Renny's
performance in tonight's concert. The kite was constructed
from every colorful scrap of material Renny had ever given
Maylee. More than anything else, Susanna thought, it reflected
the friendship of two very different—and very wonderful—
children.

Somewhere tonight, Susanna thought, *Maylee's spirit is
flying.*

Darkness had completely settled over the park when the
fireworks began to flare above the hill. Now Michael
unleashed the full force of the orchestra for the monumental
finale. The combined experience of the explosion of music and
the fireworks brought the audience to their feet—but almost
sent Susanna to her knees.

She could only stand in wonder of the spectacle playing out
before her and the thunderous riot of music under Michael's

baton. She was weeping, she was praying, she was laughing as Central Park erupted in celebration and praise.

When the music stopped and Michael turned to face his audience, he appeared dazed, as if stunned by his own achievement and its effect on those before him. His face was wreathed in perspiration and an exhausted smile, his light-weight black suit hanging limply on his tall form.

But his words came ringing out over Central Park like a holy benediction when he opened his arms as if to embrace the audience and cried, "May God . . . *forever* . . . bless America—and all her many voices!"

In that moment, that sanctified moment, Susanna's heart whispered a fervent *amen*.